Only Twice

I've Wished

for Heaven

Only Twice

I've Wished

for Heaven

A NOVEL

Dawn Turner Trice

Crown Publishers, Inc. New York

Copyright © 1996 by Dawn Turner Trice

Illustrations copyright © 1996 by Arden von Haeger

All rights reserved. No part of this book may be reproduced or transmitted in any form or by any

means, electronic or mechanical, including photocopying, recording, or by any information storage

and retrieval system, without permission in writing from the publisher.

Published by Crown Publishers, Inc., 201 East 50th Street, New York, New York 10022.

Member of the Crown Publishing Group.

Random House, Inc. New York, Toronto, London, Sydney, Auckland

http://www.randomhouse.com/

CROWN is a trademark of Crown Publishers, Inc.

Printed in the United States of America

Design by Leonard Henderson

Library of Congress Cataloging-in-Publication Data is available upon request.

ISBN 0-517-70428-5

10 9 8 7 6 5 4 3 2 1

First Edition

This book is dedicated to my sister,
Kim Denyce Turner, the little bird who flew away.

ACKNOWLEDGMENTS

I am blessed for having traveled this road. Many have helped along the way. I am grateful to my agent, Denise Stinson, for her friendship and unwavering support of this project, and to my editor, Carol Taylor, for her patience and expertise. In addition, I would like to thank the Illinois Arts Council, a state agency, for the partial funding of this project.

For their honest comments and careful reads of my manuscript, I wish to thank Anita August, Claudia Banks, Helen Benjamin, James Cox, Charles Dickinson, David Elsner, Gracie Lawson, Lisa Lewis, Mary Lewis, Laurel Mills, James Trice, Sarah Trice, Rita Whack, and Bruce Wilson.

And my heartfelt appreciation goes to my mother, Barbara Turner, and my grandmother Jennie Tucker for their life lessons on strength, perseverance, and commitment, and for their unconditional love. I admire them both.

And I am forever grateful for my husband, David, and my daughter, Hannah, whose love sustains me along the journey.

Inmate Alfred Mayes dies of heart attack

CHICAGO —Alfred Mayes, one of Illinois's most notorious inmates, died of a heart attack Monday in the Friersville Correctional Facility.

Mayes, 82, was the street preacher sentenced to life imprisonment in 1976 for the brutal murder of 12-year-old Valerie Nicholae, a resident of the affluent Lakeland community.

Warden James Delaney said Mayes's body was found by a prison guard at 8:04 Monday morning. According to the prison coroner, Mayes died in his sleep. . . .

Part I

C H A P T E R 1

Miss Jonetta Goode (that's Goode with an e):
"And the truth about Valerie's passing and Alfred Mayes and that whole mess?
Oh, the truth was buried nearly twenty years ago."

You see, I growed up in a place called Annington County, Mississippi.

In my day, colored folk up and died whenever white folk got a notion for us to. Mostly our men, but sometimes women and children. You look up one day and they gone, like a speck of dirt just blowing on the breeze. Sometimes with grown-ups, you almost had to remember if they was ever there in the first place, because you couldn't tell who was who by the graves. But with the children, there was never no wondering. People always left rocks behind, sticks, X's, half-pushed into the ground. It was parents' way of burying parts of themselves with their babies. What remained, they numbed, just to get by.

So we all learned to stand together; we learned to help one another. It was something nobody even thought about. A child needed you, you was there. You helped a little boy lean against a hoe handle until hard dirt crumbled. Then you stayed with that child to drop a seed or two inside. When a little girl was sick, you mopped her mouth and served her stew in your Sunday pot, with the biggest chunks of sausage and carrots and potatoes you could find. Wasn't no skimping, mind you. No skimping for a child. Or you hid a so-called wayward boy in your crawl space, telling him to hush up—hold his breath if he had to—until the sheriff's boots stomped off the front porch, back down that dirt road. . . . Many nights after Valerie died, I asked myself what could I've done to help her. How could I've saved that baby from so much sickness?

Down south, we worried about white folks with their shotguns and lynch ropes, which made them God. Gave them the key to a heaven my papa wasn't rushing to get his girls to that fast. So in 1932, when we came up to Chicago, to Thirty-fifth Street, I thought I was a lifetime away from all that mess. Hell, the last thing I thought I'd have to worry about up north was black folks and their guns and lynch ropes and drugs, shooting all kinds of blues in their veins. And the nasty men, the Alfred Mayeses of the world, who liked to prey on little girls.

One thing is sure, you don't get used to death. Oh no, honey. Even old, old folks want to live forever—even if before long all they can do is hang like antique pictures on the wall. Relatives come by and stroke their chin and nod and smile while looking at their old kin. Take a rag every now and then and knock dust off them when it's due. But when they leave this earth, it ain't easy to take. So you know it's near impossible to make sense of having to pat dirt onto a child's face.

I saw Valerie only once, but after Child told me the hell her little friend was traveling through, I felt like I knowed her all her days. Could say I knowed her as good as I knowed Child. Just ain't fair for one person to have so much pain. Seems like God shoulda had better sense in piecing it out like that. Seems like since Creation, God had done gave Thirty-fifth Street's children more than their share of pain. Oh, Thirty-fifth Street was a horrible mess. For the longest, even the city had wanted to forget it was there.

The mayor started by taking every city map and drawing a row of X's on the grid line between Thirty-fourth and Thirty-sixth streets. Stores hadn't been inspected in years. Mail wasn't delivered right, just left in one big pile. People never even had the dignity of a address. Thirty-fifth Street was all. Just Thirty-fifth Street. Only ten blocks made up the colored side of that street, and at every intersection, young souls was always dropping off. Like pecans from a tree. And not all of them dying in ways that call for burying, either. Sometimes that's the worst way.

So when Valerie died and the city finally got a notion to close down all the stores—to do what the street preachers had been trying to do for nearly half a century—I must admit, I was happy to get my notice. But it left a great big old hole in my heart that that damned street couldn't go up in flames without taking them two little girls with it: Valerie lifted on up to glory, and Child, who was left behind. Left to roam this here wilderness.

Every now and then, I think about the funeral, all them flowers surrounding Valerie's tiny white coffin, and a funny feeling still pass over me. Flowers are fine and good. But how come people forget to give children, especially little girls, flowers when they can enjoy them? Oh, the flower don't have to be a rose or a daisy. A flower is a "How do?" A kind word. A bouquet is no worries or cares or disappointments. It's giving a little girl a chance to enjoy a good breeze—to fix herself on a dream. And a child can't dream if she afraid to death to close her eyes at night.

I remember the day Child come running into my store, telling me a new girl come to the class. "Miss Jonetta, Miss Jonetta!" She was running so fast, her uniform had turned sideways and she was bouncing like she had jumping beans in her britches. Well, back then that wasn't nothing all that unusual for Child. She was born under a busy moon. I told her often: "Honey, us girls ain't suppose to look like something the cat drug in, like we threw our clothes up and plopped in 'em. And stop all that hopping up and down, too. That ain't right, neither. You take a chance on mixing stuff up and having them moving to places they ain't suppose to be."

But that day, I couldn't worry about her clothes or her carrying-on. "Miss Jonetta, Miss Jonetta!" she kept yelling.

"Sit down and settle yourself first, honey," I told her. She breathed in and out, swelling her chest up, like you do at the doctor's office when he say take a deep breath. "Now," I said, nearly cracking my sides, "tell me what bug done got a piece of you."

"Today . . . in school? A new girl came to class," she said. "And she sit right in front of me. She even seem pretty nice, not like the other Lakeland girls."

"I thought I told you not to worry none about them other girls," I said. "They ain't got no color is all."

"I ain't worried about them," she said. She took a peek down at those old brogans of hers like they was making more sense than me. But that day? Believe me when I tell you, nothing and nobody, not even those prissy Lakeland heifers, coulda made Child feel low.

That year, Child was eleven years old, going on ninety. She thought nobody understood her. She thought nobody understood what it felt like to want to fly somewhere and be free. That's why she wandered over to Thirty-fifth Street. She was looking for a place to run to. Her hair was too red, so she thought. Her father didn't love her anymore, so she thought. And her family had just moved to this new hankty place where she felt she didn't fit in. With Valerie over there, and me on the other side of that fence, the two of us made her feel like she belonged.

And the truth about Valerie's passing and Alfred Mayes and that whole mess? Oh, the truth was buried nearly twenty years ago. Only today it can finally be resurrected. All them years ago, I told Child that if she didn't want to tell the truth right then, she wouldn't have to. She had my hand to God that I wouldn't utter a word. But I warned her from my own experiences that secrets don't always stay down. They rise like hot bread; spread like melting butter. I told her one day she'd have to tell this thing. And it wouldn't matter if the miles stretched like canyons between us, because I would help her. One day she'd have to gather the events the way you would loose petals on a flower and piece them together again. Slowly. Into the whole story. From the day she and her family moved to Lakeland to the day that no-good Thirty-fifth Street finally went up in flames. And she and Valerie helped set all them souls free. I told her she'd have to tell it, when it was time.

It's time. So listen.

Tempestt Rosa Saville ("Child"):
"When you learn the truth."

When I was a little girl growing up on the far South Side of Chicago, my father and I would sit on our back porch—sometimes it would seem like all day. The sun would be sitting straight up in the sky and my father would be watching me chase butterflies, running from rock to rock, jumping up on the limbs of our near-dead apple tree with my hands poised, ready to pinch at their shiny wings. To this day, I can sometimes feel what was left of the morning dew squishing up between my toes, and the rose thorns and weeds scratching against my little legs. My father would laugh at me when I'd finally get tired of chasing the butterflies and I'd plop right down next to him.

Then when twilight would come and the butterflies had flown away, he'd see me smacking mosquitoes. "I hate them old ugly mosquitoes," I'd tell Daddy. "I just hate them."

One evening, he looked at me and laughed.

"You know, Temmy," he said, "you'll learn as you get older that there really isn't that much difference between your so-called pretty butterflies and your so-called ugly mosquitoes."

I looked at my father and I wondered if the sun hadn't beaten down too hot on his head. Didn't he see how light and free those butterflies were? Didn't he see how the sun fanned rainbow colors into their wings?

Well, twenty years have passed since my father and I last sat on that porch. And after Valerie died, with each year's passing, I finally began to understand what he meant.

That mosquito bites you now and it dies. It leaves a little mark, but nothing to really talk about, nothing that doesn't go away after a day or two. But the butterfly, that pretty, pretty little butterfly, bites you in another way: It makes you think life is full of color and light and easy. When you pinch its wings, it even sprinkles some of its magic onto your fingertips, like gold nuggets, making you think all you have to do is reach out for it. And you can buy yourself a forever. That's when it bites you. Unlike the mosquito, it doesn't die. But slowly you do. When you learn the truth.

Tempestt:
"Good morning and welcome to Lakeland."

I was only eleven years old but deeply rooted in our South Side bungalow when my father moved my mother and me across town to Lakeland. Our move took place in early September 1975. I remember sitting in the backseat of our well-aged Volvo, which Daddy had spit-shined himself the night before, picking at the tear in the vinyl between my legs. The more I picked and pulled at the wadding, the easier it was to forget about the itchy ankle socks and the pleated skirt my father had forced me to wear.

"Daughter of mine," he said, glaring at me over his shoulder. "Daughter of mine" was his new way of referring to me. The words fell clankety on my ears and felt completely inappropriate for two people who had swapped bobbers and minnows and base-ball cards, including a 1968 Ernie Banks number that only I could have made him part with. That particular one I kept by itself, wrapped in wax paper in one of Daddy's old tackle boxes under my bed. Though my mother never understood why a little girl would need such things—including several pairs of All Stars that Mama made me lace in pink, explaining only, "Because I said so!"—when cleaning my bedroom, she always, always cleaned around them. She also demanded that my father, from time to time, bring me roses in addition to model airplanes and finely crafted fishing rods with walnut stock handles.

"Daughter of mine," Daddy continued. This time, he squinted into the rearview mirror. "I won't ask you again to stop picking at that seat. Sit up straight, dear."

"But—"

"No buts, Temmy, and close your legs. You're a young lady. Didn't our talk last night mean anything? Weren't you listening? We're almost there now. Sit up straight, I said."

I suppose my father's metamorphosis didn't happen all at once. But it seemed that way to me. In truth, it was probably a gradual thing, like an apple left sitting on a counter. One day it's all red and softly curved and the next you find yourself slicing off sections, trying to find places the mold and sunken-in dark spots haven't yet reached. As we drove closer to Lakeland, I wanted just to shake my father, make him wake up and come back to himself. I wanted him to shave off that silly mustache he'd recently scratched out of his face and toss off that too-tight striped necktie. The house, though sold, was still empty. We could move back in, patch it up, make it pretty again, I thought. But of course my thinking was simplistic. My father would never again see the house at 13500 South Morrison Street as our home.

For me, our bungalow, our neighborhood, was the only home I'd ever wanted to know. From the day I'd learned our address and our telephone number by heart, it had become as much a part of me as my name. My parents had created a life that was sturdy and robust, existing as so much color: yellow-and-blue-trimmed bungalows that lined perfectly square city blocks; Miss Jane's red compact—the size of Daddy's hand—which Mama said Miss Jane held like a shield while sitting where the sunlight was best on her front porch, warding off the years; and Mr. Jenkins's broad purple boxers that were always line-drying on his back fence across the alley. How the prospect of ivory towers and debutante balls could ever compare to this world was completely beyond my understanding. I also wondered how my father could not only choose Lakeland but yearn for it. It was a lifestyle he'd once believed to be too "one size fits all," and as loosely woven and thin as tissue paper.

At stoplights, Daddy busied himself by flicking lint off my mother's sky blue cardigan and attempting to blot her perfectly smudged lipstick. Mama batted his hand away, warning with side glances that he was acting a fool.

"Thomas, you'll draw back a stub," she said calmly, refusing a full head turn to her left. So, after Daddy pulled the radio's knob and Mama pushed it back in (saying the static, all that popping and cracking, was trying her nerves), he folded several sheets of Kleenex and wiped his loafers. These, I must say, were the same loafers that just one year before he swore pinched his toes and were fit for nothing more than pulling weeds in our garden.

It used to be, before night school transformed my father from a cabdriver into a teacher, that Daddy watched me with a sense of ceremony as I played in our backyard. He would watch as I skipped around our partially painted picnic table and climbed the bottom branches of our apple tree. He clapped when I completed a somersault; he cheered when I shattered the Coke bottle with the slingshot he'd seen me eye in the Woolworth two blocks from our house. And with him and often my mother as my audience, that tiny backyard—with its thick rows of collards and cramped tomato vines—grew under endless possibilities. Back then, Daddy admired my socks that rarely matched, and my prickly hair, his shade of red, which he once chuckled with Saville pride was so wild, a comb would break its neck getting through.

But on that morning, when my father reached a heavy hand

back toward me, it was only to brush wayward strands, forcing them, too, into submission.

The night before our move, Daddy rummaged through the house, deciding what was fitting and proper to take to the kingdom of the drab and what was best left behind. We had packed most of our things and sent them ahead. What remained, the movers would take the following morning. There wasn't much need for furniture because Lakeland's apartments, Daddy said, were "impeccably" furnished. The only redeeming quality about that final night was that Mama allowed my friend Gerald Wayne to sleep over with me. We spent the early-evening hours in the backyard in my tent before going inside. It was one last opportunity to listen to all the crickets and grasshoppers and the pitter-patter of alley rats, whose size often put some cats to shame.

Gerald Wayne and I had been friends since the second grade. Though I had seen him often in school, we met one Saturday while he was sitting on the curb in front of Wilson's Fix-It shop, playing by himself, as he often had. (I inherited both my parents' penchant for the down-and-out.) I just happened to be walking by, when he looked up at me, smiled, exposing two vacant spaces where front teeth should have been, and said in a most sincere voice, "You dare me eat this worm?" Had he given me ample time, I suppose I would indeed have considered the question. Only he didn't. Before I could utter a word, he dangled the worm over his mouth, let the squirmy little thing stare into his tonsils, then scarfed it down. Oh, he was nasty. He didn't even flinch.

Children always teased Gerald because of his dietary habits. But he had yet another unbearable affliction: He reeked—smelled just like a goat. None of us truly understood why, especially with his family living on the west side of the el train tracks, near the old soap factory. I suppose we thought proximity alone would have an impact on his condition. Even back then, Gerald was the cutest little boy in the second grade. He had smooth brown skin, dark brown eyes that twinkled, and a smile that sometimes made even me feel faint. But he had this black cloud that formed a capsule around his entire body. It was as if no other part of the atmosphere would allow it to enter, so it clung to Gerald for dear life. It even shimmied in the moonlight. Mama said all the child needed was a bath. Daddy later obliged him with one and threatened that if he didn't make "dipping" himself part of his daily routine, he would be banned from our house. Gerald liked having a friend, so he washed, religiously.

The night before we moved, Gerald and I sat in my tent with our legs crossed and the flashlight dimming between us as we sighed, grasping for topics that didn't smack of corny recollections or mushy farewells.

"My dad said you guys are lucky to be moving to Lakeland," Gerald said, interrupting several seconds of silence. "The construction company he works for helped build it. 'Yep,' he said, 'the Savilles are some lucky black people.' "

"Oh, shut up, Gerald," I said, choking back tears. "Nobody's lucky to be going, nowhere—I mean, anywhere." Daddy had begun to drill me on my double negatives.

Outside the tent, a soft breeze nudged the wind chimes on the back porch, which alone held many of my childhood memories. It was there where Gerald helped me dig a hole to bury the horrendous Cinderella dress our neighbor Miss Jane had bought one Christmas, expecting me to wear it to church with her. Mama knew I had buried it back there. She pretended not to see one of the bells jutting up from the ground. But she never said anything, because she hated it, too. In the knotholes in the pine of the banister I had stuffed so many wads of purple and green bubble gum that after several years, they seemed to hold the old rickety thing together. And once I had even caught Mama and Daddy under that porch, moaning and touching one another in places that made me giggle.

Feeling sick, I opened the flap of the tent. I told Gerald I had to use the bathroom, then went into the house to find my father. I didn't want Gerald to see one teardrop. I don't know when it happened, but Gerald considered himself my protector, my shadow and shield. No, I'm not sure when it happened, because I was the one who often protected him. Like the day I had rubbed his head when Sandy Roberts shoved him to the ground. Daddy had told him that it was never acceptable for a boy to fight a girl, so Gerald couldn't hit her back. But I could.

In the house, I saw my father scurrying about and I wondered what was lifting him, when my mother and I felt to leave was one of the most wrenching things that could happen to us. One final box, marked Garvey, Du Bois, Merton, and Robeson sat in the hallway. My father had so many books that the movers had to make two trips for them alone. He was about to prop the box against the front door when he noticed me staring at him.

"Hey, princess," he said.

"Hey," I said, picking at the newly painted lime green wall. I unpigeoned my feet, remembering my mother's warnings about them one day turning completely inward.

"You okay? Seems like you got something on your mind. At least I hope you aren't so rude that you'd leave my boy out there by himself for nothing. Come here." He reached out to me with those huge arms of his and made me sit on his lap.

"I don't want to leave," I muttered.

"Daughter of mine," he said. "I thought we talked about this.

It's a once-in-a-lifetime opportunity, dear. There's a waiting list a mile long to get into Lakeland. And our name"—he thumped my chest, then his—"our name was pulled in the lottery. Where we're going is a much better place than this."

He brushed his hair back in frustration, revealing a row of reddish gray strands. Then he looked up at the top of the stairs, where Mama was standing, folding towels. She, too, was listening; she, too, needed another dose of convincing. At first, my father looked everywhere except directly at me. I followed his gaze to the empty living room. Without furniture, it was all too apparent the floor sloped too much toward the fake fireplace, and oddly, the room seemed smaller than it had before.

"Lakeland is a wonderful place," he said finally. "That apartment will be three times the size of this old place. You'll have your own huge bedroom with your own balcony. . . ." He paused. "Temmy, you're too young to understand this, but soon this neighborhood will have gone to pot. Already young boys are hanging out on the corners. It won't be long before this place won't be worth half of what we paid for it."

"I don't care," I moaned.

"You haven't heard one word, have you, honey?" Daddy took a long, deep breath. "There was a time, when I first met your mama, that I would never have even considered living among the 'bourgeoisie.' But there comes a time when you have to mix some ideas. You get older and understand that nothing is all good; nothing is all bad. You know why I decided to go back to school? I wanted to give you somebody who does more than drive a cab, and write letters to newspapers and hand out pamphlets in his spare time. I had to ask myself, What more could I offer my wife, my daughter? In a few months, you'll be twelve years old. Soon, you'll be going off to college. I want you to be proud of where you come from and I want you to be proud of me. I'll be a teacher, honey. Your old man a teacher at a fine, fine school."

As I walked back to the tent, I wondered what I had done. I had always been proud of my father, and I wondered when he thought I'd begun to feel otherwise.

Down the hall from the stairs was a small, pantry-sized room that my father had used as his office. There were no windows, just his cold marble-topped desk and his favorite leather chair, cracked and worn, tired-looking from years and years of our weight. Daddy had found the set in an alley in the downtown legal district one afternoon while picking up a fare. He brought it home and dusted it off, and many nights I would stop in just before bed. Though I rarely understood the depth of Emerson or Tolstoy, I knew it was nearly impossible for me to find slumber without the melody of his baritone rocking me to sleep. Those nights, I believed with all my heart that as the years passed and my legs would begin to dangle far below my father's lap, below the final bar of missing gold tacks, we would always fit into the perfectly molded cushion that we'd created. That was until my father decided to leave the set behind.

Gerald had fallen asleep. I knew this as soon as I reached the kitchen, which led to the back porch. For such a small child, he had a tremendous snore, thunderous snatches of gasping and wheezing. Mama and I stood on the porch for a second, listening to him, watching his figure, silhouetted by the light, heave up and down.

"You know everything's going to be okay, don't you, Temmy?" she asked. For years I told myself—I suppose because everybody seemed to agree—I looked just like my father. But that was because of the hair. The red hair tended to blind people to the rest of my features. The truth was that I had a lot of my mother's face, her broad eyes, olive-brown complexion, and heavy, good-for-whistling lips. That night, Mama didn't wait for an answer. I suppose she knew I didn't have one.

"Stay out fifteen more minutes, Tem," she said. "Then I'll come get you both ready for bed." She smiled at me, then kissed me on the lips.

The next morning, I awoke to the scent of my mother's country bacon. I jumped out of bed and ran to wake Gerald in the guest room. By the time I got there, he was already watching the sun rise over the Jenkinses' tree house across the alley, and the garbagemen, sweaty, their pants sliding down their butts, hurl huge barrels of our un-Lakeland-like belongings into their truck. Too soon afterward, it was time to leave. I gave him my new address and he promised to write and visit as soon as he could. From my backseat in the car, I watched my friend, hands crammed into the pockets of his baggy jeans, turn and head for his side of the tracks. I waved, but he didn't see me. Still, I continued until we turned the corner at Alexander Street, and soon the house, Gerald, the Woolworth, everything, leaned in the distance and eventually was completely out of sight.

The clock on the gate showed 10:00 A.M. when our car pulled up. My father made certain it was ten exactly. The guard said, "Good morning and welcome to Lakeland." He checked Daddy's driver's license against a clipboard of notes, then handed him a map and showed us how to maneuver Lakeland's labyrinth of twists and turns to the Five forty-five building, our new home. Finally, he opened a massive iron gate that groaned as it parted, and we were allowed in.

As I looked out the car window, my fingers began to tingle and turn cold. Let my father tell it: This place was straight out of a fairy tale. One square mile of rich black soil carved out of the ghetto. One square mile of ivory towers, emerald green grass, and pruned oaks and willows so stately, they rivaled those in the suburbs and made the newly planted frail trees in the projects beyond the fence blend into the shade. The four high-rise apartment buildings were the tallest structures I'd ever seen, and already janitors were hanging from scaffolds, washing beveled-glass windows, making sure everything shined in tandem.

Men, women, and children were out in droves, reading under the trees, sitting on hand-carved wooden benches, or walking dogs along winding cobblestone streets—appropriately named Martin Luther King, Jr., Drive, Langston Hughes Parkway, Ida B. Wells Lane. When we passed a field of children taking turns riding a pony, I got on my knees to look out the back window. Then, remembering my father's warnings, I slid back down the vinyl. I was surprised to see him smiling at me in the rearview mirror. We turned onto a path that followed the lake, and a flock of white gulls flew over the car. I scooted from one side of the seat to the other to watch their pearl gray wings stretching across the sky as they squawked like restless, hungry babies, back and forth between the rocks and a lighthouse in the middle of the water.

In Lakeland, Daddy said, was the world's wealth of top black professionals: surgeons, engineers, politicians. Lakeland had begun in the early 1960s as part of Chicago's Life Incentive Project. As an apology to the rat-infested and blighted tenement houses blacks had to endure during the migration, the mayor garnered support from the state capital to the White House to build this urban utopia. It was an idyllic community, stripped of limitations and bounds. According to the *Sentinel*'s annual obligatory article, Lakeland had every amenity: a twenty-seven-hole golf course, an Olympic-size swimming pool, coffeehouses with the classics lining oak shelves, and an academy whose students were groomed and pointed, some said from the womb, in the direction of either

Morehouse, Spelman, Harvard, or Yale. Even Lakeland's section of Lake Michigan was different from that of every other community that bordered the shore. In Lakeland, the water was heavily filtered and chlorinated—sometimes even helped along by food coloring—to look the aqua blue of dreams.

This generation of residents, once removed from salt pork, fatback, and biscuits, now dined on caviar and escargot. Neatly draped Battenberg lace scarves on marcelled heads replaced dingy do-rags and stocking caps. And plump, curved saffron to dark brown behinds that once jiggled like jelly and made little boys long to be men were now girdled and clamped down, as stiff and rigid as paddleboards.

Despite what lay outside the fence on Thirty-fifth Street, whatever the world had told black people they couldn't do or be or wish for, it didn't apply to the residents of Lakeland. Within the confines of that ivy-lined wrought-iron fence lived this elite group of people who had been allowed to purge their minds of all those things that reminded them of what it meant to be poor and downtrodden. Once here, Lakelandites didn't look back. They surely didn't want to go back. All they had to do was sign a two-part contract in which they agreed to pay a monthly rent that was lower than the average mortgage. And they vowed to put their bodies and their beliefs into this great blender and leave it there until the whitewashed folk who came out no longer resembled the pageant of folk who had entered. The women made the Stepford Wives look like members of the Rainbow Coalition. The men, with their expensive pipes, plaid pants, and stiff white collars, were about as individual as the curds in white milk.

"This is Lakeland," Daddy said, pulling up in front of our building. He beamed almost as if he had built the place, or, worse yet, birthed it.

He patted the steering wheel and told the Volvo to be nice. For his sake, even I was hoping it wouldn't sputter and spit the way it usually did when he turned it off. I was happy it didn't embarrass him. A doorman rushed the car, opening the door for my mother, then for me. Solemnly, Mama and I walked up a slight incline to the oak double doors, which led to a lobby of glittering marble and crystal. Daddy, however, floated in on air.

Tempestt:
"I spent most of the night plotting my escape."

Miss Lily's feet were epic even for a woman who stood over six feet tall in knee-highs, rolled down to her ankles. After those feet, the rest of her bolted around the corner to the foyer. Miss Lily was one of the oldest maids in Lakeland. And, as everyone in Lakeland had access to house help, she worked for residents on the twenty-second floor. We had just opened the front door to our new apartment and were marveling at the living room—big as a museum and twice as stoic—when she came lumbering toward us.

She cleared her throat and removed a rumpled three-by-five index card from her smock pocket. "Welcome to Lakeland, Mr. and Mrs. Saville," she said, reading the card. Frowning at the pronunciation of my name, she continued. "Welcome, Red."

"Thank you very much, Miss Lily," Daddy said.

"Now, I'll give y'all the tour."

As she plodded in front of my father, my mother, knowing how much I hated being called Red, placed her hand over my mouth and dragged me down the hall behind them.

Miss Lily had organized a few of Daddy's books alphabetically in a small cove in the living room. About three or four magazines with Lakeland featured on the cover were spread out across the coffee table. More of his books and magazines and articles lined oak shelves in the halls and in his office, which was nothing like the pantry office in our old house. All of his books now were as organized and neatly stacked as I had ever seen them.

We went from the living room to the dining room to the study, until we made it to my bedroom, down the hall on the right. It, like the rest of the place, had incredibly high ceilings and large picture windows. Two French doors opened up onto the balcony overlooking the lake.

Miss Lily, mistakenly—I say mistakenly because no one intentionally would dare do this to a child—had hung drapes with the motif of a black Barbie doll in all of the windows in my bedroom. The pattern conspicuously matched the bedspread, which matched the sheets. I wanted to vomit. But I just stood there, taking it all in.

M iss Lily left for a few hours and Mama busied herself by undoing everything Miss Lily had done. Mama pulled perfectly new contact paper off the shelves in the cabinets as she rearranged each one so that it was to her liking, not Miss Lily's. She put the iron skillets under the sink and moved the dishwashing liquid and scouring pads to the pantry. She put the dry seasonings on the lazy Susan by the refrigerator and moved the can goods to the cabinet over the stove. None of this made much sense, and my mother knew it. Still, she was determined to leave her mark.

Meanwhile, my father stayed as far away from us as he could. I tiptoed back to his office, where I saw him sitting at his huge new desk. His hands were folded behind his head and his large feet were propped up on top of the desk. Behind him, a picture window made the lake look as though it were a beautiful painting with the sky and the water melding into similar hues. I watched my father sitting there, staring at the ceiling one minute, spinning the globe behind him the next, then running his hands along the top of the desk as he swiveled around in his chair the way I used to when he took me to the ice cream parlor down the street.

Not long after, my father decided he wanted to visit the coffee-house down on Baldwin Crescent. The houses were renovated brownstones, where, beginning on Thursday night and lasting throughout the weekend, forums were held dealing with issues of the day: from Watergate and Vietnam to the practicality of soup kitchens and bell-bottoms. My mother didn't want to go, so my father left alone. Afterward, my mother kissed me good night and told me to get ready for bed. I didn't resist. Our bedrooms seemed miles apart, with hers and Daddy's on the north end of the apartment and mine on the south.

Before going to my bedroom, though, I walked over to the sewing room, a few feet away. Miss Lily, who'd returned not much earlier, was packing up for the night. I stood in the doorway, watching her count out bus fare from her makeshift wallet, a folded gray handkerchief with tight corners that stuck out like steel spikes. She placed some coins on a yellow tile-topped table that sat in the corner. It was where she ate her meals, portioned throughout the day from a dented metal lunch pail she now held hostage between her thick thighs.

"Are you going home?" I asked, probing in my natural fashion.

"Yes," she said, putting on her coat. It lacked buttons and the inner lining hung beneath the shell.

"Do you come back tomorrow?"

"I'm coming back," she said, "but not to work."

"Why are you coming, then?"

"For the carnival."

"A carnival?" I asked.

"You know, the back-to-school carnival?"

"Oh, that carnival," I said, lying.

"You sho ask a lot of questions for a little girl," she said, shoving her braid under her scarf. "You Lakeland people is nosy."

"I'm not a Lakeland person," I said.

"Well, you are now, Miss Sassy."

We stood in silence while she finished gathering her things, counting her pennies. She stretched out her back, her neck, brushed her hair from her face, and when she was done, she pushed past me without saying good night. I listened to her footsteps as she walked down the hall to the back door. It led to a cramped back elevator that all the servants used. Once downstairs, the elevator opened out onto the loading dock, where the maids and janitors lined up to wait for the bus that returned them to their lives on the other side of the fence.

Inside the sewing room was a tiny window. It was the only one in the apartment that actually allowed a view of Thirty-fifth Street. Although, at the time, I didn't know anything about Thirty-fifth Street, it did strike me as odd that there were few real windows on the west side of the apartment. Architects, forefathers, and the lot had toiled diligently to design a building where most of the views opened east, out to the lake. The windows on the other side of the buildings were dummies. From the inside, they were plastered over, hermetically sealed. From the outside, they were glass and looked just like the others. That they were fake would have been apparent to no one, at least no one down on Thirty-fifth Street.

After climbing on top of the table, the first thing I saw out the tiny window was the el, nearly six blocks away. In my mind, I could hear the train's squeals as it approached the Thirty-first Street platform. Sparks of indigo sprinkled into the air, then disappeared far below the tracks. I thought about how the train bisected my old neighborhood, how Gerald lived on his side and I on the other, and how sometimes when his father would come home from work, yelling and screaming at him, we would meet in the middle and wait for a train to rumble through. Then we would scream out swear words at his father. We'd curse him until the train passed and fragments of bad words shook loose from the steel beams and concrete supports, echoing off broken glass and the leaning back porches of old people too poor to move away from the tracks.

"I ain't no dumb sissie," Gerald would say with a confidence we both knew was fleeting—as fleeting as the roaring train.

"Hell no, you're not," was always my reply. Then we'd giggle at the word *hell* and flap our arms, mocking nearby ornery pigeons, and stomp our feet until our bodies ached. Small tears would sometimes well in his eyes, those beautiful brown eyes, and I'd pretend not to see. I'd pretend the tears were from the dust that flew up all around into our hair, mouths, noses, and eyes. We could taste the dirt, but we didn't care. We just spat it out. We simply spat it out. If only for a few hours, I could help Gerald lose himself in this backdrop of muted grays. The earth there always, always offered up something worthy of exploration, while graciously accepting whatever we left behind.

Boy, did I miss our old neighborhood and my friend. I wondered how he was getting along without me.

The sewing room had a phone that I supposed was for Miss Lily. When I saw the light blink on, I slowly, expertly, lifted the receiver from its cradle. And although Daddy had warned me about eavesdropping, sitting on the fringes of adult conversations, disregarding the importance of lowered voices and nearly shut doors, I decided we were under new rules in Lakeland.

"Auntie, we're here," Mama said to Aunt Jennie, my grandfather's sister and my mother's confidante when Daddy wasn't acting right. "We arrived this morning and the very first thing I did was pull the maid off to the side to let her know who's going to be running this apartment. I can tell already, these people are going to try me."

"Oh no they're not, dear," Aunt Jennie said. Her deep, raspy voice frobbled and cracked at the end of each sentence like the bones of an old woman struggling to get out of bed. "You know this life well enough to maneuver around the rough edges."

Aunt Jennie, well into her sixties, "expatriated" herself from Chicago in the fifties. She now lived in Los Angeles in her fifties-decorated condo and her hallmark black nightgown and black leather jacket. On the back of the jacket she had a tailor sew HECK ON WHEELS. Once a year, we went out to visit her, and it was always interesting to see how opposite she was of Granddaddy. When he was alive, my mother's father was part of Chicago's black elite, a prominent doctor propped up by awards, wing tips, and tailored pinstripes. She was an eccentric old woman who sported a graying globelike Afro and revved about town, puffing Winstons, on a silver three-speed Schwinn that she handled like a Harley. Mama said she fed caviar to gulls along the coast once a week, and spent any extra money from Granddaddy's stipends, doled out from his estate, on Oral Roberts and a foundation she was organizing for Eldridge Cleaver.

Though Aunt Jennie wasn't always lucid, Mama still clung to her, holding fast to what remained of Aunt Jennie's sanity.

"Auntie," my mother continued, "you know how much I love Thomas, but I will leave his ass if he doesn't hurry up and find himself."

"Thomas is a good man, sweetie," Aunt Jennie replied, her lips making a distinct smacking sound from sucking in smoke from her cigarette. "Just be a little patient."

"But I can't do this again. And I don't want to begin to hate him for insisting we move here."

Mama despised crying, but I could hear her voice quivering, losing air. "I told Thomas, I told him. I said, 'Temmy's not going to fit in here. My child's not like these arrogant, pompous little brats. She's different.' She's got far more character, she's got so many more possibilities, Auntie. A place like this can make you crazy."

"Don't I know," Auntie said, snickering. "The bridge games alone can make you feel like jumping off one."

"I'm not going to have her growing up the way I did; there's no breathing room here. When Thomas asked me to marry him, I told him I didn't want this life. I grew up in it. And he promised me he wouldn't do this."

"Now, now, dear," Auntie consoled. "I know. You know I do. But Thomas doesn't understand yet. He wasn't brought up the way you were. For some people, too much wanting can make them crazy, too. You have to remember that your father was a doctor; Thomas's father was a drunk and his mother just one day up and left him. Now Thomas is simply trying to give Temmy something Grandpa Paulie never gave him: a father who's a real man, who's dependable."

My mother was quiet for a second. "Toward the end, I started to hate Paulie," she said. "I got so tired of his promises. Pointing to maps and promising to take Temmy here and there. He would have her dressed up, sitting on the sofa, waiting for him. He'd never show. I'd wind up telling some outlandish lie. Thomas never had the heart to tell Paulie to go to hell. That's because he *is* a good man, Auntie. A good father. One who keeps his promises."

"Thomas needs to be more, Felicia. You know that. It's the legacy you inherit from the woman who abandoned you and the drunk who stayed behind. That is, if you don't fall in yourself.

Bite down, dear. You're the one who said Thomas was a man who'd been through something. This is why you love him."

"I do love him, Auntie."

"Thomas has to find himself. Give him some time. Say a year? Can you and Temmy handle that?"

The last thing I heard was "a year" before the receiver nearly fell from my hand. The words did flip-flops and tumbles in my head. A year? I wasn't sure I could take another second away from the old house, away from Gerald. A year was an impossibility.

I waited for my mother to hang up the phone before I went back to my bedroom. Miss Lily had turned the Barbie doll bedcovers back and laid out a pair of pajamas on the end. That night, I slept in my underwear—when I did sleep. I spent most of the night plotting my escape.

Tempestt:
"I strained to see the man's face, to see under his lopsided fedora with the feather that angled upward to his God, to see his eyes."

The back-to-school carnival was in full swing when Daddy, Mama, and I made it down to the south lawn. It was early evening, and autumn, though days away, teased with sometimes gusty breezes off the lake. Lakelandites huddled in long lines for rides on the bumper cars, a merry-go-round, a Ferris wheel, and a roller coaster, which sat in the middle of the carnival, lighted like a sprawling Christmas tree. And children laughed and romped as if bright, shiny tentacles reached out of the rides and from the surrounding booths, tickling them as they waited in line.

The children not in line played tag or blindman's bluff or sat in clusters around jugglers, puppeteers, and clowns, many of whom were merely costumed older siblings. Mothers gathered, sipping lemonade and fruit punch, chatting, and smoothing down windblown pleats and hair-sprayed pompadours. Fathers rolled up their sleeves to try their luck at the booths, hoping that if they threw hard enough to knock down a glass bottle or used all their might to ring a bell, they'd be rewarded with a toy gun or a stuffed animal, similar to the ones that sat dizzy-eyed on my new dresser.

"Why don't you go make some friends, Tem," Daddy said, pushing me from between him and my mother. "See all the youngsters over there? Go introduce yourself. And we'll get back together in time for the fireworks."

"I'd rather go explore," I said, staring at my All Stars.

"Tem," his voice deepened, "you'll have more fun if you make some friends while doing it. Now go on over there and talk to those kids."

I began walking in the direction of a group of kids who seemed to be about my age. As I got farther away from my parents, I looked around to see if my father was watching, and when he was distracted, I veered off in another direction, toward the fence.

I passed a picnic table of maids and janitors. They sat behind a booth in the back of the carnival, laughing and talking as the table's lone red balloon bobbed from the wind. Their children had been allowed to visit for the day and they ran around in too-big clothing, remembering to stay within the imaginary circle their parents' reprimands had drawn around the table.

"Hey, Red," a voice started from behind.

I turned around. Miss Lily was holding a child on her lap, waving me toward her with a diaper.

"Hey," I said, walking over. Off in the distance, you could hear the rom-pah-pah from the carnival and the ringmaster's calls for revelry. But it was the white gulls sitting in the sycamore overhead, chirping and singing, that nearly made it impossible for me to hear her.

"Where you think you heading off to in that direction?" she asked, an octave higher than normal.

"I don't know." I shrugged. "I'm just going for a walk."

"Well, don't go near that fence," she said. "You don't want to have nothing to do with what's on the other side."

"What's on the other side?" I asked, now more curious than I'd been before.

"Just nothing that you need to pay never-mind to." She stood, propped the baby on her hip, and waddled off to rein in some kids who were straying too far from their assigned space.

I walked over to the fence and sat down, running my hand along the ivy. It was thick and incredibly uniform, though leaves broke away freely, falling like raindrops onto the grass.

I sat there wondering what Gerald was doing at that very second.

I was about to find my parents, feign a cotton-candy stomachache so I could go back upstairs, when I heard whimpering. A dog was on the other side of the fence. I couldn't see the little thing through all the layers of ivy and I could barely hear him over the gulls. He had begun to dig a hole underneath the fence and from time to time his cute little gray paws reached through to the other side.

The ground under the fence was soft and cool. And as I watched those little paws, I decided to help him. Not long after, I was the one crawling through the concave we'd formed. The dog met my face with wild licks and kisses. He jumped all over me. I mussed his knotted fur and he continued to jump and nip at me. I rubbed and rubbed the little fleabag until I looked up and my heart rose up into my throat.

The air had changed. It was damp and smelled of stale alcohol, urine, and long-standing garbage. That's what I noticed first. Grass had dulled and in most places there wasn't any, just landscaping of cracked asphalt and pockmarked concrete. Music was louder over here, more rhythmic, like our old neighborhood. In front of me stood a twelve-story redbrick building, surrounded by a group of clapboard row houses—homes to children too numerous to count. They were sitting on front stoops, dancing in the parking lot, chasing one another in the street. To my right, about a third of a block away, was a half-dead neon sign with a flickering arrow that pointed to O'Cala's Food and Drug.

Under the sign, on a platform that abutted the building, stood a street preacher in a black raincoat. From where I was standing, I couldn't see his face; I couldn't really hear his voice, just bits and pieces of his message. People started gathering around him. Women in long white dresses and shoe boots positioned themselves next to women in too-short skirts and sagging fishnet panty hose; men in shiny polyester suits, holding Bibles, stood next to men so drunk, they teetered on the edge of the sidewalk.

The men in the suits mumbled what started as a low gutteral sound, building to a near mantra: "Preach Rev. Mayes. Tell it. Tell the story. Tell the truth to the fallen. Preach Rev. Mayes. Tell it."

A few people deboarding the Thirty-fifth Street bus at the corner walked a wide circle around the gathering so that they didn't interrupt. But many, including those driving by in cars, stopped and stayed stopped, just to see and hear this man. I walked down to the corner, then crossed Thirty-fifth Street. My little friend was afraid to cross the street, so I left him whimpering on the opposite corner.

Standing on the edge of the sidewalk, I leaned forward, stealing glances whenever there was a break in the crowd. Above us on a ledge on the brownstone, even a flock of white gulls sat in their droppings, listening. I strained to see the man's face, to see under his lopsided fedora with the feather that angled upward to his God, to see his eyes. He was a big man. A towering presence. He was bigger than my father—so tall, he should have needed a building permit just to stand there. But he didn't only stand. At times, he moved as though fire were eating through his boots. Dust danced up from the boards beneath him as he stomped every inch of the platform, then bolted like a raven in between the cars, into the middle of the street.

A white man who was driving a Budweiser truck and heading west to one of the taverns down the block yelled something before jumping down from his cab. But seeing the preacher up close, he decided not to say a word. He was even quieter when four young boys pimped up to him, snatched his keys and his silver coin dispenser, and slid open the back of his truck. Beer cans started flying from hand to hand and rolling down the street. It was the only thing that for a moment stole the attention away from the preacher. The white man jumped back up into the cab of his truck, locking both doors, hoping the beer would render him invisible, I suppose. Three of the four boys stuffed as many cans as they could carry into their coat pockets and left. The last boy, whose two front teeth were the size of two large sugar cubes, joined the people on the corner. He, like the rest of us, watched the street preacher take his place back on the platform in front of the little drugstore.

When enough people had gathered around and all that remained in the back of the beer truck was a rising cold mist, the preacher officially began his sermon. And he began as if he were a sculptor laying out all his tools, preparing to pull from his ragged Bible, then create something from nothing. Shape, mold with those hands.

I watched his hands closely, nails bitten down to where they were supposed to bleed. I watched him bow his head and pray silently over a purple-and-gold Crown Royal bag that sat atop the garbage can, along with a muddied Dixie cup. I watched his rings—wedding bands on each finger—as he removed a gallon of water from an A&P bag behind him and filled the Dixie cup. When he anointed the crowd, his rings, a cheap yellow gold, caught the light from the neon sign. People moved back as he sprinkled water their way. They even moved sideways, but they didn't leave for good. I moved around the crowd until I was standing at the top of O'Cala's steps. That was where I could see him best. I had to get closer to him. I began to wish Gerald was with me, because a secondhand description wouldn't do Alfred Mayes justice. How could I explain this man to Gerald? He was God-like in stature and form. He was an explosion, all-consuming and equally devastating. Just the thought of being so close made me shiver.

"They call me the Reverend Alfred Mayes. And me and my New Saved congregation would like to welcome y'all tonight," he said. "We, the New Saved, have been on this here corner for many, many years, brothers and sisters. Why? 'Cause we on a mission from the Almighty. You see, y'all just don't want to act right. You been frequenting this little store behind me for the happy juice, thinking it'll save your poor souls, set you free. But I'm here tonight to tell you only God got the power to set you free."

Members of the congregation, now peppered throughout the crowd, echoed vehemently, "Only God got the power to set you free."

"Only God can give you peace," Mayes said, shooting his finger to the sky.

"Only God can give you peace."

The crowd moaned out a couple of amens and a few approving grunts. The boy with the big sugar-cube teeth lifted his beer can to the sky and took a sip. He then let out a foghorn burp that made several people jump, including me. Alfred Mayes turned slowly to look at him, then shook his head. Then an older woman, oblivious to the young boy, screamed from the back of the gathering. She stood hugging herself, rocking on her heels, snapping her head from side to side. "My son," she cried up to the platform. "I don't know where he is. He gone again. Help me find him. Help me. He somewhere along Thirty-fifth Street. I hear he's in O'Cala's." Her face was slick with tears and she held out her hands, trembling. And the reverend stepped down from the platform to stand by her side.

"You believe this store and all the others is Satan's work?" he asked.

She nodded.

"Will you help me and my New Saveds close it down? Close all of Thirty-fifth Street down?"

She sucked in two short breaths and nodded again.

And he said, "Peace," promising it to her as if it were this hawkable commodity, prepackaged and accessible to all. But only through him. Alfred Mayes helped the woman bow down before him. She smiled at his touch, into his hands, visibly humbled by his rings. And the two prayed right there on that sidewalk, mumbling quietly while everyone watched.

I turned around to look at the little liquor store that was the focus of so much discontent. It was in the basement of an old brownstone. The arrow on the sign did its best to point it out so the world wouldn't miss it, though the Reverend Alfred Mayes and the other preachers were doing their best to will it away. About five superclean steps led down to the entrance. And there was a picture window with cardboard signs advertising the day's sales on all kinds of sodas and juices and health tonics. One sign, cocked sideways just below a bullet hole, offered HOT COFFY 5 CENTS, although Miss Jonetta later told me hot water hadn't made its way down to that store in years, let alone hot coffee. She said anything hot was hot on its own accord and didn't need help from electricity.

Alfred Mayes once again returned to the platform. The woman

looked peaceful and ordered, as though she'd indeed been touched by God. Once more he raised his eyes heavenward, this time promising, "No more crying or hard times. No more heartaches or hurt feelings. I was a sinner myself."

The congregation sang out, "Well." They sang it as though they had no more words inside them, and to sing it made them rise on the balls of their feet and stretch their bodies to the reverend in a force so strong, we all were pulled closer toward him.

"I was lost in this hell along Thirty-fifth Street," Mayes said. "And Jesus found me. I've been a pimp and a hustler." With each word, he stooped, carrying a heavy load. "I've been a gambler and jailbird. A cheat." He then stood straight, suddenly free of his burdens. "But the God I serve—I said, the God I serve, the God of Abraham, of Isaac, of Moses—can change that. All you need is a little faith. God said a faith even the size of a tiny mustard seed, and he'd give you peace!"

His voice was so powerful that it echoed throughout your chest and your palms began to feel hot and sweaty and your eyes began to see but not see. Every face and every body, every upturned hand and outstretched soul belonged to Alfred Mayes.

And then, when he knew he had us in his grip, when nothing short of a storm could rip us from him, he cried out, reared back, and started spinning around and kicking with those jackboots at something or someone only he could see. Unintelligible words spit-fired from his mouth. Many of the people standing around were even dancing with him in the street, bottles flying and burdens lifting. Every now and then, Alfred Mayes stopped dancing, just long enough to catch his breath and some of the pages flying from his Bible.

A few of the people were reaching into their pockets and throwing dimes and quarters up on the platform. Again he'd stop long enough to pick up his earnings and drop them into his Crown Royal bag. All the while, I watched every move he made, every twist and every turn. I must admit, I, too, was taken in. I could hear my heart pounding in my chest. I swear I felt the sidewalk shift.

And then he walked over to me. He knelt down on one knee. I stepped back a bit. He held out his Bible and I looked into his eyes, red and deeply set, glowing from the sweat dripping off his brow. He told me to place my hand on top of the Bible.

"Don't be afraid, little sister," he said. "The Lord don't want you to be afraid."

The glint in his eye grew wide. He pushed back his hat, wiping his brow with the sleeve of his jacket. I noticed a long, fleshy scar, shaped like a lightning bolt, that ate into his hairline and shot down just above his left eyebrow. Staring into the scar, I was about to reach out to him when someone grabbed me from behind. It was Miss Jonetta. That was how we met, and she scared me so bad, I nearly wet my pants.

"Child," she said, "I wondered who them rusty legs belonged to. I saw you up here out my window and I wondered. Honey, I won't bite. Come visit me for a while."

"But . . ." I said, still looking into Alfred Mayes's eyes.

"You just come here and visit with me for a while," she said. And she grabbed me by the hand. "Wind too strong out here for a little girl."

She guided me by my shoulders, leading me down the stairs. I tried to turn to look back at the reverend, but she made me face forward. She pushed open the half-glass, half-aluminum door, then looked over her shoulder at Alfred Mayes, still at the top of the steps, kneeling, holding out his Bible. She gave him a piercing look. I could see her reflection in the door just before we entered and she slammed it behind her.

The store itself wasn't bigger than my new bedroom. But, unlike the rest of Thirty-fifth Street, it smelled wonderful, a mixture of heavy rose perfume and lemon oil. As soon as I crossed the threshold, she nodded for me to wipe the mud off my All Stars on a welcome mat by the door. When they were as clean as I could get them, I looked up and saw the barrel of taffy candy. Never mind that *1 cent a piece* was scribbled on the side in shaky chalklike lettering. Miss Jonetta saw the way my eyes widened and my lips curled, and she handed me one of the purple wrappers. In the center of the store were two aisles of the freshest bread around. Miss Jonetta said it was fresher than the bread at the Jew-owned bakery down the street and so fresh that customers sometimes complained it tasted a little strange and caused stomach cramps. The bread occupied shelves with jars of maple syrup, molasses, and strawberry preserves. Next to the first aisle was a floor display of Kotex napkins, carefully stacked into a cinder-block pyramid, which, she said, her brave male customers often leaned against to show how manly they were. On the west wall was an elaborate oak cabinet filled with everything from vodka to Rip-ple to castor oil. In front of that was the cracked checkout counter and the cash register with the stiff buttons. On the east side of the store sat a wobbly old table with four equally wobbly old men. Two were playing checkers, the other two watching, refereeing. And in the back of the store was a vomit green Philco refrigerator that smelled funny and spewed frost on the upright piano and Victrola at its side. Above all that, on the wall, hung a yellowing Pepsi-Cola clock, which Miss Jonetta said had "sometimey hands."

Miss Jonetta pulled a stool up in front of the counter for me. She stood behind the counter and grabbed a white cloth from underneath and started wiping it down, though it didn't need it.

She was a fair-skinned woman with satiny black hair, pulled into a bun so tight that if a bobby pin got loose, it would take your eye out. I didn't mean to stare, but it was those ruby red lips, that oval ebony mole on her right cheek, and those long "they're mine because I bought them" eyelashes that batted and winked and fluttered at will. I knew she was about as old as Miss Lily, but Miss Lily didn't look anything like Miss Jonetta Goode. Miss Lily didn't have it in her.

"Who that you got there?" one man called from the table.

"Just mind your own business, Chitlin," Miss Jonetta said.

"You hear 'bout President Ford, young lady?" the man yelled. He removed his white earplug from his ear and pushed his transistor radio to the center of the table. "I don't like him much, but I sure don't want to see old paleface dead." This time, Miss Jonetta gave the man her bullet stare, then went back to wiping down her counter.

Because I noticed her hemline, and only because I noticed, she feigned modesty and adjusted her well-fitting purple skirt to midthigh. Then she adjusted her pale pink sweater with the pale pink and white bows that saluted every man who entered the store. Miss Jonetta believed wholeheartedly that clothes weren't only meant to fit; they were meant to belong.

"So, Miss Ma'am," she said to me. "What's your name?"

"Tempestt," I answered.

"Tem who?" She stopped patting down her skirt and looked at me out of the corners of her eyes.

"My name is Tempestt Rosa Saville, ma'am."

"My Lord. Umph. I'm not sure what kind of pains your mama was having when she came across that name."

"Ma'am?"

"Never mind, Child. Don't mean no disrespect to you or your mama, but that ain't no name for a pretty little girl. And while we're on it, this ain't no place for a pretty little girl. What you doing out so late by yourself?"

"It's not late," I said, watching the hand of the Pepsi-Cola clock approach 6:30.

"Honey, I know late when I see it," she said. "Where you from, Child?"

"Over here." My voice was hesitant.

"You ain't from over here."

"Uh-huh." I nodded vigorously, hoping that would convince her.

"Child, don't you know I know things you too young to even think about? I can look at you and tell when you're lying, and I know you ain't from over here. Now spill it, honey."

"My family just moved across the street, ma'am."

"Don't lower your eyes, honey. Lakeland?"

"Yes, ma'am."

"Well, Lakeland ain't no place to be ashamed of. People over here would sell they mothers to live around all them famous, important people." She looked over both shoulders and moved closer. Speaking just above the jingling of her gold, silver, and bronze bracelets, she whispered, "By the way, you can drop that *ma'am* mess, honey. That's for old ugly women. Call me Miss Jonetta. That'll do just fine."

Her voice raised again and she said, "Oh no, Child, Lakeland ain't no place to be ashamed of. Lord, I remember when them buildings was being built. You wouldn't believe the projects was built around the same time, would you?"

I shook my head just to be doing something.

"Well, when they finished, the projects was the same old red-brick mess. One squat-ugly building. But your Lakeland? Oh, I ain't never saw them put nothing up so pretty. Each building seemed to rise out of the ground. They was so white and spotless.

Honey, they made the sun jump back and take notice. Prettiest things I ever saw. They was like soldiers in snazzy suits and brass medals, standing taller than anything connected to this earth, making God proud of black folks. Yes, Lakeland was something to behold.

"But, those of us along Thirty-fifth Street here was allowed to see it just for a while. Not long, mind you. Because after they put up that fence, each year the ivy got thicker and thicker, a tied-up, tangled-up mess, so bad, we couldn't even see them anymore. Couldn't even wave a 'How do?'"

She brushed my bangs back down on my forehead and wiped my face with an unused section of her white towel. But she never mentioned the color of my hair. Never. And I didn't fight her the way I had most people who touched me as though red hair gave out privileges black and brown didn't.

"Well, enough of all that," she said. "Now, this is what I want you to do."

Just then, one of the men at the table jumped up from the game of checkers and yelled, "Well, shut my mouth wide open. King me, motherfucker. King me." He clapped his hands and did a little fan dance around the table until the floorboards creaked and fluttered.

"Excuse me, honey," Miss Jonetta said. "He don't win too often, and when he do, he tends to get a little stupid in the head." She placed her hands on those hips. "Fat Daddy, didn't I tell you to watch your words in my store?"

He didn't answer, just kept smiling at the checkerboard.

"I told you us girls got delicate ears, damn it. Us girls don't need to hear all that mess. Us girls is ladies and wants to be treated as such. This place may be a hole-in-the-wall, but it ain't no gutter. And take your hat off in my store."

She took a deep breath as she beckoned for the man sitting next to Fat Daddy. His name was Hump. Miss Jonetta walked over to the window, pushed back off-white sheer curtains, making sure Alfred Mayes had gone. Dusk had layered the sky crimson, purple, and a navy blue, and without distractions up on the sidewalk, it was clear to see the mud splatters on the window.

Miss Jonetta told Hump—Mr. Hump, I called him back then—to take me home.

"Now, grab her hand," she said, "and don't let it go till you get to the gate way down yonder. Now don't let it go, I said. I'm gone go to the corner and watch y'all till I can't see you no more."

To me, she said, "It was nice meeting you, young lady. You stay over there, honey, where it's real safe. 'Tain't safe over here on Thirty-fifth Street. You understand? 'Tain't safe over here at all. You just stay your cute little self right on the other side of that fence. Okay?"

I smiled and nodded, knowing full well I'd be back as soon as I could break out again. When Mr. Hump and I reached the sidewalk, I could see the light from the el a few blocks down. I remembered it from the night before. Only this time, I could hear the train's squeals. As I steered the old man back to the opening the dog and I had carved out of the ground, I thought about Gerald, the el tracks, and my plan to run away. I hated Lakeland already. That was clear. Didn't care for Miss Lily much, either. But I decided my plan could wait a few days. As much as I missed my friend, I had to come back to Thirty-fifth Street. I had to see Miss Jonetta again, and even more I wanted desperately to see the Reverend Alfred Mayes.

CHAPTER 6

Miss Jonetta:
"Me and the regulars would keep a watch over her."

I was sixteen years old when I first set foot on Thirty-fifth Street and first saw Alfred Mayes. And when Child came that night, I knowed exactly what she saw while staring into his old devil eyes. I had saw it myself, lo them many years ago. Honey, them eyes could cast a spell. They invited you in. Told you to make yourself at home, and then before you got comfortable good, they done grabbed hold of the corners of your soul and shook till your whole being was shuffled in the darkness, till you hardly could speak your name. Child didn't have sense enough to be scared for herself, but I was scared for her. The Right Reverend Alfred Mayes and me went back a long way.

As I finished closing the store that night, all I could do was think about that little girl—her pretty red hair, her cute little crooked smile, the way she walked holding Hump's hand, looking over her shoulder, waving back at me. There was something about Child that was special. I saw that the moment I laid eyes on her, just like I could tell she was coming back no matter how I warned her to stay away. When she nodded, even after I asked her if she understood it wasn't safe over here, I knowed that nod was a lie.

Like I said, I was sixteen when I came to Thirty-fifth Street and first saw Alfred Mayes. It was the summer of 1932. And I don't mind saying I was fine, long black hair, with an even finer waist. Everybody say I looked just like my mother, a cross between Mahalia Jackson and Bessie Smith. But high yellow as honey dew, with big dimples and green eyes trimmed in amber. My mama died birthing me, so I never got a chance to see her. I had to take everybody's word. I still keeps a photograph in my pocketbook that shows me in my fine days, though. It's of me and my big sister, Essie, sporting Sunday flop hats with wax sunflowers and gingham dresses, looking cleaner than the board of health (even though there was a few holes here and there we tucked out of view).

The night we made it to Thirty-fifth Street we'd been in Chicago a couple of months. Essie and me waited for everyone crowded in that old tenement house we was staying in to fall asleep. We was two young girls sneaking out our bedroom window like two men tipping out on their wives. We had on the same Sunday dresses and hats we had on in that picture, and some fresh-from-the-kitchen bacon grease that we spread across our legs and elbows to get rid of the ash. We thought this was a occasion to be fancy.

I was the one that wanted to go to Thirty-fifth Street. Poor Essie, I just drug her with me. She was three years older, but I always led the way to the fun stuff. I probably wouldn't a gave a hoot about the place if Aunt Ethel hadn't warned us to stay away, hadn't slapped our faces with her old gnarled hands with that warning. My face carried her whole handprint; Essie was much darker, so her print went away faster. But the hurt was something neither of us could easily rub off.

"It ain't nothing but Satan's Row, a hole that shoulda burned down when the rest of Chicago was on fire," Aunt Ethel told us, making a ugly face, worser than the one God left her with. "The only good thing about it is the New Saved preachers. And all the good work we're doing to try to lift it out of darkness. Now, I want you girls to stay away, you hear? Your papa works too hard for you to not mind."

Then the old heifer fell to her knees, with her lace handkerchief pressed against her flat chest, and baptized us in her spit. She yanked us to our knees and mumbled all kinds of prayers, trying to protect us, she said. All the while, she pinched and tugged our ears, making sure we heard what she said, what God said. Oh, she was full of horse hockey and evil as hell, which is now her final resting place. We found out later that the money Papa was giving her to feed us, she used to boost her tithes at that New Saved church, instead of putting food in our bellies.

Anyway, I came to Thirty-fifth Street that night the way the three wise men came following that star. The bright city lights called me. (They was lamps, but any light is bright when you from the country.) And when I got there, Lord, the street, all that mud, was soft as sweet cream and seemed to mold to my feet—my old, tight, run-over shoes. And the people? Ladies, beautiful ladies, in feathers, around their sleeves, around their necks, and dangly wanna-be pearls and diamonds. White satin gloves and expensive slippery dresses that knowed when and where to hug, and when and where to flow. Fine, fine men, coffee black, coffee creamed, coffee in-between, in suits with fat wallets and shined shoes and processed dos so slick, they glowed in the dark.

I looks back now and have to chuckle to myself because I remember Essie and me walking so close to each other and holding on so tight, you woulda thought we was in a wind tunnel. I don't know which was opened wider, our eyes or our mouths. You see, Thirty-fifth Street was like something you see in a picture show or only hear about when some crazy uncle gets too drunk to keep his business to himself.

Folks was everywhere. Yelling from the windows, high over the street. I remember one woman standing in nothing—I mean *noth-ing*—but her corset and garters and holding a glass of "feel-good," toasting to the full moon. Young boys our age was swinging from the fire escapes; some was sliding along the sidewalk, in all kinds of fits; another group was roasting a pig, or what we hoped was a pig, over a bonfire in the alley while basting themselves with the contents of three slop jugs.

Each old brownstone we passed offered up something different, so we had to stop and take a gander into the large windows. There was a jazz joint—Club Giovanni, they called it back then—smoke-filled and dark. It headlined a woman in a tight, velvety, berry red dress who was singing some hootchie-cootchie number, running her hands up and down her thighs and in between her legs, across the dollar bills in her cleavage. She rubbed as she wig-gled in front of this dude on the sax. When she passed, shaking those ripe tomatoey hips, his old horn wailed out kisses and spoke in tongue, honey, hoping she'd tarry for a while. (Essie and me almost fell out, because the closest we ever came to something like that was Sister Pearl at the AME church down by the river in Annington County. Some Sundays, she would sing "Amazing Grace," then get the Holy Ghost and rub herself with the tam-bourine in ungodly places. Even Papa said she was nasty. And in God's house.)

The club was so dark, Essie and me could hardly see, but we saw one other thing before moving on. We saw Alfred Mayes. At the time, I didn't know what I was looking at, or I surely woulda ran as fast as I could back to Aunt Ethel's. They say the devil you know is better than the one you don't. But, at the time, all I could see was this tall, fine black man. Built like a African warrior. He had shoulders from sea to sea. Regal. Cheekbones carved out like mountains. He was dressed in a bright yellow suit trimmed in black, shined from head to toe. He rose slowly from a round table in the front of the club. If there was a spotlight, it woulda crowned him king. The way he strutted up to that woman on that stage made my thighs shake and my ankles sweat. When he touched her, it was like she was a ruby ring he had took off for a while to let sparkle and now was about to wrap right back around his little finger. She stopped singing, stood jellylike. I stopped breathing. He grabbed her waist with one hand, pushed up on her breasts with the other, loosening the dollar bills in her cleavage. Then that sister climbed Alfred Mayes like he was a mighty oak, planted by the river. Green leaves falling all over. She grinded her body into his. And he grabbed her fanny and they squeezed and hugged and touched each other as they did a slow, nasty dance. I started to wiggle with them, hips moving from side to side (a little number I'd put together in a barn back home). Essie slapped me on my fanny. Soon every man in there who had blowed her a kiss or offered her a ride home got the message—a beep, beep, beep from Western Union, honey—that she was off-limits. She belonged to this big dude Alfred Mayes.

Essie grabbed my arm and shook her head. "Johnie," she said, her voice a near mumble, "we ain't suppose to be seeing all this." Well, I knowed that; still, I didn't want to uncement my feet. I was sixteen years old and stupid, caught up in that tingling feeling women know from experience and little girls only giggle about. I didn't see Alfred Mayes leave Club Giovanni right then that night, but it wasn't because my fool eyes wasn't looking hard enough.

Next door to the nightclub was the policy house. The men was sashaying out with pocket change spilling over the sides. I ain't never seen so many colored people with so much money in my life. I wanted to hang out there for a while, too. But Essie pulled me away when this young boy came flying through the door and landed near our feet. Pockets turned inside out. Somebody had mashed his head good. Razor marks slit across both his cheeks. He crawled into a vestibule, licking his wounds like a old dog that'd met up with a coyote in the middle of a field.

Two doors from that was this long line of men and boys, some pressed, others dirty and dusty from a day's work at the stockyards and steel foundries. The line whipped nearly around the block. White police officers walked past twirling their sticks; some stopped to get in line. Essie and me was so green, we thought this was an example of what Papa meant about the long lines of men and boys that form during wartime—men and boys in line, signing up for tours of duty to serve their country. Ha, wouldn't be no war for another ten years! These men was all waiting for some service, uh-huh. Rationed if need be. This was the whorehouse, biggest, finest brownstone within miles. Even had a wraparound porch that the women wrapped themselves around like tinsel and holly. But that was at night. During the day, they was nowhere to be found because the first floor doubled as an insurance agency.

Rumor had it that Robert "Mr. Ribs" Price, the first colored to own a chain of restaurants in Chicago, opened a ribs joint next door so that when the dudes finished their business, they could walk a few paces and grab a rib, with a smile on their face. Business got so good, I hear told, that—with the help of some mob money—Mr. Ribs bought the whorehouse and opened the tunnel underneath the two buildings. Police had closed it down during Prohibition, when people was trying to haul bootleg from place to place. So, with the tunnels open, some men's wives never saw them again. Wasn't no need to go home for dinner, or anything else.

Papa used to say for every left there's a right and for every up there's a down. Well, Thirty-fifth Street was no exception. Because that night, for every sin we saw committed on that street, for every house of ill repute, there was at least one street preacher running interference, trying to wash everybody white as snow. At the corner of Thirty-fifth and Bernard Street stood the neighborhood's one storefront church. Every breath that came in and out my aunt Ethel's body had something to do with that church. She loved it so much. Its members called themselves the New Saved people and they just kept churning out New Saveds all night, left and right. Left and right.

You think the so-called sinners cared? They knowed getting in most places meant getting past them preachers, their bug-eyed stares, their questions. But everybody came ready for the fight. And them New Saved preachers was pretty uppity, mind you. What made a bunch of men with gold teeth, dressed in Crooks Brothers suits and wide-brimmed hats think they had something to say about getting into heaven, nobody knows. Seems to me most people on Thirty-fifth Street had already found heaven, one way or another. Or at least thought they had.

But them church girls surely stood their ground behind their men. They was on firm footing—with gold teeth, tall white wigs, bleached and starched white dresses that swung below their knees, and shoe boots with ties—belting some tune, maybe good for my soul but hell, fire, and damnation on my ears. Lord, them New Saved women couldn't sing. I don't care how new and saved they was supposed to be. Essie and me couldn't believe it. When they was done, everybody hummed, and not long after, Bibles and wigs soared toward the heavens. And them white pigeons overhead cried out, too. Flapping here to there. All that bad singing got on their nerves, as well. Didn't help much, being a bird.

Essie and me didn't stand long around them preachers. There was more of this place to see. We did feel a tad guilty, mind you, so we dropped a penny in one of their gold-plated canisters. Then we scooted past them to the cute little drugstore on the corner, O'Cala's Food and Drug.

The first thing that hit us as we walked down those steps and opened that creaky door was the smell. That steel window fan mixed up some stuff—cigarette smokestacks, stale bread, cheap cologne, and at least five or six behinds that were old and cried out for a bathing. But for the people who made it inside, the regulars who came to play cards as well as those who came down just long enough to get medicated, none of that mattered.

At first, Essie and me stood in the doorway. I was just a-gaping. I watched the woman behind the counter, watched her pretty red fingernails plunking the cash register. Essie was too busy trying not to rub against the walls, holding herself like something was about to jump out and bite her and she didn't want to get bit. When everybody started staring at us like we was crashers at a party, I throwed my head up and switched on up to the counter. I kept my arms close to my body, stifflike, in case Essie had a mind to grab at me, pulling me back. I stood between two men who to this day I still ain't sure knowed I was there. And I listened like they did as each time somebody placed an order, the doors of the cabinet let out a pop, then a swish. Each time, I swear, a little dude at the table in the corner just rocked back and forth in his chair, his rusty body moving like the clapper of a dinner bell.

When it was my turn, I said to the woman, "I'd like me a bottle of White Pork, please." I said it the way I'd heard the man in front of me say it.

"You sure?" the woman said, twisting her mouth.

"I am," I said. I reached up my dress, pulled out my nation sack, and cut my eyes over to Essie. Poor thing was two steps from fainting. We both knowed wasn't no money in it. And in lifting my dress, I'd showed too much leg and too many patches for her liking.

"Is this for here or for walking?" the woman said, reaching for a sheet of newspaper that she used to wrap up people's business.

"Uh," I said, searching my nation sack. I giggled and fanned myself with my hat, like you do when you surprised to see something you ain't supposed to see. "Silly me," I said, "I plumb forgot my money." I backed away from the line.

Before Essie grabbed me and pulled me out the door, I touched the clover leaf wrapped in satin hanging over the threshold. I ran my hands through it the first time because old people used to say satin brought you a lifetime of luck. The second time was because it was soft to the touch.

It's a funny thing what patches can and can't do. They can cover up the holes in your clothes, but they don't do nothing for the ones in your heart. Especially if the person sewing can take you or leave you. And even more if the person sewing hates the very path that led you to her door. A little girl wants to know she belongs. And my own aunt Ethel made it clear I didn't.

That night we walked back to Aunt Ethel's house, I felt so light. It was like every hole in my old dress was suddenly patched over with satin cloth. And the threads that hung beneath the hem had been seared off from the heat of Thirty-fifth Street's lamps. At the time, they made me feel safe and warm. I skipped half the way and Essie skipped only to catch up with me. I lifted my dress, twirling as I walked, flinging my braids from side to side. Then I slipped into a switchy walk and pretended I was wearing one of those feathery things the women carried on their shoulders. I pretended my ugly shoes was high heels, and my worn socks was silk stockings dark enough to cover belt-buckle scars.

When we got to Aunt Ethel's, we tiptoed around to the alley to the fire escape, where we'd hid our nightgowns. We climbed it, changed clothes, and when we tried to sneak back into our bedroom window, lo and behold, Aunt Ethel was sitting on our bed.

"Just come on in," she said, that black belt snaking around her fat folded arms. "Just bring your no-good selves right on in."

Essie froze at first and started shaking, poor thing. Shaking and shaking. Then she slid on over the windowsill, flipping one leg over the other. I followed right behind her. We both stood for a second side by side, in front of Aunt Ethel. Nobody saying nothing. Nobody even blinking. Then it hurt my heart to hear the pee drops plopping to the floor. Essie was that afraid. It hurt me even more when she bowed down and crawled across the splintery wood over to Aunt Ethel's wide feet. "I'll be good, Auntie," she cried. "I'll change my wicked ways."

Before I knowed it, I was jerking at my sister's arm. "Get off your knees," I said. I pulled her over to the window and I began throwing the few things we owned into a brown paper sack. All the while, I kept my eye on Aunt Ethel. "C'mon, Essie," I said. "You gotta come with me, now. We don't belong."

At first, Essie just sat by that window like my lips was moving and there was no sound. Then every time I tossed something into the bag, she took it out. We kept pushing and pulling stuff until Aunt Ethel stood up and yelled, "Enough!"

Seeing me still gathering my things, unmoved by the force of her voice, she said, "Where you think you going?"

"I'm leaving this hellhole," I said. I stood up straight as I could.

"What you say in God's house?"

"This ain't God's house," I said. "You starve us and call us nasty names. And you beat us like we dogs. You ain't new or saved."

"What you say? What them half-white lips of yours say? Is this the thank-you I get for taking you in? Nobody else wanted you." Her voice got real low and she got quiet for a spell the way animals do before a great storm. "Essie is fine, 'cause I know she belongs to my brother. She can't help it 'cause y'all's mama was a lyin' whore. We all know no two blue-black people can make a white."

"I ain't white," I said, clenching my teeth. "And Mama wasn't no whore."

"We all know no two blue-black people can make a white."

Then she came toward me, balling her fists up, that old belt sliding to her feet. She walked real close in my face, reared back, and hit me so hard, I fell on the bed. All kinds of purple started whirling in front of my eyes. Essie ran over, but she couldn't help. Aunt Ethel's stare made her freeze before she got to me.

"Go get me a glass of water," Aunt Ethel said to Essie. Aunt Ethel liked to dip the leather belt in some water when she really wanted to make the lashes suck our skin up through the holes.

But Essie didn't move.

"Go get me a glass of water, I said."

And when Essie, poor thing, still didn't move, Aunt Ethel pushed Essie out of the way and went to get it herself. I tried to hurry to talk some sense into my sister. "Essie, ain't you tired of getting hit upside your head, being beat everywhere but the soles of your feet? Essie, ain't you tired of being told you no good? Essie, ain't you tired of bedding down hungry, your belly aching? Mouth so dry you ain't got enough spit to spit. Essie, honey, ain't you just tired?"

But she didn't want to leave Papa there in that wilderness. So I told her I was headed for the big time; hell, I had seen the light and Alfred Mayes! "I'll come back for you," I whispered to her. Didn't take the bag. Just took what was on my back—that nightgown I had on—and my raggedy dress and them old muddy shoes

waiting for me on the fire escape. "I'll come back for you, Essie."
One leg was hanging out the window, the other still in that god-
forsaken room. There was a bright white moon that night in front
of me, so big, I reached out for it and it took me by the hand.
Why it later left me, all by myself, I don't know.

For me, leaving Papa wasn't too hard because him having to
work three jobs had turned him into a monster, yelling and
cussing people when he was at home. Through the years, I realized
the pain he musta felt. While down south, he thought "up north"
was a step away from heaven. Only when the train made that final
stop, he learned quick that "up north" had to go some more
before it got anywhere near glory. He, like many others, thought
"up north" meant he could be a real man. Could take care of his
two girls without having to bow to the white man. Could tell them
without lying, without having to go off in a corner to cry about
that lie, that they could be somebody. But then he got to Chicago
and couldn't find a job for the longest, had to move in with his sister and leech. Then had to work piecemeal work instead of using
the training he'd got from forming and laying bricks. Well, his
pride was stung real bad. And that was worser than any whipping
any white man coulda laid on him. It even left deeper scars.

Like I said, leaving my father wasn't as hard as it shoulda been.
The problem was leaving my sister. Because that was like leaving a
part of me. I saw her through the years, but we never got close
again before she died. Now, when I think back, I don't know
which one of us was better off. Me with Alfred? Her with Aunt
Ethel? Oh, honey, sometimes hell just ain't got no one particular
address, especially if that address is anywhere near Thirty-fifth
Street.

But I tell you, I wasn't about to let Child fall into the wrong
hands. By 1975, it had been forty-three years since I stepped

onto Thirty-fifth Street. And the place hadn't changed. Sure some of the buildings, like some of the people, had crumbled out of existence. And Lakeland now took up more city blocks than you could count on fingers. But the same cloud hung over that street and darkened everything connected to it.

I knowed there wasn't a word I could utter that woulda made Child change her mind about coming back. That's why I sent Hump to stand near that fence every day about the time I thought school would be out. I wanted him to watch her walk over. I wanted him to make sure she made it to the store safe. I told him not to follow too close behind. Just close enough to make sure some nasty old bastard wouldn't snatch her from herself the way Alfred Mayes had sopped me up. Me and the regulars would keep a watch over her. Because I wasn't gone let no somebody lay his hands on Child.

CHAPTER 7

Tempestt:
"Peace."

I spent the entire weekend thinking about returning to Thirty-fifth Street. I wanted to see Miss Jonetta, but I wanted even more to see Alfred Mayes. By Monday morning, school was to begin, and I lay in bed still thinking about him and his shopping bags of peace offerings. I had decided that the contents of his bags would allow me to find peace, by allowing my family to return to our life before Lakeland. Peace was me flopping around our old wooden floors in my father's boots, my big toe sliding down into the concave his had made. Peace was my mother and me in his arms.

I lay still under my covers until I heard a faint clicking sound outside the French doors. From the window, I saw my father sitting on the balcony off the living room. Plants with wilting flowers swayed back and forth above his head, but he didn't notice them. It was a cool, damp morning, so I wrapped myself in the Barbie doll curtains as I peeped carefully. I didn't want him to see me. He was sipping his morning coffee. Steam rose from his mug to meet his breaths, which were slow and deliberate. As he bent over, shoulders sagging, he rested his elbows on his knees and stared into the waves, the rocks, and a red-gold band of sky that stretched far beyond where, even at twenty-two flights up, we could see. The horizon was interrupted only by the lighthouse, sitting far off in the middle of the water.

In our old house, my parents often awoke together to watch the sunrise from the kitchen window. They'd stand over that drippy faucet, watching daylight climb the Jenkinses' tree house across the alley. They'd wait until columns of white light poked through the eyes of a cardboard owl I'd made in school and Mama had hung in front of the window. Then they'd call me or come wake me for breakfast. Many mornings, I'd pretend to just be rolling out of bed. After the Donaldsons' house was bulldozed and the lot left vacant, my parents' view of the sunrise also included a group of boys who gathered there from morning to midnight.

My father said this was evidence of the direction in which our neighborhood was going: straight to hell. Like the one of his childhood, which he'd never seen change from good to bad. By the time he was born into Chancey Park, he said, it was already a slum. No place for a child.

At about seven, I heard Miss Lily's keys jingling outside the back door. When she entered, I saw the light from the sewing room pass under my door. I tiptoed over to see what she was doing.

"Good morning, Red," she said. Her back was to me and she was smoothing her stockings up her legs, twisting a knot around the top. She then sat down at her table to read her newspaper. Though Mama wouldn't allow her to dust, vacuum, or make the beds, Miss Lily still had to spend the time. "I hear you sneaking up behind me," she said. She spread the newspaper out before her and snapped the pages. "Got eleven kids, so don't think you doing something I ain't seen before." She turned around. "Didn't I lay some nightclothes out for you? What you doing naked?"

"I'm not naked," I said, looking down at my underwear.

"Yes, you are," Mama said, walking up, patting my behind. "Is that clean underwear or dirty?"

I looked down at my undershirt again. "I could probably get another day out of it."

"Temmy, I wouldn't start if I were you," Mama said, making a fist and rubbing it against my nose. "Now you get your little self in that bathroom and wash your privates and change your underwear."

"But I don't feel so good. My stomach is woozy."

"Little girl, there's nothing wrong with your stomach but a case of butterflies. You'll be just fine. Now get."

While I was in the tub, my mother peeped into the bathroom and hung on the back of the door one of the most god-awful sewn-together pieces of material I had ever seen. It was a brown-and-beige plaid jumper dress with a white blouse for underneath. To complete the look was a pair of white ankle socks and a pair of black shoes with big steel buckles, anchors for the unduly rambunctious.

"Mama," I said, nearly choking on my words.

"It's ugly, I know," she said, kneeling by the side of the tub. "But don't come out without it." She took my face towel from my hand, lathered it, and began to wash my back. Lowering her voice, she said, "Your gym shoes are in your book bag. If somebody turns you in, I'll have to pretend like I didn't know. Understand?"

I nodded, smiling.

"Hurry," she said, standing. "Breakfast will be cold soon."

When I walked into the kitchen, Daddy stood. "Never seen you prettier," he said, pulling the seat out for me.

"Thomas, there's no sense in lying to that child," Mama said, rolling her eyes.

I sat down, first staring into, then picking over the muffins, scrambled eggs, and my father's favorite fried catfish that Mama had prepared. I suppose I was nervous about my first day, but I was also trying to force a response from my parents, who sat quietly clanking their silverware against their plates. This wasn't the normal raucous scene that met us for breakfast every morning: Daddy kidding about how Mama burned the toast, me pretending to keel over from food poisoning. This morning, we sat around like mannequins, stiff and terribly uncomfortable.

Before Daddy left to meet his class, he sat me down on his lap on the sofa. He looked out the window, and I could sense a speech coming on about how he was depending on me to be a good little girl today. But he didn't say anything. He gave me a hug and a kiss, told me to have a wonderful day. Gave my mother a dry peck on her forehead. And he walked on out the door.

Lakeland Academy sat midway between Lakeland's northern and southern borders, but just steps away from the lake. The school's design was meant to reflect its importance in the community. In short, its off-white facade looked like city hall, white columns, broad, sweeping steps, perfectly round hedges, and large windows, tinted green.

When Mama and I arrived at the academy, kids were lining up in neat little rows to go inside. Boys checked the knots in their ties; girls tucked socks and fluffed the pleats in their jumper uniforms.

Before going to the office to enroll, we saw Daddy and his class of eighth graders standing over by a group of rocks and a totem pole that each graduating class was allowed to decorate as sort of a rite of passage. I lifted my hand to my cheek and waved at my father, and he barely waved back with his ruler. In the old neighborhood, he'd have needed that ruler to beat the natives, but in Lakeland, corporal punishment of any kind, including a tug on the earlobe, was not acceptable, deemed too barbaric, uncivilized.

I watched my father until he gave his class the signal, a conductor's swoop of the arm, and they all marched through a set of double doors.

Mama held my hand as we walked up the stairs to the registrar's office. After entering, she walked up to the counter and rang the bell. I sat down on a wooden bench by the door. A woman came out from a room behind the counter. They talked for a minute; the woman nodded, then handed my mother a folder with a set of papers. Mama began filling them out.

Not long after, a girl about my age burst through the door. She wore no socks and her shoe boots were smeared with mud in a feeble attempt to polish them. As she ran up to the counter, stretching her thin body forward on tiptoes to ring the bell, I noticed her worn slip and her uniform, which clung too tightly around her chest and bunched up too much around her waist. Conscious of the misfit, she nervously pulled at her hem. The woman who had helped my mother was now on the telephone in her office, and she peeked outside the glass portion of her door. Holding her forefinger up to the little girl, she said, "Miss Nicholae, just one moment, please."

Finally, the girl stopped ringing the bell. She turned and paced in front of the counter, unfurling an envelop from her side pocket. She held it in her hand as though it were a jewel she'd shined all night.

"Good morning, Valerie," the woman said, approaching the counter. "I take it your father signed your letter?"

"Uh-huh," Valerie said, nodding. "Yep, he sure did."

Valerie handed the letter over and the woman told her to have a seat. She walked over to the bench where I was sitting and plopped down on the opposite end. At first, we took quick, polite glances so that no one could accuse us of staring. I looked down at her ashy ankles; I know she looked up at my red hair. But we said nothing as we tried to avoid each other by surveying my mother, the yellow, red, and orange cutout leaves pasted around the office, and the welcome banner that stretched between two fluorescent lamps, which hummed when the room was quiet.

"You new?" she asked, scratching her head and jostling two sandy-colored braids that draped over her shoulders.

"Uh-huh," I mumbled, scratching my knee, which didn't itch, and remembering to unpigeon my toes.

"I was new last year," she said, moving closer. "This year I'm old."

"Oh," I said. We were quiet for several more seconds as we watched the minute hand on the broad-faced clock across from the counter tick toward nine. We both jumped when the bell rang.

"I saw you at the carnival," she said, moving even closer and lowering her voice. "First I saw you talking to the fat maid; then I saw you crawling under the fence. I ain't told nobody, *yet*. Gimme a quarter and I won't tell."

"I don't have a quarter," I said, scrunching my face. "And if I did, why would I give it to you?"

She scooted over once more, until she was nearly sitting on my hand and I could smell the sour milk odor in her uniform and see the sleep crusts that stuck to her long eyelashes.

She looked over at the counter, somewhat distracted when the woman closed her door. Then she lowered her voice some more. "I was sitting on the grass, 'cause the Ferris wheel made me dizzy and sick. John told me not to go up so many times. He said I was showing my color. . . . But that's where I was when I saw you. You looked funny. Just kidding about the quarter. I ain't gone tell nobody." She crossed her heart, letting me know she meant it. "John is the head laundryman in the Five thirty-five building. We stay in a garden apartment in the basement. What building do you live in?"

Just then, the woman opened her door and walked back out to the counter. "Miss Nicholae," she said. Valerie got up slowly, as though she knew the news wouldn't be good. As she walked closer to the counter, she tugged on her dress, just one side, leaving the other side hiked up and lopsided.

"Sorry, Valerie," the woman said. "We need your father's signature, and this looks more like yours."

"But . . ." she started, staring at the returned letter lying on the counter. "But school start today and you want me to go to school, don't you? John say I could sign his name. He say it's okay. He ain't got no time, he said, 'cause ya'll rich folks working him to death. So he said it was okay if I done it."

"I know, Valerie, and I'm really sorry," the woman said. She looked over at Mama, who had stopped writing. "But we really need your father's signature. I just tried to call him. . . ."

"He doing his rounds," Valerie said, still staring at the letter, her voice nearly a whisper.

"Well, I'll try him later, and you come back tomorrow. Okay? Tell him how important it is for him to sign this."

She took the sheet of paper and a deep breath before turning around to leave the office. Her shoe boots made weird suction noises as she walked over to the door. Again, her uniform bunched up around her waist, but this time, she didn't bother to pull it down.

By the time I arrived in class, students had begun telling tales of their summer vacations. When I walked in, Mrs. Jackson, the sixth-grade teacher, interrupted a boy to introduce me. She turned to the blackboard and said, while writing my name, "Please welcome Miss Tempestt Saville."

And the class chimed, "Good morning, Tempestt Saville." Mrs.

Jackson directed me to a seat in the back, near a window overlooking the lake.

Students had come prepared with items from their trips. The boy resumed his story about how he'd spent several weeks hiking in the Grand Canyon. Another eager child passed around a train ticket from a vending machine in Japan. Another showed a tarboosh, a veil, and a bag of kola nuts from a caravan ride across the Sahara. Another displayed a string of worry dolls he had gotten from a pen pal who visited from Guatemala. He said legend had it that if you put the dolls under your pillow, your worries would go away. (I thought about the girl in the office as well as my parents and wondered if it was worth taking a chance on stealing the dolls.)

When it was my turn, I stood and told the class how I'd spent the earlier part of my summer eating gallons of ice cream because I'd had my tonsils removed. I'd become an expert at hurling wads of blood and flesh several feet into my grandpa Saville's spittoon. I told them how proud my father was that the spittoon had been passed down to yet another generation. Grandpa had used it for snuff (he'd also mistaken it for a urinal a couple of times, but I didn't mention that); Daddy had used it to gather fish scales when he cleaned his catch.

"I have my tonsils in a jar at home," I said, smiling and wishing I'd known the assignment a day earlier. "I can bring them in tomorrow if you want to see."

After looking out onto a group of students who sat with their faces balled up like clenched fists or their mouths hanging wide open, Mrs. Jackson said that wouldn't be necessary. And my account became the final one of the morning.

We spent the rest of the morning talking about one of Lakeland's most important social events of the year: the debutante ball. Although we sixth graders were too young to "come out," there was a part of the ceremony where we would prance around, curt-seying and smiling, just for the cameras and proud parents sitting on the sidelines.

My classmates stumbled all over themselves, trying to assist me in signing up for the to-do. "Mrs. Jackson, I can show Tempestt where the auditorium is." "Mrs. Jackson, Tempestt can practice marching out over at my house." "Mrs. Jackson, I can show Tempestt how to pick the proper gown."

But of course, during lunch, the niceties displayed in class didn't translate out on the playground. The little tribal rats were such snobs and had well-established klatches. The one among the girls was headed by Natalie Hubbard, a round-faced, breathy child with knock-knee. When she walked, her legs moved like scissors. The girls stood over by a small pond, their bodies staking out their territory.

I walked up to the group and said, "Hey," and Natalie looked over her shoulder and turned around.

I was sure she'd misunderstood me or perhaps hadn't heard, so I said, "Hey" again. She said, without turning around, "This is a private group." Then she did turn and she looked at my hair, say-ing, "What color is your gown for the ball?"

"I don't know yet," I said.

"With all that red hair, if I were you, I wouldn't choose green." She laughed and the other girls laughed. "You'd look like a Christ-mas wreath!"

Well, having not been born in Lakeland, my thinking was not to respond with equal glibness. I drew back to punch Natalie right in her fat snout. Fortunately, I thought about my father and how I didn't want to disappoint him. So instead of punching her, I gave her the finger and walked away to the sandbox, where I sat alone until the one o'clock bell sounded, ending the lunch hour.

The rest of the afternoon moved much like the first part, too slowly. We read, we wrote, and at three the bell rang, ending class.

Instead of students leaping from their seats and running to the coat closet, the way I was accustomed to doing, the class sat quietly and allowed Mrs. Jackson to finish her thoughts—even though her thoughts ran a five full minutes beyond the bell. She dismissed everyone except me, telling me that she hoped I enjoyed my first day. My mother was waiting downstairs for me, she said, and I should check with my mother before joining my class in the library, where all the students spent a couple of hours after school.

"Has anyone told you about library time, Tempestt?"

"No, ma'am," I said.

"Well, you're going to love it. Library time is your time. You sign in, then find a study carrel where you can read whatever you want for two hours. Or you can go into the theater and watch an educational movie. The topics are posted outside. We'll see you tomorrow."

I smiled and ran down the stairs.

The air had turned colder and the sky combined a harvest-wheat hue with an overcast pale blue. Mama was waiting on the steps for me with a sweater and an umbrella she had brought along because Miss Lily forced her to. Though the air was damp, mostly due to the lake, Mama said Miss Lily's back told her rain was on its way.

"How was your first day?" Mama asked.

"I hate it here," I said, staring at those blasted shoe buckles.

"It's only your first day," Mama said, hugging me. "Don't worry, Tem, everything'll be fine. And don't forget to mind your manners. I'll be back at five-thirty."

Mama kissed me and turned to walk back to the apartment. I waited until she was out of sight before I ran back up the stairs to the library and signed in. I found a study carrel in the back of the room, changed into my All Stars, and sneaked out when the librarian left her post. I ran outside the building, running low, like a little prisoner, all the way back to the south lawn where that little dog and I had dug the hole. The dirt blended well with the brown and beige in my jumper dress as I crawled under and ran as fast as I could to O'Cala's Food and Drug.

If I'd had more time, I suppose, I would have stopped at the top of those steps to try to think of a legitimate reason for returning to the store, especially since Miss Jonetta had warned me against it. I looked down the street, neck straining, eyes bulging, in search of Alfred Mayes. But the only New Saved preachers I saw were testifying about having realized the prophecy of the generation before them. Lost souls were soon to be saved, they said. Their voices screeched over the microphone, and their Holy Ghost stomps echoed off the platform. It had taken years, blood, and tears, but lost souls were soon to be saved. Sinners were about to bow down, beg for forgiveness. They could feel it, they said. That little liquor store and all the other places of ill repute along Thirty-fifth Street were about to face the wrecking ball, God's holy pendulum. And they dared anyone to doubt them.

I was on O'Cala's middle step when the door flung open. Miss Jonetta, standing in the entrance with Hump, saw me, half-smiled, and shook her head.

To Hump, she said, "Now, I know I told you I liked your cologne yesterday, honey. I don't mean no harm, but today you done drowned yourself in it. Like I said, it's too strong, Hump. Now you just sit out here and dab some of that off. Retha Mae won't be here for a while. Don't worry about her. You just dab some of that off and let this breeze stir around you for a spell. In fact, why don't you walk over to the pile to get my mail?"

Then to me, she said, "I thought I told you 'tain't safe over here? Maybe I didn't make myself plain enough?" She reached up, grabbed my hand, pulling me toward her. "Maybe I should speak louder, because I reckon you don't hear too good. You got some type of hearing condition?"

I shook my head.

"Of course you don't," she said, trying not to smile. "Just stubborn, I suppose." In the store, she sat me down on her stool behind the counter. While she tended to a few customers, I looked at the shelves underneath and saw several folded white towels, a stack of brown paper bags, a pair of pink fuzzy house slippers, many cartons of Kool, Newport, and Raleigh cigarettes, and a cigar box of Raleigh coupons.

I tugged on her arm. "What are these for?" I asked, pointing to the coupons. Daddy had turned me into an expert at saving coupons, especially S&H Green Stamps.

"They for some tangerine satin sheets," she said, "seen them while flipping through the catalog and took a liking. You know what satin is?"

"Uh-huh," I said. She could tell by the way my eyes shrunk that I wasn't really sure, so she pulled a red makeup bag from under the counter.

"Just to refresh your memory," she said. "Feel how silky smooth that is."

"Oh, now I remember," I said, smiling, holding the lumpy bag.

When the customers had cleared, she unfolded a towel, shook it out, and began wiping down her counter. She paid particular attention to a few scratches from old coins, paper clips, safety pins, which came from customers who emptied their pockets of every item including lint and clumped-together pieces of peppermint in search of enough money to pay for their cough syrup. Cough syrup was what Miss Jonetta said was in the bottles in her wall cabinet and the jug under her counter. Thus, O'Cala's Food and Drug.

"Hump's gone ask Retha Mae to marry him," she said, cleaning the buttons on her cash register. "That's why his nerves is bad. You'd think at sixty-two years old a man would be past jitters like that. . . . Pacing, spilling a whole bottle of cologne on himself. With all that cologne, Hump was about to choke us out of this little store. And, honey, this place can only stand one person at a time trying to smell good."

She looked at my uniform and said, "This your first day at school?"

"Yes, ma'am," I said.

She gave me another look, jogging my memory. "I mean, yes, Miss Jonetta."

"So how was the first day?"

"I hate it," I said, which apparently wasn't the right thing to say, because she stopped wiping down the counter and put her hands on her hips.

"What?"

"I don't like it there."

"And why not?"

"The girls don't like me. I don't like them."

"Why don't they like you?"

"I don't know."

"Why don't they like you?" This time when she asked, she was looking out the window at Hump. He was still pacing in front of the window, the shoelaces of his old lace-up oxfords beginning to untie.

"Because I'm new and different," I said.

"How different?"

I pointed to my hair as one obvious answer. And she pretended to be shocked by it. I told her that I wished my hair was the same color as hers.

And she said, "Child, between you and me, this is black number five from a bottle. It's been so long since I seen my real color, I wouldn't know it if it walked up beside me on a street corner. And don't waste your time worrying about them girls."

She smiled, leaned forward to look outside the window at Hump again. "Listen, them girls just got eyes full of envy is all. You'll learn as you get older that you could have crossed eyes and a harelip and somebody'll still find a reason to be jealous of you."

Flinging her towel over her shoulder and jerking her head in the direction of the table, she said, "You see them old men playing checkers? Let me tell you about each one of them and how different they are."

First, she pointed to a caramel-skinned man who wore a pair of dark gray work pants with suspenders and a red plaid flannel shirt.

"His name is Judd," she said. "I met him about forty years ago. He owns the ribs joint down the way. He used to stop by just to bring me a order. But since he retired about a year ago, he come every day. People could look at him and say he different. Don't look like he got much to offer beyond fixing a slab here and there. But every now and then, he goes back to that dead piano. And, honey, Judd, and only Judd, can thump it and make it rise up and talk. Oh, that thing's been out of tune for as long as you been on this earth. And he got another talent. I won't tell you what it is. But one day, Child, you'll walk in here and you'll hear him."

She looked up out the window again and I began to wonder why she was so concerned about Hump. She then pointed to the little man, barely taller than I was, who was sitting next to Judd. Wearing an out-of-season seersucker suit, Mr. Chittey, or Old Chitlin as Miss Jonetta called him, was puffing on an oversized cigar and impatiently searching for a static-free station on his AM-only transistor radio.

"Old Chitlin there is the owner of the building," Miss Jonetta said, smiling. "Mr. O'Cala left the building years ago when he was sure black folks was here and staying longer than a stopover. O'Cala did like the other white owners of the stores—just left. And everybody, including Chitlin there, got them a nook and took over. Ain't nobody got a mortgage."

"Somebody talking about me behind my back?" Mr. Chittey yelled from the table. "Got something to say and can't say it to my face?"

"Ain't nobody talking about you, Chitlin." She moved closer to me and lowered her voice. "Can't see a Mack truck, but he can hear better than two dogs. Anyway, Child, he got more money than the government. And is he tight? Whew! Got a '60 Le Sabre that ain't got nothing but twenty thousand miles on it because he afraid to run out a tank of gas. And you know with gas being as high as it is these days, he ain't about to go nowhere." She nudged me and laughed. "Don't know how he made all that money; just know he used to drive a ice truck in the thirties. And one of the people on his route was Al Capone. Now, I won't lie to you, he got a spot of hell in him, but he won't hurt you. It's just that men his size, who ain't never growed pass looking like a homely ten-year-old playing dress-up, tend to hold too much in. And they pop, from time to time. He keeps a twenty-two in his boot. Well, it starts the day tucked into his pants, but by late afternoon it done slid off his puny hip down to his boot. He pulls the little thing out every now and then, but it ain't loaded. Really, Child, so don't worry.

"You met Hump. Like I said, he about to propose. We call him our man of few words. He may pass you a note when he got something to say. And if he don't, well, then, just assume he done said all he wanted. The only other thing I can say about Hump is, I owe him my life." She stared off into someplace far away, then batted her eyes, returning to where she'd left off. "So the last one is Fat Daddy. Right across from Old Chitlin. We call him Fat Daddy to get around calling him his real name: Rooster Tucker.

He owns the pool hall on Grand. And if there's ever anything any-body needs, he can find it like nobody's business."

"Why is he called Fat Daddy?" I asked loudly. Fat Daddy heard his name and ran a welcoming finger along the brim of his hat. So I whispered, "He's skinny as a pole."

Miss Jonetta snapped. "Look, that ain't important," she said. "Just stay in a child's place. Understand?"

It would take me at least a couple more years to understand the abruptness of Miss Jonetta's answer. But I got it. It dawned on me one day as I reflected on Fat Daddy's swagger, his conked hair under his many hats, his three-piece wrinkled suits (which Miss Jonetta said made a liar out of permanent press), his kelly green elf boots, and his crotch, which looked like a few pairs of socks had been thrown in for good measure. Enough said.

Miss Jonetta looked out the window again; this time I'm sure she had forgotten she was talking to me. "Some so-called educated people might look at these men and think they ain't got nothing to offer because they look a little different," she said. "They sit around all day playing checkers, fussing, and cussing. Fat Daddy do most of the cussing. But I'll be the first to tell you, I'm grateful for their differences. Lord knows, they've helped me through the years."

"How?" I asked.

"Just know they have is all. Each of them in they own way. And do they have character? When the good Lord call them home, he gone be scurrying to find replacements.

"And I'll tell you another little story, Child, and this is some-thing I don't want you ever to forget: One day, years ago, I was down at Sarah's Beauty Shop with some other ladies. We each was getting a touch-up or some color. Well, we had all been talking about men, what we take, what we give. You know, girl talk, mostly telling lies. Anyway, we was about to leave, so we each put on our scarves, because the last thing you want after spending your last dime for your do is the wind to mess it up. Well, all of us put on scarves except this new lady, Lucinda, who had fit right in up until then. While we was tying the knots in our scarves, she politely pulled out a pair of stark white panties and draped them across her head."

"Panties?" I asked, eyes straining wide.

She nodded. "Panties, Child. I must admit, them was the prettiest panties I ever did see, nice little embroidery around the edges. I swear the store's owner, Sarah Ann, almost fainted. I may be crazy myself, but I have to downright admire a sister who can situate a pair of drawers over a press and curl like she just been crowned queen of England, grab her pocketbook, and flag herself a cab, like nothing happened . . . and never look back. So that's what you gotta do."

"Put a pair of panties on my head?" I asked, laughing.

"No, Child," she said, head tilted a bit. "You got to decide who you gone be, how you gone be it, and then don't look back, no matter who might say otherwise."

And with that, she smacked the counter and looked back up at the window. This time, Hump had fainted. Thick froth was bubbling up around his mouth.

"Lord," she said, "I was hoping this wouldn't happen. Judd, Fat Daddy!" She rushed from behind the counter. "Go get Hump. Look at him."

Fat Daddy said, "Shit," drawing it out like a song. Then both he and Judd jumped up from their seats and brought Hump in and sat him in a chair by the table. The chair's legs started to chatter against the floor with the twitching of Hump's body, and he immediately slid out of it. So Fat Daddy and Judd stretched Hump out on the floor.

Mr. Chittey grabbed his transistor radio, his cane, and hobbled over to me. He told me not to worry. "He does this all the time. Got something wrong with his brain," Mr. Chittey said. "He waits until I'm about to win my game, too. Ain't nothing but a spell. They come on when he get nervous or when he forget to take his pills." He leaned against the counter next to me. "I hear you live across the way, behind the fence. We ain't never had nobody from behind the fence here before. What's it like around all them important folks?"

Miss Jonetta interrupted, "Chitlin, ain't you got nothing better to do than bother that child?"

Mr. Chittey said, "Humph." He reached into his pocket and pulled out a handful of candy. "I know you people over there have fancy candy, but if you want some of ours from time to time, the barrel is over there," he said, pointing a dark wrinkled finger across the floor. "I just reaches in a couple of times a day. Ain't supposed to 'cause I got sugar. Red ones taste like medicine. So you don't want them. But the purple ones so good, they make you hurt yourself." He handed me two purple wrappers under the counter so Miss Jonetta couldn't see.

I smiled and shoved them into a secret pocket I'd made by converting a tiny rip into a major hole. Mr. Chittey didn't say anything further. We both watched as Hump flipped around the warped floorboards while Miss Jonetta tried to keep something shoved into his mouth and Judd and Fat Daddy struggled to hold him down. "Hang in there, old dude," Fat Daddy said. He fanned Hump with a loaf of bread with one hand, held on to his hat with the other. And after Hump's eyes rolled back in his head, flickered on and off like the neon sign above the door, it was over. Fat Daddy and Judd helped Hump back into the chair, where he sat slumped over, looking lost and disoriented. Miss Jonetta stood over him, wiping sweat from his brow and neck with one of her white cloths.

Then Fat Daddy loosened his belt to push his shirt back down into his pants. He straightened his suit jacket. "I told you that bitch Retha Mae's got some hoodoo on her," he said. "Hump ain't had a spell in over a month. I told you he shouldn't marry her, Johnie, 'cause she got a hex across her pussy that's worser than a black cat crossing your path. I know." He paused. "I mean, I hear told."

"Child," Miss Jonetta said, punching Fat Daddy in the arm and hoping to water down a word I hadn't heard referred to anything but cats until Gerald's mean father used it on him. "Judd here is gone walk you back home. Grab her hand, hear, Judd?"

Judd put on his army jacket, walked over, and took my hand.

"But I don't need anybody to keep walking me home," I said, frowning.

She raised her eyebrows and said, "Honey, I don't remember asking you what you needed. Now, I guess I'd be wasting my breath if I told you not to come back. So I'll just say I'll see you next time I see you. And be careful crossing that street, hear? Look both ways. And come straight to this store, if you must. Don't you take your fanny nowhere else along Thirty-fifth Street. Understand? And if you see that man from the other night, you just run, you hear? Run as fast as them little legs'll take you."

"But why do I have to run?" I asked.

"Honey, you the nosiest child God ever gave breath to. Must you know everything?" She paused when I didn't answer. "Well, let's just let this thing be a wonder."

I didn't press her further because, truth is, I would have agreed to anything so long as I could return the next day. Walking out the door, I could tell Fat Daddy had set Miss Jonetta off. I wanted to stay and watch, but according to the Pepsi-Cola clock, I had just enough time to make it back to the school and to my carrel in the library before Mama would start out to walk me safely home.

CHAPTER 8

Tempestt:
"Good morning, Valerie Nicholae."

We were all seated, heads down, reading, when Valerie arrived at class the following morning. I snickered when she walked in. I'm not sure why. But I stopped when I realized more heads were turned toward me than to the front of the class, where Valerie was standing.

Mrs. Jackson rapped her desk at the noise I made. "Class," she said, "you remember Valerie Nicholae from last year. Please welcome her back."

"Good morning, Valerie Nicholae," our voices droned.

First, Valerie stood in front of the blackboard, on display, as if she were a model. She only needed to twirl, but she didn't. She stood there for a few seconds, smiling brilliantly, before sauntering to her seat in front of me. She was completely undaunted by the way the class glared. And to prove it, before she sat down, she stuck her tongue out at Joel Russell, seated to her right. He was the only one with the audacity to visibly turn his nose up. As she settled into her seat, I was sure she smiled at me. I was hoping she had remembered me as I'd remembered her from the day before.

Natalie raised her hand. Mrs. Jackson said, "Yes, Miss Hubbard?"

"Can I show Valerie the reading assignment?"

"Yes, Miss Hubbard," Mrs. Jackson said, taking her seat at her desk.

Natalie got up and started over to Valerie, but Valerie said, "I don't need no help," and began flipping through the pages. Her voice was rough and indelicate, and, worst yet, she didn't even look up.

"Don't you want to know what we're reading?" Natalie asked, head tilted slightly askew as Valerie's rejection slapped her in the face. "Why, last year you had a hard time finding your place because you missed so many days."

"It's right on the blackboard. Ain't it?" Valerie said, still looking down into the book. "Chapter two, page sixteen. Time's up at noon."

"Oh," said Natalie. She smoothed her pleats, jerked her head around, and returned to her desk.

After that, it was impossible for me to read. I kept sneaking peeks at Valerie. She was a fast reader, briskly turning pages, running her fingers along the lines. She concentrated. And from time to time, I could hear murmurs of her struggling to pronounce a word. The words left the quiet of her mind, spilling out like clumsy table manners into the silence of the room. The class stirred a bit but continued reading. And so did Valerie as she scratched her scalp often, sending white flecks onto her shoulders and the farthest edge of my desk. Once, she reached back to adjust her undershirt strap and I got a glimpse of her hand, the red-tinged scratches, a tiny heart-shaped tattoo, and her untrimmed fingernails, razor-thin and browning.

I kept up my inspection until the noon bell rang, at which time

Mrs. Jackson told us to close our books and place them in the right-upper-hand corner of our desks.

"Rise and line up by the door," she said. Then we marched down to the dining hall.

The first thing everyone, children and adults alike, noticed upon entering the dining hall was the playground just beyond the bay windows. The monkey bars were out of this world—gleaming steel, bright reds and blues. A swing set had *all* the seats. The sandbox had a banana yellow merry-go-round in its center, and sand inside, not rocks, not slivers of glass.

We took our places at a round mahogany table; a total of twelve tables were arranged in a circle around an ornate rug. Under each table were ten high-back mahogany chairs with maroon cushions, and on top of the tables were ten place settings and a large parsley-garnished bowl of salad that served as the centerpiece. Because there were eleven of us, one person too many, Valerie sat with Mrs. Jackson at a different table and Mrs. Jackson assured Valerie she could sit with us next lunch period. Valerie frowned as she walked away.

The kids at my table started chatting. I watched Mrs. Jackson leaning forward, hands folded, itchy-fingered, talking to Valerie. She kept reaching over to pluck lint from Valerie's hair; then she removed Valerie's linen napkin from her cotton blouse and placed it in her lap. And when Valerie forgot to say grace and immediately reached for the rolls, Mrs. Jackson tapped the top of Valerie's hand. Slowly, Valerie pulled it back. When we were served, Valerie chewed quickly. She drank an entire glass of milk in what seemed to be a single gulp and wiped her face with her shirtsleeve, leaving a white streak across her cheek. And when Mrs. Jackson turned to talk to another teacher, Valerie stuffed a handful of table crackers into her pockets before running outside to the playground.

She tried to play with everything, to touch everything. And for the longest time, the children inside watched as she played alone. They whispered and they laughed as one by one they lined up to scowl at the little girl who was spoiling their precious toys. Valerie leapt from one piece of equipment to the other, swinging boldly, like a madwoman. She was pumping harder than I'd seen Gerald pump that day I dared him to flip over. He did. She didn't. Though I thought she might. She soared so high, kicked her heels so hard. When she was nearly out of breath from that, she ran over to the monkey bars, climbed up, jumped down. Then she hit the sandbox and started hand-shoveling sand. She created a one-person dust storm, whipping plumes of grit into the air, onto the sides and the seats of the nearby seesaw. Finally, she did a Frankenstein walk through a flock of gulls and sent them scattering off into the sky. Resting on moss-slicked rocks, she sat facing the water.

"Hey, Valerie," I said, skipping across the grass.

She had removed her shoe boots and was pouring sand from them and scraping mud off the bottoms when I ran up beside her. Looking over her shoulders, she squinted until I moved into the sun. "Hey," she said, quickly turning back to her shoe boots. "You're the one from the fence. I didn't know you was in my class. I can tell you everything you want to know about anybody in the class, since I'm old and you're new. What's your name again?"

Sitting down and remembering to close my legs, I said, "Tempestt, but everybody calls me Temmy. I hate it here. You?"

"It ain't that bad," she said. "Better than some places I been. I been around here long enough to know how things work." She rubbed her eyes with the back of her hand, then pulled out one of the crackers she'd stolen. Squeezing it into a palmful of bird food, she tossed it onto the rocks in front of her.

"You from Thirty-fifth Street?" she asked. We both paused to watch the gulls lower themselves onto the rocks, fanning cracker dust into the wind. "That's why you went back over there?"

"We didn't move from over there," I said. "I just found it by accident. It's much better than over here."

"No it ain't," she said. "When John got the job last year, only me and him moved. Mama stayed behind and I visits her after school. If she wasn't there, I wouldn't never go back. Mud always sticking to your shoes. People just as soon cuss you as look at you."

"Why'd your mother stay behind?"

"Because she part of Rev. Mayes's New Saveds and Mama's got more good work to do, saving others over there in the projects and along Thirty-fifth Street. She sings in the choir. Got the prettiest voice you ever heard. I help her after school. But if I didn't have to, I wouldn't never go back."

"I saw Rev. Mayes the other night," I said. "He was wonderful. Do you know more about him?"

"Not a whole lot," Valerie said. "Only that Mama says he's a bright star to lead Thirty-fifth Street out of the darkness. You know, stuff like that."

Valerie looked over her shoulder to the playground. She moved closer to me and began to whisper, though nobody was around to hear. Her eyes widened. "You see that woman over there with the dog?" She pointed to a thin woman wearing a near-blondish wig and a white caftan. She was talking to Mrs. Jackson. "That's Natalie Hubbard's mother. Can you keep a secret?"

I quickly nodded. I loved secrets.

"I saw her with John last spring before school was out. They was in the basement behind the elevator shaft." She paused, looking over her shoulder. "They was doing it."

"It?" I said.

"Uh-huh," she said, nodding. "Nobody knows but me. I walked in and they was under a brand-new rug somebody had throwed out because of a red mark. A itty-bitty red mark. Can you believe that? Well, Mrs. Hubbard was breathing real hard and grunting like this." Valerie started panting like a dog and she began to growl instead of grunt. "Then Mrs. Hubbard let out this big scream that made me jump back against the garbage can. John called out, 'Who dat?' but I didn't say nothing. Just ran back fast as I could. So now you can't tell nobody, either. Promise?"

"I promise," I said.

Valerie grabbed my hand and wrapped my little finger around hers and twirled it in an around-the-world circle to cement the promise.

"My friend Gerald and I once walked in on his cousin and her boyfriend," I added, giggling. "They were doing it, too. Gerald said she's done it with everybody. Even Taylor Davis, and he looks like a frog."

"A frog?" Valerie asked.

We looked at each other, leaned back on the rocks, and laughed up at the gulls dodging in and out of the clouds. Since I'd been behind the fence, I hadn't laughed so hard or felt so free.

In return for Valerie's gossip and friendship, I also wanted to tell her about my secret place, O'Cala's. I wanted to invite her to come with me one day after school, but the bell rang and the students began lining up to go inside.

"By the way," she said, standing, brushing off her clothes, "you ain't got to crawl under the fence."

"What?" I asked.

"Nope," she said. "There's a little gate that mostly the janitors know about, 'cause when they have extra garbage during the week before throw-out day, they go over there and dump it. All you have to do is count five trees from the lake and feel through the leaves for a latch."

"Five trees?" I said, smiling as we ran to get in line.

"Uh-huh," she said. "Five trees. Five fat trees from the lake."

When the day ended, the class marched single file down to the library. Valerie stayed with us until we made it to the second-floor landing, where Mrs. Jackson smiled at Valerie, signaling for her to step out of the line.

"Go on to the library, class," Mrs. Jackson said.

I walked along with the others but turned around several times. I even stopped a few times so I could see better. Mrs. Jackson and Valerie stood stone-faced at the top of the stairs until our line managed the corner to the hall, leading to the library.

I ran and signed in, found a carrel, then searched for a window that looked out onto the front of the building. I got there just in time to see Valerie running to a yellow Nova parked at the curb. She cradled her books as she ran and pulled up on her falling slip. The car door sprung open for her and she jumped inside. Within seconds, Valerie and a woman I guessed was her mother pulled off, slowing winding along the cobblestoned streets of Lakeland until they got beyond the church, the Five forty-five building, and a group of benched Lakeland biddies. After passing through the front gate, I'm certain the car markedly picked up speed.

M iss Jonetta, Miss Jonetta!" I yelled, pushing open the door. I was unable to stand still. I had run to O'Cala's that afternoon faster than ever. I was so happy that I'd found the gate. Just as Valerie had said. Concealed under all the ivy was a latch that once had had a padlock but now remained open because the janitors must have thought the ivy had hidden it well enough.

I was moving so fast that that day the peppery smoke from

Judd's ribs house a few doors down didn't make my eyes watery or my nose itch.

Miss Jonetta was in the back room behind a red velveteen curtain. She had placed two Tupperware bowls of quartered finger sandwiches on the end of the counter. A plate of the same sat in the center of the table. Fat Daddy, Mr. Chittey, and Judd tore through the sandwiches and kept tiptoeing up to the counter, winking at me and sneaking extras.

"Child, is that you?" she called from behind the curtain. She then peeped out. "Is everything all right?"

"Yes, Miss Jonetta," I said, nearly ripping my windbreaker pull string out of its slit. I dipped my finger into her mug under the counter and ran the yellow liquid across my tongue. I frowned and tried to bury the cough in my sleeve. "Okay, then," she said, "take a seat and I'll be out in a minute."

I walked over to the table, twisting from one side to the other. Mr. Chittey was about to jump one of Fat Daddy's men. "Come over here, little girl, and give me some of that Lakeland luck," Fat Daddy said to me. He had only two men left on the board against Mr. Chittey's three kings.

"Now if I move this man here," he said, thinking out loud, "ol' Chitlin'll jump me sho as my name is what it is, and the game'll be over. So I can't move that one." He placed his hand on his chin and shook his head.

"But if you move this one," I said, pointing to the board, "Mr. Chittey can jump you this way, too."

Fat Daddy looked up at me with a fake scowl. "Well, shut my mouth wide open. I guess with friends like you, I don't need enemies, huh?"

Judd said, "Man you should learn how to play and you wouldn't have to worry about friends or enemies. If I told you once, I told you a million times, watch your back row. You can't be in such a hurry to get rid of that back row. Then Chitlin can move in for a king."

Just then Miss Jonetta came from behind the curtain with a young girl who was carrying a suitcase.

"Miss Jonetta, Miss Jonetta," I said running up to her.

"Sit down and settle yourself for a minute, honey," she said to me. And she continued toward the door with the girl. "Now, Diana," she said, "since you don't want Judd there to take you to the station, the cab is waiting right outside." Miss Jonetta turned to the cabinet, reaching into her bosom. "Here's a piece of change that'll keep you for a while, till you get situated in Detroit. I'm gone write to you once a week. I want you to do the same."

The girl nodded. Tears began to stream down her face. "Honey," Miss Jonetta said, hugging her, "I told you we wasn't go do all that crying. Make you look too old." Smiling, she held the girl by her shoulders and looked into her eyes. "Now you can start over. You hear? I want you to start over."

When the door closed behind the girl, Miss Jonetta wiped her hands on her apron. She turned to look at me over her cat woman eyeglasses. "Now, Miss Ma'am," she said, smiling, "tell me what bug done got a piece of you."

"Today . . . in school? We got a new girl named Valerie Nicholae. Well, she's not new, but this was her first day back. And she sits right in front of me. She used to live over here; her Mama still does. And she's not at all like the other Lakeland girls."

"I thought I told you not to worry none about them other girls. They ain't got no color is all."

"I'm not worried about them," I said.

"Well, you better not be. Them girls just stuck-up."

"But you should see Valerie, Miss Jonetta. She's got lots of color."

"I'd love to see her, Child," she said, "but truth is, you ain't really suppose to be here yourself. I don't reckon it's wise to bring another child in here."

I nodded and she wiped her hands on her apron again and said, "Did you try my horsederves? Retha Mae said yes to Hump's proposal, so we gone have a hitching, a real jump-the-broom ceremony, right here. Next month. I told them not to worry about nothing. Long as it's not a Sunday night, I'm fine. I don't let nothing get between me and my Lawrence Welk show. I like to see the girls dancing in them pretty ballroom gowns. And they can sing like angels."

She leaned closer to me, smiling. "Hump was sweating like a pig on the blocks when he passed her the note."

"A pig?"

"A pig, Child. Got down on one knee, too, right here in the store. That was my suggestion. Nobody had to help him up, either. Retha Mae fanned herself, rubbed that old mangy squirrel she wears around her neck, and acted like she had to think it over. I said to myself, You older than Methuselah, girl. You better snap that man up like he the Last Supper. And when she said yes, we all hugged and kissed and I told them not to worry about nothing. So I'm trying out some different recipes for the horsederves and tea cakes. And I'm gone decorate real pretty. Gone make Retha Mae a nice bridal wreath. Close the store down for the whole day and piss a whole heap of folks off, but they'll get over it." She looked up at the ceiling, drumming her fingers against the counter. "Come to think of it, the last time I closed down the store was in '66 for Li'l Row's rent party. Nearly started a riot. Anyway, Jewel down the way planning on baking a rum cake. I got to watch her, though, because she'll pack a heck of a lot more rum in it than cake and we'll all be talking to ourselves and wondering why. . . . "

Miss Jonetta looked out the window, over her glasses, and I suppose she didn't want me to meet the young boy who belonged to those unbuckled galoshes crossing the window, coming down her steps. So she sent me to the little back room behind the velveteen curtain and told me stay until she called.

"There's a light back there," she said hurriedly. "Pull the cord and there's some old society magazines. Just flip through them till I'm done. Won't take nothing but a minute. Now move, Child."

The young man who came through the door wore a heavy wool coat and skullcap. He was the same boy with the two sugar-cube teeth I'd seen that first night, robbing the white truck driver and burping in front of Alfred Mayes. Those teeth made it impossible for him to keep his mouth fully closed.

Miss Jonetta stepped from behind her counter, and when Judd saw who entered, he shot up from the table and walked closer to the aisle with the bread and strawberry preserves. He put his hands in his pockets and leaned against the metal shelf. Every now and then, he'd look down at some of the bottles, pretending to read the labels. But mostly, he kept a guarded eye on the lady of the store.

Miss Jonetta placed her hands on her hips. "You open the door and ain't no telling what'll walk in," she said. Her voice was low and heavy. "Li'l Beaver, I thought I sent your ass to the A&P last week to get me a chicken."

"I got sidetracked," he said, holding a handful of her mail and placing it on the counter.

"You got sidetracked? Negro, the store is right across the street. Where the Sam hell is my five dollars?"

He shrugged and shook his head, dug into his pockets, turning them inside out. And Miss Jonetta patiently waited for him to say what she knew all along. "Last thing I do," he said finally, "I'ma pay you back, Miss J."

"You on that shit again, ain't you, boy?" she asked. "You lied to me. You took my money, looked me right smack dead in the eye, and lied to me. Told me as God was your witness you was gone get clean. Well, let me tell you something: I'll be able to do two skips on a rat's ass before I believe a word out of your lying lips again."

"I'ma do better, Miss J.," he said. He removed his hat, running his fingers through hair that was parted in the middle and hadn't been combed in days. "I just got sidetracked."

"Honey, have you looked in a mirror lately?"

When he shook his head, Miss Jonetta asked Judd to look under the counter for her purse. She took out her round gold compact and handed it to Li'l Beaver. "Look at yourself, boy. Come in here looking like death riding on a soda cracker. Look at your eyes. Look at all them stick marks on your hands, honey. You done run out of space on your arms, now you using your hands. When was the last time you ate?"

Mr. Chittey looked up from the game. "Hell, when was the last time he soaked his ass in a bathtub is what I'd like to know."

"Hush now, Chitlin. This don't concern you," Miss Jonetta said. She walked around with her hands returned to her hips. "Judd, take what's in my coin purse and go down to the funeral parlor and get this boy some soup. I reckon that's all he can stand on his stomach right now."

Judd put her purse down and shook his head. "I got money," he said, disgusted. Judd walked over to the table and whispered something to Hump, who repositioned himself in the aisle.

"I wouldn't give that dumb nigga one brown penny," Mr. Chittey muttered, scooting his hat back to scratch his forehead. Then, with a perplexed expression, he said, "Judd's going to the funeral parlor for some soup?"

"Yeah," Miss Jonetta said, "Buck fired Miss Jean from the diner yesterday because she kept forgetting to stretch the eggs with a cup of milk. So she got herself a hot plate and Mr. Felix at the parlor gave her a nook. I told her I'd send business her way when I could."

She turned to Li'l Beaver. "What you laughing at? Something funny? She working for a living. You?"

He shrugged and made his face go blank.

"Now, this is what I want you to do," Miss Jonetta said. "I want you to walk three times around the block before coming back here. And while you're walking, I want you to think long and hard about what you did, Li'l Beaver. Think about all that talent you got and think about why you want to throw it all away. Don't even want to see your seventeenth birthday. Think about why you'd rather die for a high."

"I don't want to die," he said, frowning at the ceiling light.

"Yes, you do, goddamn your soul, boy!" She walked closer to him, looking as though she couldn't decide whether to shake him or hold him. He took a step backward. But she didn't touch him. Instead, she said, "Li'l Beaver, you'd just as soon limp through this life than try to walk through it like a man."

When the door closed behind him, Miss Jonetta stopped for a second. She shook her head at the cabinet, the wall of liquor; then she grabbed her bottle of rose-scented perfume from her purse and sprayed the area where Li'l Beaver had just stood. She told Fat Daddy to hurry and retrieve me from behind the curtain.

"Take that little girl to the fence, you hear? Hold her hand, and don't let one word drop from your old gutter mouth. Not one word."

"Ah, Jonetta," Fat Daddy said, jumping up from the table. He took a minute to button his wrinkled olive green suit jacket and brush bread crumbs off the plastic flower in his lapel. He turned to the wall to comb his hair back before cocking his lemon-colored hat sideways on his head. "What you think I am?"

"A bad influence, that's what," she said, smiling. "Now go 'n before Li'l Beaver comes back."

As soon as Fat Daddy and I left the store, I started doing everything I could to get him to talk to me. "Who was that boy?" I asked. When he kept staring straight ahead, I said, "I'm sorry I wasn't lucky earlier for you in the checker game. I don't know what happened. My father says I'm always lucky for him when we go fishing. You fish? Daddy catches some of the biggest trout and catfish when I'm sitting next to him." Still, Fat Daddy didn't say anything.

When we got to the corner, we saw Li'l Beaver sitting on the curb, smoking a cigarette.

"Well, shut my mouth wide open," Fat Daddy said. "Bucky, didn't Miss Johnie tell your ass to walk three times around this block?" Fat Daddy had forgotten he was holding my hand, and he started gesturing too much. He lowered his voice. "I ain't told Miss Johnie yet, but they tell me that monkey on your back 'bout growed into a gorilla."

The boy stood quietly, not taking his eyes off Fat Daddy.

"Man, get on around that block before I put a hummer on your head."

"What's a hummer?" I said, smiling up at him.

"That's something nice, little girl," he said, his tone smooth as a nursery rhyme as he reached into his pocket. He pulled out a quarter, tossed it up into the air, catching it over his shoulder. "And as far as Miss Johnie goes," he said, flipping the quarter to me, "I ain't said a word. Got it?"

He winked. I winked back, all the while watching how the silver sparkled in my palm.

C H A P T E R 9

Tempestt:
"Because when Judd's fingers touched that dead piano, joining in the melody of
his humming, it was as though he was digging out buried treasures,
breathing life from his very soul."

Valerie came to school that one day, but she didn't come back for the next two days. I kept waiting for her to return, watching the empty wooden chair in front of me, trying to will it to slide back and bump against my desk. I was afraid I wouldn't ever see Valerie again. During the days she wasn't at school, every time the classroom door opened, I hoped she'd come through it. When Mrs. Jackson stepped outside the room to talk to another teacher, I hoisted myself up from my seat, leaned forward, trying to listen. Maybe she'd say something about Valerie. While in line marching to the dining hall, I peered into other classrooms. While eating, I counted heads at surrounding tables. I listened for her gruff voice. I waited for her on the rocks, smashing ants and pressing their bodies into moss-lined craters.

Then, when I had given up looking at the door and my heart had refused to flutter with excitement when somebody walked through it, Valerie returned.

I didn't notice her at first because I was staring out the window, concentrating on the lighthouse across from the pier, playing a game with the blinking light that sat atop the tower. Despite the buzzing of the lawn mowers and blades clicking below (Lakeland was always in a perpetual state of upkeep), I was trying to focus on timing the opening and shutting of my eyes so that when my eyes opened, the light would be on. Each day, this was becoming a game of skill as well as a way to avoid thinking about how my father was leaving earlier and earlier for work. And more and more, my mother and I were sitting at the breakfast table alone.

"Eat your food, Tem," Mama had snapped at me that morning when she caught me watching her pick over her own breakfast. She was stirring aimlessly in her bowl, smashing oatmeal lumps. I was sure she was thinking about the night before. Daddy had walked out for some air. That's what she told me when I ran into her room after hearing the front door slam. She told me to close her door and go back to bed. But I didn't. I left the door ajar and I watched her spread out across the bed, kicking my father's pajamas off the end as she dialed Aunt Jennie.

"Auntie," she said, "Thomas just stormed out of here. I don't know where the hell he went."

She uh-huhed a few times and wiped her face on the bedspread.

"When he comes back, I'll just let him choose my outfit. Yes, something that petty. But I tell you, this is the last compromise. He's been second-guessing me on everything lately. Far be it for me to embarrass him at the cocktail party tomorrow night by wearing the wrong thing. Hush, no. Okay, okay, I'll be good. Hold on for a second, Auntie." She cupped her hand over the phone and yelled, "Tem," making sure I wasn't eavesdropping. When I didn't answer, she continued.

"The invitation said seven, but of course everyone will have to be fashionably late. So while Thomas is pissing on himself, wringing his hands about being on time, I'll be on my fifth martini, maybe too drunk by then to care. Okay, I'll be good, I swear. One martini. A big one."

That morning, seeing Valerie made me feel better.

Valerie looked the same as she had the first day I saw her. In fact, she almost looked like she'd never gone home to change. When she sat down, I wanted to tap her on her shoulder or pass her a note asking where she'd been, but Mrs. Jackson paced about the class, asking us if we had any questions about the reading. I was forced to wait until noon.

After lunch, I spied Valerie sitting on the rocks. As I was walking toward her, I saw my father sitting on a bench by the dining hall door. He was talking to one of his girl students. She sat erect, with one leg crossed over the other. And she had breasts— big ones, the size of navel oranges, that poked through her wool blazer. I walked over and wedged myself between my father and the girl, paying particular attention to step on her toe as I scooted her out of my way.

"Hi, Daddy," I said, showing every tooth in my head. I grabbed his arm and looped it around mine. "Are you having a good day?"

"Tem, this is a private chat, dear," he said. "We can talk at home." He peeled my arm off his and dislodged me from the curve in his midsection. The girl was now standing, hair blowing in the cool wind, arms folded, eyes poised.

"But, Daddy," I said, rubbing his arm, "I have something very important to tell you."

"What is it, Temmy?"

"It's a secret," I said, and I formed a ten-finger cavern around his large Saville earlobe and whispered, "You don't want *her* to hear our secret, do you?"

He looked up at the girl, then back at me. "Temmy," he said, "we can talk about this at home." He took me by my elbow and lifted me up from the bench. Tapping me on my behind, my father told me to scoot, as if I were some common, bothersome tick.

I was mad. Who did my father think he was? He was my father, not that girl's. I was the only little girl in his life. And my mother was the only person with breasts allowed to sit so closely. I wanted to cry. And I had completely forgotten about Valerie until she ran over and grabbed me by my hand.

"Hey, Temmy," she said. "Come look at this."

She dragged me over to two large rocks. A mound of sand was stuck in the middle and she reached her thin hand down to scoop out a fistful before slopping it onto the rock. She began spreading the wet sand out like a pancake until all kinds of worms, green bugs, and other wet-winged insects appeared. She brushed everything out of the way, discovering a quarter.

"Where've you been?" I asked, still angry at my father.

"Out," she said, amazed by her find. "I'm just gone take this and put it with my others. Got a whole box full of quarters in my bedroom. Would have been full a long time ago if John hadn't found it and started dipping in it. When it's full, I'm going on a trip."

"Another trip? Is that why you haven't been to school?" I asked again.

"No, I had to do something."

"And you could stay away from school?"

"John don't care," she said. She looked out into the water, then handed me a sugar cookie from her side pocket that she'd taken off the table. Crumbs and sand from her hand stuck to the tips of my fingers. "You know Joel Russell in the third row?"

"Uh-huh," I mumbled, biting into the cookie.

"Well, last night it was real late. And, where my room is, there's this pipe that lets me hear things. And you know what I heard?"

I shook my head, still crunching.

"I heard Dr. Russell come in and Mrs. Russell say, 'You been gone for two days, Paul. Where you been?' Come to think of it, she said it like you just said it to me. 'Where you been, Paul?' Then Dr. Russell say, 'I had something to do, so don't start with me, Patty.' And she kept on talking; then I heard a loud thug and Mrs. Russell was crying all night long. I could hardly sleep. I think he whacked her. You?"

"Sounds like it." Changing the subject and lying, I said, "My mother says you can spend the night sometime if you want. Friday or Saturday nights are good. We can watch *Creature Feature* and eat popcorn. If John says it's okay."

"It'll be okay," she said. Once again, she squeezed a cookie and threw it over the rocks. And once more the gulls came. "We can sit up late with the lights off and talk about the deb ball. Y'all got a maid, don't you? She gone help you with your deb dress?" Her face was expectant as she slapped her hands together, ridding her palms of the crumbs and sand.

"Miss Lily's everybody's maid on the twenty-second floor," I said. "Not just ours. Besides, Mama won't let her clean our house. So she just sits around, reading the newspaper and drinking coffee."

"We ain't even got one that does that," Valerie said. "Even though John's the head janitor and all, we still poor. John says, 'Here in Lakeland on a shoestring.'" She cocked her head to the side. "You sure don't act like the other girls, to be rich enough to have a maid. I bet your deb dress is gone be beautiful."

"We're not rich," I assured her. I was almost angry that she could think something like that. "We're not rich at all."

Several seconds of quiet allowed us to hear the kids behind us in the playground and made me appreciate, once again, that Valerie was with me on the rocks.

"Sandy Christianson and her family got kicked out of Lakeland last year," she said. "John said Mr. Christianson gambled away the rent. When they left, they threw away her deb dress. Boy, was I lucky when I found it. I dug it out of the garbage, brushed it off, and hung it on the pipe in my room. The hem was loose, so I sewed it up. A button in the back was missing, so I went to the boutique on Main and yanked one off another dress. When I got caught, I cried and cried till I made this old man feel sorry and he had to let me go. My dress been hanging for the longest, just waiting on me to wear it. I look at it every day when I go home. Aren't you excited about the young deb's part of the ball?"

"Not really," I said, glancing over at my father.

Valerie moved closer, "Last year, I was too young to go to the ball. But John had to deliver a tuxedo for Mr. Richardson. So I followed along with him. John told me to stand in the back of the kitchen behind a tray of little sandwiches. But I didn't. I peeped out the door, and you should have seen all the pretty dresses. The yellows and blues and pinks. The girls walking out on their father's arms. The mothers standing and taking a bow when their daughters came out. All night long, them girls danced and twirled with their fathers on this big stage and everybody took pictures. There was so many lights from the pictures, I was almost blind when John came back. That's how he knew I didn't do like he told me to."

"The girls danced on their father's arms?" I asked. "All night long?"

"Uh-huh," she said, shaking her head vigorously. "All night long."

As we had on that first day, we leaned back on the rocks, resting our heads on our arms, our elbows barely touching. I'm not sure what Valerie saw in the clouds. But what I saw was a possibility. Somewhere along the clouds, I saw me and my father dancing.

Suddenly, there was hope in debutante balls and frilly dresses after all.

The bell rang and the afternoon played out similarly as it had earlier in the week. We had class. I passed Valerie a couple of notes, asking when she thought she could spend the night. I gave her a couple of choices and she shrugged off both. When the day ended, we all lined up. This time, because it was Friday and there was no library time on Friday, Valerie didn't step out of line. We all marched down the stairs to the double doors.

That's when I noticed Valerie had started to change—stiffen. As we walked, I tried to pass her a note, but it slipped right through her hand and fell onto the floor. "You okay, Valerie?" I whispered. She didn't say anything. Natalie Hubbard even cut in front of her and she didn't seem to notice, or care. She didn't giggle, or even fidget.

In her silence, I could better hear the suction noises her shoe boots made. It was a sound that was often lost in all her chatter. Once outside, Valerie didn't stop to talk as the other students did. She ran through the crowd, right to the yellow Nova waiting at the curb. I called her name, then ran after her. But by the time I reached the curb, she and her mother were pulling off down the street.

Mama wasn't home when I got there, and I decided it was better to avoid my father. So I told Miss Lily, who was in the sewing room reading her newspaper, I was going down to the playground.

I headed to O'Cala's.

Once outside the fence, I leaned against the ivy, wondering on which floor in that muscle-bound building Valerie's mother lived. I looked through the sea of battered cars in the parking lot for the yellow Nova, but it wasn't there. So I watched a group of wild-haired girls jump double Dutch on the sidewalk leading up to the entrance of the building. Did Valerie know them? I loved the way their entire world hinged on "Hey Miss Bee and the Bibety Bop." And I loved the way the rope danced along with them as it slapped against the concrete. It sounded like two spoons smacking together or an ensemble of clapping hands, cheering on stomping, stinging feet.

That afternoon, four street preachers were on the corner in front of O'Cala's, and I jogged toward them, once again hoping one was Alfred Mayes. But as I got closer, I realized he was nowhere in sight. No crowd had gathered and cars hadn't clogged the intersection. They were barely slowing at the blinking red light.

A woman in an apartment of the brownstone over O'Cala's raised her window and yelled down to the preachers. "Y'all can go to heaven or to hell," she said. "Doesn't matter to me. Just go soon, please." She slammed her window and pulled her curtains together.

But the preachers weren't disturbed in the least. Their voices grew stronger, more resonant, as if bolstered by the woman's disrespect. And they continued to pull Jonah from the whale, follow Moses down the *Dead* Sea, preach about Job's problems, complaining his was nothing compared with theirs. Despite a body of boils, they said, Job didn't have to preach over a slobbering and belching congregation that shouted from overhead and shifted underfoot. And brother Job, with all his misfortunes, didn't have to tread through puddles that would have made even brother Moses wince. Only in front of O'Cala's Food and Drug.

When I entered O'Cala's, a woman was standing at the counter with Miss Jonetta. She smelled of mentholated salve and was dressed in white from head to toe—definitely one of the New Saveds.

"Hi, Miss Jonetta," I said, flopping down on my stool.

"Child, you look like you got something weighing heavy on your mind," Miss Jonetta said. She placed her hands on my shoulders, settling me in gently, the way you'd slow a top from spinning around. "I see you changed outta that uniform," she said. "But into blue jeans? A pretty little girl like you should be in a fine lace dress, not them denims."

The woman looked me over with a mixture of contempt and pity, then added, "That's right. My Bible says little girls ain't got no business in any kind of pants, dressing like little boys."

"Oh, she'll be just fine," Miss Jonetta recanted, leading me to the red velveteen curtain. "The Lord ain't got time to be studying about nobody's attire."

To me, she whispered, "If he did, he'd a struck her and her preacher friends down a long time ago. That much white, especially them bonnets, could make you blind."

She muffled her laugh and said, "I got some new beauty magazines behind the curtain. Miss Sarah won't be here but a minute more. Lord, no. Then you can come visit me for a while. And we can talk about what's on your mind."

Miss Jonetta yanked the string in the middle of the ceiling, turning on the light. She sat me down on an old ironing board she had recently straddled over two thickly insulated pipes. She handed me a magazine. The way she had straightened the little room, brightened it a bit, added a shelf with bottles of fingernail polish and tubes of lipstick, along with a couple of cookbooks, told me I'd be spending a lot of time back there. When she left, I peeked from behind her carefully pulled curtain.

I couldn't hear their voices well. That Miss Sarah really knew how to whisper. She did most of the talking at first, before Miss Jonetta started turning red. Then Miss Jonetta talked as she wiped down her counter, her cash register, her cabinet. Everything within arm's length got dusted, except Miss Sarah.

Then Mr. Chittey yelled over, "Sarah Ann, why don't you just find a hole to slide into, you old snake."

"Now, Chitlin," Miss Jonetta said as the woman pulled her collar around her neck, "this don't concern you."

When the woman left, Miss Jonetta propped open O'Cala's door with a wooden crate. A stale breeze gushed inside and I could barely hear the preachers' voices. They had gathered their things and were spreading the Word farther down the street. Miss Jonetta came to get me, walked right back behind her counter, and began fanning herself.

"Sure is hot in here," she said, loosening a purple scarf she had looped around her neck and draped over her right shoulder. "Whew, Child."

She was fanning and patting her foot. The rhythm of the rat-scratching-like tapping of her royal blue pumps against the counter made the men really quiet. The temperature in the store hadn't changed, I was sure of that, but I wasn't about to tell Miss Jonetta.

"Whew, I'm hot, too," I agreed, fanning along with her. I placed my elbows on the counter and rested my chin in my palms.

"You okay, Child?" Miss Jonetta said. She removed her compact from her purse and blotted her forehead, then the area with the tiny crow's-feet under her eyes. "You look like you got something heavy on your chest. You need to shake it off?" She peeped around her mirror.

I was quiet for a moment. Not very long. Then my stomach began to feel sour and bubbly, and for the first time the rose perfume and the lemon oil in the store combined to make my lunch rise up and burn my throat. Before I knew it, the words just slipped out: "My father doesn't love me anymore." I was suddenly both afraid and ashamed of what I had just said, though I had been thinking it for some time.

Miss Jonetta pinched the tip of her purple scarf thoughtfully but didn't say a word.

"He's different," I mumbled. "Ever since we moved across the street. Even before. He's wearing funny clothes. We don't go fishing. . . ." My bottom lip began to quiver, but I stopped it. It took all my might.

"Oh, Child," she said, putting her arm around me, "your papa ain't stopped loving you. Sounds like he just going through a stage is all." She lifted my chin and made me look into her eyes. "Listen to me, honey: A man is a weird animal. You'll find out as you get older. He can go for years—day in and day out—doing the same thing. Then one morning, all of a sudden he'll wake up, stumble to the mirror, and decide he don't like what he sees. So he'll try to disguise himself is all. He may pencil over the gray strands in his mustache or he may sit for a complete makeover. But if you give your papa some time, Child, and the proper breathing room, he'll begin to come back to you.

"That man moved you over there seeking the good life. He ain't meant no harm. No sir. I suppose he just gone have to learn for himself that everything that looks good ain't, and every itch ain't meant for scratching, no matter how easy it is to reach. But until then, don't you ever think your father don't love you. Ever."

With her thumbs, she lifted my face into a smile, careful not to scratch me with her nails. Then she bent down and hugged me tightly until my T-shirt, normally scented with Popsicle juice and sweat, held a hint of her rose perfume.

Sometime during Miss Jonetta's talking, Judd had moved away from the game of checkers to the piano bench. I hadn't noticed until he struck a key haphazardly, just as anyone would who happened to be walking past. His back was toward us, but we all knew his eyes were closed by the way he leaned his head to the side and by the way his broad shoulders arched, then softened beneath his flannel shirt. Miss Jonetta smiled and began to trace the top of her mug. Normally, it sat in obscurity on a shelf under her counter. But this afternoon, Miss Sarah had made Miss Jonetta bring her cooling-down juice out of hiding.

Funny thing was, no one came in the store. It was like at some churches when during Communion nobody is allowed to enter or leave.

All of a sudden, the store got scary quiet. I started looking around, wondering what was wrong. Fat Daddy and Mr. Chittey stopped playing checkers in mid-game, leaving a couple of kings stranded on several corners of the board. Hump got up and moved to the vat next to the piano.

Miss Jonetta whispered, still smiling. "Remember when I told you Judd had another talent?"

I nodded, not really remembering.

"Well, you about to see what I meant."

It was so quiet all around us. Even outside. You could hear the cars whizzing by and footsteps from people on the sidewalk. No sermons, no cussing, just the destination-bound shuffling of battered stiletto heels and clogs, run-over platforms and work boots.

Judd leaned back and rocked a few times on the piano bench. He removed his hands from the keys and folded them in his lap. And then, as if given a permissive nod by a choir director, he began to hum. In the beginning, the sound didn't seem capable of coming from one man, or from such a cramped area by the back wall, under that Pepsi-Cola clock. In the beginning, the sound seemed to be helped along by a bass trumpet no one could see— the melody building, then surging in his chest, rising quickly like a just-popped balloon, before slowing to dip down into a special place. It was a tucked-away place where Miss Jonetta said grown-ups didn't get to visit too often. And those who did visit there weren't always equipped like Judd to stir up life's heartaches and set bits and pieces of them free.

Not long after, the room began to vibrate. The ceiling light swayed a tad. You had to look closely to see it. The cabinet glass trembled. And in deference to a special combination of lows and highs, Fat Daddy lifted his hat and sat it atop the checkerboard. This was the first time I'd seen him remove it without caring about his bald spot. He propped his elbows on the table, rubbing the deep, crooked creases in his forehead, as if to flatten or erase every line.

We all sat very still—silent—as we listened to one man put birds and beautiful wind chimes to shame. Nobody said anything for fear that Judd would end too soon and O'Cala's and Thirty-fifth Street would return to normal. But within seconds, I learned there could never be a normal again. Because when Judd's fingers touched that dead piano, joining in the melody of his humming, it was as though he was digging out buried treasures, breathing life from his very soul. Miss Jonetta had told me only he could really force that old thing to stand upright and dare it, at least while he was sitting there, to slink again.

When it was over, Judd got up from the piano and walked back over to the table. Nobody said a word to him. No pats on the back, no thank-yous, just worn handkerchiefs returning to pockets and feet shifting, chairs scooting back under the table. When I was certain it was over, and only then, I asked, "What was he humming, Miss Jonetta?" My eyes wide open, I said, "Boy, I wish I could do that."

"No you don't," she said abruptly. She hesitated for a minute, stretching a piece of taffy candy until it resembled a purple hair ribbon and finally snapped in two. She handed me half, saying what Judd had was special but not to be fooled, because it was a beautiful gift wrapped in bows of suffering—something you don't envy, just simply enjoy. She said you don't envy it because without Judd having lost his whole family—a wife and two kids, in a house fire years ago—he wouldn't have a hum like that. It would be simple and ordinary. "Like the preachers on the corner," she said. "All that moaning and groaning, and the result ain't never been much more than bad breath whipped into a frenzy." What Judd had was God's way of letting us know how pain and talent come together. "They lace themselves like clasped hands in prayer," she said. "And sometimes, if we're lucky, they unfold into truly miraculous things.

"As far as the tune, Child? It ain't nothing you heard before." She shook her head, patting the soft bed of my palm. "No, Child, you ain't lived long enough yet. Just wait your time."

Miss Jonetta:
"Hump walked Child back to the fence that night and I was about to lock
up early when I could still hear Judd's humming. Seems like pieces of it was
hanging on to the cobwebs, afraid to let go."

Judd's humming was beautiful. Had healing properties, like a balm you rubbed all over yourself until you sure enough felt like flying, when without it, what you really wanted to do was cry. About old wounds. Or just being old.

I was standing at my counter thinking about what Sarah Ann had said. Sarah Ann used to do hair Monday through Thursday. On weekends, she prophesied on the side. Told fortunes and lies. She was one of the New Saved people and part of the street ministry: a group of ladies who'd done spent most of they lives flipping they legs open to whoever had the change; cussing people and cutting throats. Then old age caught up with them and they decided they wanted to be new and saved before they met they Maker. I had been knowing Sarah Ann for as long as the sun and stars been taking up room, and she was the only person I knowed who could turn a two-minute conversation into a life sentence. Never got to the damn point. Well, that afternoon she asked me if I was doing the right thing by letting Child hang around somebody like me. That's what the heifer said. "Somebody like you, Johnie."

She said, "Johnie, I'm not one to butt into other folks' business . . ."

"Yeah," I said to myself, "and I'm the President of the United States."

"But, dear, you can't take care of every good-for-nothing along Thirty-fifth Street. The Bible says, 'They that wait on the Lord shall renew they strength.' We got to be patient and wait on him. What is best, is you stop trying to save all these young girls all by yourself and send them our way so they can learn the Lord's will."

"His will?" I said.

"Yes. Let the Lord save these chil'ren from drowning in sin. You can't call yourself saving somebody and at the same time you selling Satan's juice."

"Oh hell, girl," I said, pointing to my cabinet. "You know more water in them bottles than anything else. People don't come here for a high, Sarah Ann. They come 'cause they ain't got no place else to go. No clean place, that is. They been told they ain't no good, made to wallow like pigs in all that dirt out there. I make them feel like they belong."

"Dear, what you think the preachers for? Let God make them feel they belong. We're trying to save souls and your establishment is just undoing all our fine work. Like Rev. Mayes says, you can't talk one life and live another. What people here need is some soul saving. . . . And now, amongst all this deviling in this store, I see you got a child on the premises?"

"Listen here," I said. I swear I was this close to popping her in the mouth with one of my towels, but she did my hair, so I held my hand and my tongue a bit. "You know how much religion I think Alfred Mayes got. You know how much I think of that dog. As for the rest of them preachers, they been here for as long as I can remember, and all they do is pray and rub roots and burn candles. And look at this place, Sarah Ann. If y'all'd get them white outfits dirty, get in the trenches, maybe y'all could really save some souls, instead of flapping them jaws."

"Johnie Louise Goodings!" she said. (She was one of the few people who knowed me before I got tired of my name and changed it.) "You done found the devil's high horse and you sitting right proud. But with all your high-and-mightiness, you think that little girl in that back room should be hanging around somebody like you?"

"Somebody like me?"

"I don't mean no harm, Johnie, but somebody like you? The right example?"

"Why don't you go 'n and say it, Miss Sarah Ann?" I said. And I looked at her the way you'd stare down a rabid dog and dare him to take a second snip. "Ain't no need in beating around a bush with me, honey. You talking about my past. Now, let me tell you something. I want you to listen good because I don't feel like repeating myself: I ain't ashamed of what I used to be. Truth be told, I'm right proud of my past. Wasn't built to clean nobody's toilet or pick nobody's cotton. Besides, I was one of the finest girls that ever worked Thirty-fifth Street. Finer than your ass ever was. And as far as Child is concerned, all I can tell you is that she'll be far safer with a sinner like me than with any one of you New Saveds. Because I'm gone keep a watch over her. Ain't gone just pray over her and send her on her way. I'll tell her what she needs to know. All the rest, I'll leave alone. You hear me, Sarah Ann? I'll leave them whispers about my past alone. I expect you to do the same."

Oh, she got in a huff and walked out. And not before it was best. Afterward, I must admit, I remember looking across at Child and wondering if I was doing the right thing. Of course, I wouldn't give Sarah Ann the pleasure of knowing I had second thoughts. Fat Daddy and Judd had asked me the same thing about

Child coming to O'Cala's. Unlike Sarah Ann, they wasn't concerned about her being around me. They worried about her just being on Thirty-fifth Street with the righteous as well as the sinners. Truth was, by being at the store, Child had heard too much, seen too much. Still, I couldn't turn her away. I won't lie—a part of me just loved having that child in my store. That little redheaded girl had a smile like sunshine peeping through a rainbow. In my heart, I pretended she was Chloe, my own little girl. I suppose Child came to me at a time in my life when all I did was think about my daughter. Each time she came to my store, plopped down on her stool, my heart got happy just to see her, each time she opened that door.

Hump walked Child back to the fence that night and I was about to lock up early when I could still hear Judd's humming. Seems like pieces of it was hanging on to the cobwebs, afraid to let go. It took me back to the morning Chloe was born, a time I don't visit too often because it brings too much pain.

I locked the door and looked out my window, around them signs, and I could see myself the night I ran away from Aunt Ethel's house. I could see my scarred, skinny legs running past. Could see the hem of that dress and my old tight, run-over shoes. I remembered how hard it was to fight the crowds; how I kept getting tangled up in arms and elbows, and kept getting my hat knocked sideways; how my head was still spinning from Aunt Ethel's punch. I finally got tired and took me a sit-down on the front stoop of the ribs joint. I sat there for some time, watching and waiting, plotting my next move. People just kept going in and out of that place, slamming that screen door with the knotty strings for hinges. Above it some dude had done strung some floorboards together and called it an awning. It was something to see.

I was waiting, minding my lonesome, when lo and behold, guess who walked up out of the barbershop? Alfred Mayes. He strutted up to me, big as the Lord himself, with an equal following—but of pretty women. He called them his "peaches." Waving them off, he introduced himself, then asked me, "What's a pretty young thang like yaself doin' out so late? You lost?"

"No, sir," I said, standing so fast, I nearly knocked my own self off balance.

"Waitin' on yo man?" He grabbed my braid and twisted the tip. "If I was yo man, I wouldn't keep you waitin'."

"No, sir," I said, and I pulled my hair back. "I got friends I'm waiting on."

"Uh-huh," he said. Looking me up and down, he took a toothpick out of his breast pocket and began flipping it around his mouth with the skill of a root man waving a wand. He had so many rings on his fingers and everything shined—his lips, his hair, which had been slicked down and curled at the end. His mustache and eyebrows were arched like the spine of a black cat and trimmed to a razor point. A piece of gum-wrapper tinfoil was folded and stuck behind his ear. It caught the light from everything, the streetlamps, the marquees, and even the stars.

I put on my tough face, but he saw right through it. He was seasoned, all right. He told me that if my friends didn't show up and if I needed a place to hang my hat for the night, he had some contacts. He wrote his name and the address of a friend on the inside of a cigar band. He gave it to me and told me, "Ask for Bea, and tell her Scooter sent you. She down the street." Then he winked and smiled, wiggling that toothpick up and down.

"Thank you kindly, sir," I said. "But my friends'll be along in a while." I rolled the paper so that it curled around my fingers; then I throwed it on the ground. He walked away, parting the crowd like it was the Red Sea until it folded around him, until he was out of sight.

I waited—on what, I don't know—for another hour. All the while, I watched where that little piece of paper tumbled, mind you, in between watching that full moon and the crazy men under it. Men wrapping rubber bands around they arms before turning down into the alley. Others throwing up so hard, I thought they was about to die. The preachers circling around them like vultures, saying those dudes was just getting the devil out from on they soul. But that didn't last long, honey, because as soon as they could, they was clearing their throats, preparing to hitch him back on.

A couple of hours passed and I was tired—feeling light-headed from a empty belly—and fishing that piece of paper out from under all the trash on the steps. Before I knowed it, I was standing at Bea's door, peeping in her curtains, through the keyhole, trying to get up the nerve to knock. When I did, Bea welcomed me with open arms. She hugged me like I was kin, a cousin just up from the South or a old friend. It was early morning and she was dressed in a bra and garters, wide awake, but that didn't mean nothing to me. She gave me a big pretty room to myself with a lock on it. Sheets was clean. Spread had pretty fringes, the kind you braid when you bored. Furniture was polished and shiny. Sturdy, not that rickety mess Aunt Ethel put us on, expecting us to get a good sleep.

"Girl, you hungry?" Bea asked me.

"No, ma'am," I said. Still, she brought me a whole fried chicken with some corn and some potatoes on the side, and she knowed I'd lied to her by the way I gobbled it up. "Thank you kindly, ma'am," I said. "Thank you."

During the first couple of weeks, Alfred Mayes treated me like a princess. Nobody knows what that means to somebody who been treated like a loose penny, like they don't count. He told Bea to wash my hair and let it hang real pretty. And she did. He told her to bathe me, which she did. Then she taught me the proper way of sipping champagne as she painted my toenails and finger-nails scarlet red. Sprayed pretty rose perfumes on me and wiped my body down with sweet-smelling orange and lavender oils. Gave me talcum for my panties. Gave me pearls and dangly earrings and feathers and fitted me for all kinds of flowy dresses with beads and sequins. Bea put a floor-length mirror in front of me, called Alfred Mayes, and told me to twirl...and was I pretty? He agreed and tipped his hat. The dress hugged my thin waist and ballooned out like a burst of fresh air. And Alfred Mayes stood behind me, hugging me tight, his hands pressing all my tired pieces into a whole.

When Bea left the room, he started kissing all over my neck, nibbling up and down my ear. I was visited once again by that feeling I'd had when I first saw him rubbing on that woman in the red dress. He grabbed me up and took me right there on the sofa. I watched him do his work in the long mirror. He was like a beautiful butterfly—silky smooth, soft to the touch, flitting around. I held on. I squeezed him the way he squeezed me, rolling my tongue around the peppermint taste in his mouth the way he did mine. Then he put his tongue in my ear, the way you'd ease a dainty foot into a glass slipper, and Lord, I felt a flash fire shoot from that ear straight to my groin, it did. I can still hear his belt jingling to the ground as the other hand tapped out *I love you* on the small of my back. He moved his hips up; I moved mine up. He moved them down; I moved mine down. Then he showed me how to do it right, and I didn't want to let go. I felt like flying away. Lifted up on his wings. When it was over, he told me he loved me like he ain't never loved nobody. And I believed him.

I swear to Jesus I was so green that I didn't know what was going on until the next night and that first white man came a-knocking on my door.

"White men kinda rough on colored girls," Alfred Mayes whispered, licking his finger to smooth my baby hair down. "But you so light, they might go easy. If they don't, just rub yaself with some cinnamon and honey in between. Take a shot of whiskey. And it won't hurt so much as you can't stand it."

"But I ain't that type a girl," I told him.

"You ain't, huh?" he said. He took those hands and massaged my shoulders. "So I guess you ain't the type who likes fine thangs? You ain't the type who likes to please her husband-to-be?"

"Husband?"

"Sho, sweet thing. I thought you knowed that. I belongs to you and only you now. Look a here, you won't have to do this long. We'll make us some change, get hitched, and go live somewhere pretty. Somewhere pretty like you. You'd like that, you think?"

My smile musta been broader than those shoulders of his.

"It won't be long, sweet thing, and you'll be the Mrs. My one and only."

Well, many nights followed, and Alfred ain't never said another word about getting married. I never saw any of the money. And all the while, the white men kept coming. Then one day, my monthly stopped. Didn't think nothing of that, either, until my belly started to swell and Alfred got mad because I was sick all the time. I told him the baby was his. He was the only one I truly let inside me. Inside my room. My private room. Who I let run from corner to corner, unlocking all the doors, opening all the windows. Playing so much pretty music. I told him the baby was his. But he didn't believe me.

Soon all those men just became ghosts floating in and out of my room. When they finished they business, I blanked them from my memory. I wiped down my sheets, then washed their nasty hands off my body and their grunts and moans outta my mind. Many nights, I'd lower myself into that bathtub with the nice curvy legs and dip my head under the vinegar water and stay there for a while. Many times, I surely wanted to stay under. I wasn't much on praying, mind you—Aunt Ethel had fixed that—but there was nights when I hurt so bad, I prayed to God to just allow me, sir, if you please, to stay under. Wash myself right out of this world. And try this life all over again in a man's shoes. Men didn't have to wear high heels and fishnets and prance around. Men grunted and felt good, let all their worries spill from them like a running faucet. Us girls wasn't no more than dirty drains, hollowed to catch all kinds of mess that you never, no matter how much soapy water you use, completely clean out.

In about my sixth month, I could feel Chloe kicking around in my belly. Chloe is the name I gave her almost as soon as I knowed she was there. I don't know how, but I knowed my baby was a girl. I loved feeling her in my belly, moving around, playing. At night, I would lie in bed, lift my gown, and watch her just go, turning my stomach into peaks and valleys. Seem like sometimes she was running around a wide-open field in there. I imagined lots of daisies and berries and wild roses.

In about my eighth month, Alfred put me out. Oh, he apologized first. Said I was taking up too much room but that I could come back if I couldn't find no place else to go. It was cold outside. That year, Chicago got about ten inches of snow that didn't want to melt or I swear I woulda had Chloe in a alley full of rats rather than go knock on Aunt Ethel's door again. To have to stand underneath that torn green-and-yellow awning, snow falling through it, made me sick. To have to beg her to take me back made me even sicker. But I did it for Chloe. Woulda walked through hell for that little girl. Might say I did.

That night, Aunt Ethel looked at me the way you do a old dust rag you not sure whether to launder or throw away. It was Papa who told her to let me in. Then he closed up like a trap when I walked through the door. It had been near a year since I seen him last and he looked tired and sickly. Had gone to ashes, poor thing. Didn't look like my papa at all.

"Thanks, Papa," I said, walking past him, trying to suck in my belly. But he didn't even look up at me. He was sitting in his chair, smoking his cigar and reading the newspaper. He never said a word to me. Aunt Ethel relayed his messages, or what she said was his messages. The first was: "Your father say he ain't never been more disgraced or 'shamed of nobody." The second: "Your father say you the one that shoulda died at birth 'stead of your mama." Then Aunt Ethel led me down to the basement, where she made me a nook.

It was damp and cold down there. I'll never forget how cold, even though she shoved me next to a radiator. All day and all night, the pipes made all kinds of fuss. And the mice made more noise than men. No peace at all. Every time Aunt Ethel came down those rickety-ass stairs to bring me food, she made sure I understood that this housing was only temporary. As soon as the baby come, I'd have to go again, she said. And she also made me promise to stay away from Essie or she'd make me leave no matter what Papa said. Baby or no baby.

I talked to Chloe to keep my mind right. I told her about Annington County and how Essie and me used to run through the fields, through rows of briar and wheat. Pollen thick as cotton. Chasing one another like crickets and sucking on lollipops from the five-and-dime in the next county. We would walk for miles to get to a place where nobody knowed us, because there I could buy all kinds of penny candy and they'd let me because of my color. Then we'd both run back home through the old cane fields and dirt roads, rolling in our penny candy. The clouds used to layer one on top the other; then just as you thought it was about to pour down raining, the sun would come peeking out and color the wheat a fine whiskey yellow, the grass a 7 Up bottle green and the sky a pure powder blue. I told Chloe that I'd of gave anything to be able for the three of us to run through those fields right then. Nothing else would matter.

One night I was half-asleep and shaking from the cold, and I heard footsteps coming down the stairs. "Essie, is that you?" I whispered. Then I got real quiet, fearing it was Aunt Ethel coming to change her mind about letting me stay. It was dark and the only light came from a kerosene lamp sitting on the steps. As I turned over, I got a sharp pain in my privates. I felt around and I was wet; my water had broke. Then I felt a cold hand on my forehead just before a heavy blanket fell over me. It surely felt good. That cold hand touched my forehead again and then a pair of chapped, shaky lips kissed me on my cheek. It was so dark, I couldn't see. Couldn't see a thing until I looked toward the kerosene lamp and saw my father's worn hunting boots going back up the stairs.

The next thing I know, the baby coming. I cried out and Aunt Ethel came running. She ripped my undies off and there was so much pain and blood. But not long after, the baby came. Oh, Chloe had a good holler on her. A strong baby, I said to myself. I wanted to see her. But Aunt Ethel wouldn't let me. She whisked Chloe off up the stairs. Didn't say a word. I fell asleep. I don't know for how long, but Aunt Ethel came back after a while and woke me and told me my little girl didn't make it. What? I said. How could that be? And more bad news. Papa's heart gave out on him overnight. He was gone, too.

"But I heard the baby cry," I said, barely catching my breath, not really hearing the news about Papa.

"It was her last," Aunt Ethel said. She was looking down into her old crooked hands. Couldn't look me in the eyes. "She was too spare and came too soon was the problem."

"Where is she?"

"We done took care of her."

"Where is she? I want to see my girl."

"We done wrapped her up in some newspaper and put her away. Now get some sleep, Johnie, because you got to leave soon. This is best for us all."

Best? Oh Lord, I screamed and I cried out. My insides began to ache and ache. "I want to see her!"

Aunt Ethel kneeled beside me and started praying, "The Lord is my shepherd; I shall not want. . . . "

"I want to see her," I kept saying over and over. "I don't care if she wrapped up; I want to see her." I tried to move, but I was too weak. "I'll be good, Auntie," I said, rubbing her gnarled hand. "I promise I will. I'll change my wicked ways. I just want to see my little girl." But that mean bitch just kept right on with that Twenty-third Psalm like it was gone make me stop wanting. Make my insides stop wanting what had done come from me, was a part of me.

Then something just shut down in me. Everything turned black.

When I came to myself, I was in Hump's kitchenette apartment. Hump's real name is Herbert Fastile Porter. He introduced himself and said that was his fourth time doing so since he found me a week or so earlier curled up in the alley under his window. To this day, I don't know how I got there. I don't remember a thing.

On a crumpled sheet of paper, he wrote out, "People call me

Hump." He wore baggy overalls and didn't say one word. Just wrote everything down on that rusty hand-size clipboard. "Want another blanket?"

I was laying in his Murphy bed that came out of the wall. Hump, poor thing, had slept in his rocking chair, watching me the whole time. Feeding me. Here I am this stranger he found curled up in the alley. And he cared for me. A stranger. When he left for work, he even asked his landlady, a Miss Clarice, to look after me and to clean me up. One day, she had me in the tub, soaping my privates, and she realized the blood wasn't stopping, my fever wasn't cutting, so she made me lay down in the bed. I remember her saying, "Child, you gone die soon if I don't git this stuff out of you. Ain't gone feel too good," she said. "But I gots to do it." She rubbed and pushed down on my stomach. Rubbed and pushed down, saving my life but ripping the rest of my baby's afterbirth from me. Laying on the bed, willing myself in and out of this world, I reached between my legs. Then I dabbed some of the blood for safekeeping on one of Hump's handkerchiefs. I've kept that handkerchief for so many years, watching it blacken and wear thin, stored away in the zipper part of my pocketbook.

Hump ain't never been much on words, mind you. So when I came to for good and had to tell my story, had to throw it off me, he sat over by a fire and listened. I cried and cried so hard that I could hardly think or move or feel at times. How could God be so cruel? I asked him. Taking my baby. My papa. But Hump offered no answers. He'd just hand me a towel from the bureau to wipe my face. Didn't come too close doing it, either. Never tried no funny business. Went back to his seat and he listened. Rocked in that chair, embers floating around them old brogans.

I was at Hump's place until mid-spring, and he never said one word. Most days, I'd clean that room, fry him some chicken, then prop me a chair by the window and look out onto the alley. As the snow melted and the weather got warmer, more and more I started seeing little girls, running half-naked through the alley. I'd raise the window, throw something down or just yell to the men, "I'ma tell your wife." And then nasty men'd jump off the garbage cans, yank their pants up, and run. Lids rattling to the ground. The little girls didn't know no better. They'd look up at me and cuss me because sometimes they had lost they meal ticket. So they'd run after them men and find another alley or vestibule, offering them half their money back—pennies, nickels, and dimes—just to keep up a good business. I know I don't always explain things clear enough, but that's what I was trying to tell Sarah Ann the day she saw Child. I had to learn it myself: Yelling, whether Bible verses or anything else, don't do no good lessin you give a child a safe place to hear it in. It's like scattering fresh seeds on hard concrete and expecting a miracle. Them girls, most of them, was no more than fourteen, sucking, and doing things to nasty men who was old enough to've knowed better. But all them men cared about was feeling good and getting lost in that feeling as they lay back on them garbage cans, fixing their no-good eyes on them white pigeons or the clean laundry that hung on lines, stretching from one building to the next.

I don't know if it was from Hump's landlady or somebody saw me going for groceries or what, but word got to Alfred Mayes that I was staying near Thirty-fifth Street in Hump's place. One evening, I was fixing dinner and I got a knock on the door and I thought Hump had lost his keys.

But that night, it was Alfred coming to visit, big as he pleased. I wouldn't let him come in. So we stood out in the hallway. He told me he was sorry about the baby. So sorry. He flashed some bills in my face, moving them from one pocket to the other, and flashed that $5 million devil smile. He pulled me close to him and he rubbed his hands up and down my spine. "So sorry," he said, "about the baby. Sorry about your papa. Didn't mean to put you out, sweet thing, but that was only business talking. I was out of my head. Forgive me," he said. Even had the nerve to drop a tear. And that little scrawny piece of salt water fell like a sledgehammer upside my head. "Give me a second chance," he begged me. He even bent down on his knees.

"You'll see, I'm a changed man. You don't have to work no more, just be my woman by my side."

Now I was seventeen at the time, and after a year, you woulda thought the little green fool had ripened, wised up. But I hadn't. Wanting to be loved, taken care of, held tight, told I belong surely made me stupid. Here was this six-foot-tall pile of horse hockey, standing in Hump's doorway, and I was blind to it. My papa always said you can dress it up, put a shine on it, and it can fool you from far away. But up close, you shouldn't have to rely on nothing except your nose. Well, good sense failed me. I wrote Hump a note, thanking him for all he done. I had two dresses and a pair of shoes that I tucked under my arm; then I left with Alfred Mayes.

Alfred took me into his house on Thirty-fifth and Bernard Street. Opened the door for me. Led me into the living room by my arm like I was a princess, again. He kissed me on my cheek and hugged me tight. Told me he wouldn't touch me in that other way till I was ready and not before. "You can sleep with me in the bed, Johnie, if you want. Or I can take another room." He held his hands up, palms facing me, and said, "It's your call. You makes the rules, sweet thing. You makes the rules."

Alfred slept on that hard floor the first night. He was in the bed with me the next. The sun hadn't come up and set a good two times before Alfred decided to show his ass. He came home that third night complaining about his girls being sick, either knocked up or clapped up.

"Maybe you should look for another line of work, Scooter," I said. Then he started fussing about how he ain't never had no support. Daddy died too early. Mother was a whore, working more than she was home. The black man ain't got no support, he said. "I'm losing money. All kinds of money. Johnie, baby, honey, sweetie," he said, "you know I don't want to ask, but . . . You know I said you ain't have to do this no more, but . . . You know how much I love you and if I didn't have to ask I wouldn't, but . . ."

"Alfred, I can't go back," I said.

"Don't tell me what you can't do," he said. He walked over to me and put his hands around my neck, rubbing, pinching, scratching with those rings. "Johnie, get dressed. One time is all I need to make it right." He kissed me on my neck, pulled me close.

"Alfred, I can't go back."

With those words, the old dog reached around and slapped me so hard, I fell across the dining table. Now, living with Aunt Ethel had taught me how to take a punch like a grown man. But after what I'd been through, Chloe, Papa, Essie, I didn't feel like being hit again. He walked up to me a second time, grabbed me, digging his nails in my throat. And he started shaking me until his arms got weak and he pushed me back down on that hard table.

And I swear something came over me. It was like I wasn't even there no more. I was this rag doll with the insides spilling out. Body tired of being shook and thrown from here to there. It took me a second or two, but I grabbed that heavy candleholder on that table. And all I did was hit Alfred one time. He hit his head on a rusty pipe that jutted out the wall. It had always snagged my hose.

When it was done, I stood over him a couple of seconds. A

jagged gash split his forehead right down the center. I watched him bleeding, turning blue-black, his body shaking out of control. I stumbled out of my heels and ran to the bathroom to throw up. Lord, I got scared then. I thought the Negro was dead. I shoulda knowed hell wasn't ready for that old dog just yet. I bent over the washbasin to splash cold water on my face, and when I looked up in the mirror, I was so confused. The person wielding that candle-holder was gone. And the little naïve fool was back, scared and crumbling. How could I've been so stupid to believe he had changed? I remember reaching for Alfred's razor. I remember holding on to the pearl handle, bowing my head and wishing for a heaven. Wishing hard that there was such a place I could hang my hat. Wishing the way you do when you ain't got nothing else to reach for and you find yourself sinking into a hole so deep and dark and cold. Well, that night I thought, Lord, what a fine time to join Chloe and Papa, the onliest two people that could love such a fool. What a fine time.

And I swear I was about to take that blade . . . when I heard a husky voice. I looked around that bathroom and I was alone, but my papa's voice came to me just as plain as if he was standing in front of me today. These was his exact words: "We ask the Lord to deliver us from the fiery furnace and when he do, we jumps right back in, headfirst. There's a field out there, Johnie, cool and open and light. Go run through it. Run as fast as you can and don't look back. Run, child."

I think about it now and chuckle to myself, because I didn't know these feet could move so fast. I woulda outrun the 7:26 to Memphis that night. I grabbed my pocketbook and a few balled-up bills Alfred Mayes kept hidden in a shoe box under a floor-board. I started running and running. I ran past the hardware store on Gordon Street, past the Palace Theater, where folks was dolled up, waiting in a long line. I hopped over the railroad tracks. Kept going past the carpet warehouse, the whorehouse, the ribs joint, the fish market. And as I ran, stuff just started falling off me. You wouldn't know it by looking at the bruises Alfred had just gave me or all the mud covering my feet and legs. But I hadn't felt that good in years. Tears rolled down my face and I could feel the pain balling itself up into a form that could fit into the palm of *my* hand, and nobody else's. I don't know what all I lost, but I didn't go back looking for it. When I finally stopped, I ended up on the steps of O'Cala's. Them pigeons was making a fuss overhead. Always making a fuss. And a bunch of preachers was outside, huddled around a collection plate, singing off-key: "If you get to heaven before I do, Lord save a seat for me—save a seat for me."

I bowed my head and said to myself, Papa, take care of Mama. Tell her I look forward to meeting her someday. Watch over my precious little girl, Chloe. Tell her I love her, oh, how I do love her. And if you please, sir, save two seats, one for Essie and another for me. I'll be there one day, I told him. I'll see you again someday, I promise, Papa. But not until the good Lord calls. Not until he calls and calls.

Part II

Tempestt:
"It was big and fat, lumpy and red."

Three weeks after we arrived in Lakeland, I hauled off and sucker punched Joel Russell. I remember it was three weeks, because my father kept mumbling it over and over later that night when I arrived home.

"Daughter of mine," he said, teeth clenched so tightly that he could barely speak, or breathe, for that matter. "We've been here three weeks. Three little weeks and already you're acting up. Didn't our talk mean anything? I told you there were different rules in Lakeland. Didn't I? You can't just knock the hell out of somebody when you feel like it."

"It was for a good reason," I offered down to the shag carpeting.

When I glanced up at him, I noticed he was looking at me so sternly, I was afraid to meet his eyes. Then, to add to the indignation of having been pulled out of class and forced to hold Mrs. Jackson's hand clear to the office, then returned to class and *encouraged* to apologize to Joel, my father spanked me—three swift and precise slaps on my bottom. Oh, it wasn't the spanking that hurt me. Daddy had never hit me hard, at least never as hard as I knew he could. What hurt was that my father lifted his hand at all, especially when he was the one who had taught me how to bob and weave and hold my guard properly. And he was the same man who had stormed out of our old house countless times in retributive searches for neighborhood bullies who had given his only child black eyes, fat lips, and scraped knees.

"Now Joel's father is talking about suing," he said as we both sat on the edge of my bed.

"Oh, he's not going to sue," Mama said, now standing in the doorway.

"I know that Felicia, but it's like we've been branded. The Saville family: barbarians."

"Sounds like that little Joel boy is the one who's been branded." Mama snickered. She joined us on the bed and wrapped her arms around me. "He's going to have one monster of a lip for a while."

"Shit, Felicia," Daddy said. "What's the point?" He spurted up from the bed and the next thing we heard was his office door slamming behind him. A fierce thunderclap shook the tiny chandelier outside my door, reverberating throughout the apartment.

Later that night, I lay across my bed, thinking about my father and how he had totally disregarded my reason for punching Joel. He wasn't even willing to hear my side of the story. Hadn't he always said there were two sides? "Sometimes," he'd said, "you even have to stand back to look at a situation. Sometimes you have to stand back to see what up close tends to distort."

And now my father wasn't the least bit willing to understand, listen to, or look at my situation at all. In truth, it wasn't that that day had been much different from any other. There had been several occasions since arriving in Lakeland that I'd felt the urge to strike somebody. But I had restrained myself, primarily because of him. But that day, Joel had assailed Valerie, and Valerie was my friend. I hit Joel because of what he'd said to her.

By October, I'd learned that Valerie would come to school no more than two or three times a week. So every time I saw her, I was determined to make the most of our time together. Normally, nobody disturbed us as we spent the majority of the lunch hour sharing her secrets and pouring playground sand from her shoes and feeding the gulls.

But that particular afternoon, Joel had decided to ruin it all. He was the type of child who could find pleasure in swatting down a bird's nest or destroying a spider's carefully threaded web. I had seen the little coward and two of his friends approaching out of the corners of my eyes. I hadn't said anything to Valerie because I was hoping the three would continue on down the shore.

"Valerie," he said, walking up. A sudden shadow fell over us, as if the sun had fallen from its trusses. "Your father's the head laundryman in our building, right?"

Valerie nodded hesitantly.

He cocked his body sideways, pointing to his hip pocket. "I think he missed a spot on my pants."

Joel and his friends laughed, a sickening outburst that made the hairs on my neck shoot up. But Valerie didn't say anything, even though I fully expected her to mention Joel's father's temper and his mother's bruises.

"Boy, this spot is a stubborn one," he said, scratching at his pocket. "You think you could lick it off?"

I stood. "Take that back, Joel," I said. "Take it back or I'll give you a lick, all right." I could feel my hand curling into a fist, more of an involuntary movement than anything else. I knew it well, and I also knew that once the process began, rarely was it ever possible to reverse it.

"Take what back, carrottop?" he asked, picking up a small rock and aiming for one of the gulls.

"Temmy, I ain't worried about him," Valerie said. She tugged lightly on my arm.

We stood there staring for a minute. There was something about Joel's smirky face that didn't set right with me, then the cavalier way he extended his chin and folded his arms over his chest. He didn't push me, although it felt like he had. So I hauled off and punched him. Right in the mouth. He fell backward, arms splayed while his friends looked at me as though I were some kind of lunatic.

"My tooth," Joel cried, lisping. "I think she's loosened my tooth." His friends huddled around him on the ground, looking into his mouth, around that rising dollop of flesh.

In class, Mrs. Jackson asked me why I'd hit him. "Because he disturbed our peace," is what I wanted to say. But I knew she wouldn't have understood that, so I shrugged and followed her down to the office, watching my knuckles swell as she dialed my mother, then called my father—over the intercom—to come retrieve his daughter.

The day after the incident with Joel, I sat on my stool in O'Cala's, explaining to Miss Jonetta why my knuckles were red and my fingers stiff, and why I deserved her sympathy rather than her admonitions against girls fighting. Unlike my father, she listened intently, even though she interrupted me every now and then to drum her fingers along the Formica countertop or twist her white cloth into a knot so tight, you could almost see the fabric fraying.

All the while, Mr. Chittey was listening. Finally, he hobbled over, concerned about one thing only. "Did you bust that nigga's lip good?" he asked. His ears perked up and his neck protruded like that of a nosy chicken.

I looked at Miss Jonetta, then back over at him. Slowly, I nodded.

"Well, what'd it look like?" he asked.

I thought for a moment, though it wasn't necessary. The memory of Joel's lip had been indelibly burned into my brain. "It was big and fat, lumpy and red," I said.

At first, I was leaning against the counter, resting my chin in my hands—Miss Jonetta said I was looking "sorrylike." But when Mr. Chittey's eyes widened, lifting his little body with every question, something inside me started stirring. I sat up straight, the tips of my toes barely touching the wood-plank floor.

"Did he bleed good?" Mr. Chittey prodded.

"Like a faucet," I said, half-smiling.

"Chitlin!" Miss Jonetta said, placing her hands on her hips.

"Did he fall to the ground?"

"He sure did," I said. "With a thud."

Smacking his thigh and laughing, Mr. Chittey said, "Hot dog! They gone throw you out of Lakeland and send you over here to us. For good."

"Chitlin!" Miss Jonetta said again. "Little girls ain't supposed to be fighting."

"But it was for a good reason," I reminded her.

"It was for a good reason," Mr. Chittey said, looking more serious than I did.

"Honey, ain't no good reason," Miss Jonetta said to him. "She could fall and damage herself for life. Get a big old ugly scar and nobody would ever look her way. Besides that, she takes a chance on making her insides jump around to places they ain't supposed to be. If he didn't hit her, ain't no good reason, Chitlin."

I left the store that day feeling nobody, not even Miss Jonetta, could ever have understood.

CHAPTER 12

Tempestt:
"I've got a secret."

W e had been gone from our old house a little over a month
when Daddy, Mama, and I drove up in front of the yard.
An early snow nearly camouflaged the cement blocks that Daddy
had used to buttress the sagging front porch. Though we knew we
couldn't go inside the house, I think the feeling—that breathless
feeling—we each shared was one of coming home.

"Doesn't look like the same old place, does it?" Mama said to
my father while picking at the short hairs on the back of his neck.
It was a nervous habit my mother had adopted from my father,
though she often batted his hand away when he did it himself.
Those days, their relationship—as well as my father's and mine—
was as unpredictable as the weather, ebbing and flowing between
the warmth and love that we'd lived by in the old house, and one
of distant familiarity, something quite specific to Lakeland.

"They've gotten rid of my shingles. And, look there," Daddy
said, pointing to the side of the house along the driveway.
"They've taken down my trellis." He looked at Mama. "You
remember how long it took me to put that thing up?"

"I do," Mama said, smiling. "And I bet it came down a whole

lot faster." Mama patted his arm and turned to greet Miss Jane, who lived two doors down and was now walking up, pushing a shopping cart full of groceries.

"Since when they let you take one of them things home with you?" Mama asked, lifting herself from the car.

"Since they started charging seventy-nine cents for a homely pound of beef that should cost half as much." Miss Jane stopped her cart and extended her arms. "This here is what you call a fringe benefit, girl! Come here, Felicia. How you been?"

"I'm doing fair to middling," Mama said, embracing the woman Daddy said was too nosy for her own good. "How you like your new neighbors, Janie?"

Miss Jane tipped her head back and pushed up her nose; this was her way of saying they were too uppity. Then she bent down to peep inside the car window. "Well, if it ain't Thomas Michael Saville and my little Tem-Tem." She leaned forward for a kiss and her huge lips looked like two saucers hurtling toward me. So I scooted as far across the seat as I could. My mother sang out, "Tempestt!" But Miss Jane was unaffected. "Come here, baby," she said as she grabbed my arm and sucked in my face. "You all taking care up there on the hill?" she asked my father. "How much one of them apartments costing these days?"

"Oh, they're not bad," he said to Miss Jane while turning the ignition. "Not bad at all." To me, he said, "Tem, what you say we go around and pay Gerald a visit?"

Nodding hard, I leaned forward, resting my head on folded arms over the front seat as he waved at Miss Jane. I could smell English Leather, two face slaps' worth, which earlier that morning I'd watched him work into his hair and his new mustache. I'd even waited until he left the bathroom and then dabbed a bit on my wrists.

As soon as we turned onto Cottage Grove, we saw Gerald and

some other boys playing a game Gerald and I had perfected. The boys were taking turns, waiting for cars to pass so they could latch onto the rear fenders and glide on their skateboards down to the Woolworth and back. As we pulled up, Gerald had just grabbed onto a car and was about to go sailing down the street. Unfortunately, he saw our Volvo, let go too soon, and skidded into the sidewalk.

Daddy stopped the car and jumped out. "I don't have to ask if you all are crazy," he yelled. "You could kill your fool selves." Every one of the boys, except Gerald, snatched up their skateboards and tore through Gerald's front yard to the alley. Gerald just sat there, stiff as roadkill, hoping to fade into the black-and-gray speckles in the asphalt.

"Gerald, you know better than all that foolishness," Daddy said, walking toward him. "I turn my head for a minute and you turn into a retard?"

"Mr. Saville, uh . . ."

"Don't Mr. Saville me, buddy." Daddy pulled Gerald close to him, knocking his baseball cap sideways. I jumped out of the car as they walked to the front stoop and sat down.

"I don't want to catch you doing that nonsense again. You hear me?" Daddy said.

"Yes, sir," Gerald muttered.

"You sure you hear me, son?"

"Yes, sir," Gerald said much louder.

"Hey, Gerald," I said, running up, adding a half wave.

He looked up at me, then smiled at his skateboard. "Hey, Temmy."

I was happy to see he hadn't completely reverted to his old ways. Though his pants were a tad muddied, that was from the game. And a few lint-clogged curls lined the nape of his neck, but he smelled fine. I looked at him closely and there were no half-moon purple scars under his eyes or red licorice stick welts across his arms and fingers. In fact, he said there hadn't been many since the afternoon he came over to our house looking like he'd been chained and dragged through the alley. That day, Daddy had jerked Gerald by his hand and stomped over to Gerald's house. I followed, jogging now and then to catch up. Mr. Wayne was sitting on that very stoop in his oily jeans and T-shirt, smoking one cigarette and thumping his pack for another. "Tell the person," Daddy shouted to Mr. Wayne, "the animal, who did this to this child that if it happens again, he'll have to answer to me. Then the authorities." Daddy turned Gerald loose and told us to go play. I don't know what was said further, but Mr. Wayne thought twice about hitting Gerald real hard again—at least so hard that he left marks.

But during our visit that evening, it was apparent that even without me or my father, Gerald was doing well.

"How's school?" Daddy asked, beginning his drill.

"Fine," Gerald said. "Got a *C* in English, but all others was pretty good."

"Well, that's good," Daddy said. "You'll just have to work on bringing up that *C*, right?"

Gerald nodded.

"How's your family?"

"They're fine. Auntie's been cooking and cleaning and straightening things out. She said since she's going to be here a while, she wants to make the place more hers."

Daddy smiled. "Is your aunt in the house now?"

"Yes, sir," Gerald said.

Daddy tugged on the bill of Gerald's baseball cap. "Visit fast," he said to me. "It's not fair to leave your mother with Janie for too long."

When the storm door slammed shut, I moved closer to Gerald.

"I've got a secret," I said, arching my spine, trying to imitate the way Valerie launched into her tales. "A few weeks ago, you know what I saw?"

Gerald shook his head.

"I saw a man standing on the street, preaching the Gospel!" I stood up, clapping my hands, now trying to imitate the Reverend Alfred Mayes.

"He was running to the left and to the right, flapping his arms. He was as black as Jimmy Parker, maybe blacker. And he had a long scar in the center of his forehead. Like that." I pointed to a rock on the sidewalk that was nearly split in two, held together by the strength of overgrown prickly weeds. "He was even taller than my father."

Gerald grimaced. I was sure he didn't believe me. So I crossed my heart and turned facing north, in the direction of the cemetery, a few blocks down. I swore on his mother's grave. And he stood up because he knew then I wasn't lying.

"He was how tall?" Gerald asked.

I stood on the side railing of the stoop and measured over my head. "You should have been there, Gerald," I said, jumping down. "That man even came over to me. He picked me out of the crowd of people standing around, just watching him go." I lowered my voice. "But you can't tell anybody because it's a secret. And I've got another secret."

"You do?" Gerald asked, frowning, wondering how I could possibly have another.

"I got a friend named Valerie. You'd like her a lot. She's in my class. And I got another friend named Miss Jonetta. She's old, but she doesn't seem real old. She works in this store where funny people come and go. I sneak over there some days after school. She keeps a jug under her counter. I took a sip once when she wasn't

looking. It made my face do like this." I twisted my lips like I was
sucking a lemon.

Gerald then tried to compete by telling me how he and my for-
mer classmates were preparing for *Blacks Around the World and the
Bicentennial,* a play in recognition of Black History Month as well
as the country's upcoming two hundredth anniversary. When Gerald realized he had begun to bore himself as well as me, for his
stories paled in comparison with mine, his voice trailed off into a
fog of cold, settling beneath chocolate-colored leaves that he himself had raked into a pile in the center of the yard. After a few seconds, we both found ourselves staring into the pile.

With little else to talk about and even less time, we ran around
to the alley behind Gerald's house to the old mattress on the side
of the garage. He and I used to play on it, jumping up and down,
pretending to be weightless astronauts on the moon. Because
nobody else wanted to touch it, neighbors had often called the city
to have it removed. Rats had nibbled straight through to the
springs and all the alley cats had peed on it at least once.

Off in the distance, we could hear the train coming to a halt on
the Washington Street platform. And as we tossed ourselves into
the cold, metal-tasting air, we watched the train, first out of the
corners of our eyes, then straight on. We watched the cabin lights
coming toward us, moving slowly at first, then weaving lightning
white lines through old houses and barren branches until red
lights faded out down the tracks and out of sight.

Sitting down on the edge of the mattress, gasping for air, Gerald said, "I've got a secret."

"No you don't," I said, flopping down next to him.

"Uh-huh," he said. "Promise not to tell?"

I nodded.

"Your father's come by a lot since you all moved. . . ."

"What?"

"Uh-huh," Gerald said, slowly shaking his head. "Mostly on weekends. Sometimes after school. At first, he'd just drive by slowly in front of the house to say hi to me. Then he started coming in to say hi to Dad. He told me to keep it under my hat. I think that's why my aunt moved in."

"You swear?" I said.

"I swear," he said, raising his hand, turning slightly in the direction of the cemetery.

"Well, shut my mouth wide open," I said under my breath.

As I was sitting there, trying to digest this, my father called. Gerald and I raced each other back to the front of the house. Mr. Wayne, Gerald's aunt, and my father were all standing around the stoop. A dim yellow light on the front porch shone on Mr. Wayne, and smoke from his cigarette wavered in the thick air, creating lassos as he talked and gestured toward the old willow in front of him. He and Gerald had begun to cut it down. Seeing Gerald and me, my father reached out to shake Mr. Wayne's hand. And as they wound down their chat, I stood beside Gerald for as long as I could, staring at my father, at how he stood a whole head taller than Mr. Wayne and at how the crooked limbs of that nearly dead tree cast shadows across his face. I knew right then as we walked back to our car that I'd ask him to hoist me onto his shoulders so I could touch one of the remaining leaves or run my fingers along the crumbling bark. I knew, too, that I didn't care one bit about that old tree—the way it felt or leaned or waved. All that was important was my father lifting me, a thousand feet into the sky.

CHAPTER 13

Tempestt:
"God said, a faith even the size of a tiny mustard seed."

By October, it had become a loosely held secret among the maids that if they wanted rest and relaxation, they could lie and say they had work to do in the Saville apartment. Our apartment had become a sort of refuge, especially as everyone was preparing for the debutante ball. At first, Miss Lily had held her afternoon "teas," as Mama called them, in the sewing room. But when the room started to get too cramped, Mama invited Miss Lily and her friends into the kitchen. Miss Lily's friends feared that joining in with the lady of the house could cost them their jobs. So they stopped coming by. But Miss Lily didn't. Every day at about noon, she'd huff and puff her way through the back door to lunch with my mother. And eventually, it was my mother who was doing all the serving. After the appropriate amount of time had passed, Miss Lily felt comfortable giving Mama a list of her favorites. "Coffee calms my nerves," she said. "So does tea. A doughnut every now and then gives me a boost, and scones, I found out, make me regular." And Mama shopped accordingly, all in exchange for the conversation and friendship she needed when Aunt Jennie wasn't readily available.

The morning following our visit to the old neighborhood, I was about to tell my mother I'd cleaned my room and was going outside, when I stopped by the kitchen door to listen.

"You don't say," Mama was saying over and over. She was staring at my father, who was sitting at the breakfast table, determined to be more interested in his newspaper and coffee than in Miss Lily's and Mama's conversation. "You don't say," Mama said again, louder and in a more prodding tone. "A swamp? Lily, you're lying."

Miss Lily leaned forward, shaking her head into her coffee. As a matter of habit, she dabbed at the two permanent coffee dribbles on her smock before adjusting her big breasts onto the table. "Girl, I was born under the sign of Gemini and we don't lie."

"But how could that be?" Mama asked.

"I don't know," Miss Lily said. "But, here's my hand to God. Somebody filled in a swamp. Most of this land. All of Thirty-fifth Street. That's why there's so much mud all the time. But this is how the people here came to know about it.

"About two years ago, Mrs. Hubbard wanted to have a spring fund-raiser for the NAACP on the east lawn. So she came to me and told me to help organize everything. She wanted a big canopy, had to be yellow and white. Big enough to cover about fifteen tables. She wanted the finest china, silver, crystal glasses, the works. All that was fine until she told me she wanted me to cook her up some sweet potato pies because Mrs. Coretta Scott King—coming all the way from Atlanta—loved her some sweet potato pies. Only, Mrs. Hubbard wanted them on the bland side."

Mama frowned, still staring at Daddy, who hadn't turned the page of his newspaper since Miss Lily started her story.

"Bland, girl," Miss Lily said, looking into my mother's face. "I said to myself that if I even thought about cooking a sweet potato pie without the proper amount of cinnamon, honey, lemon rinds, nutmeg, and sugar, Mama Lilian would jump up out of her grave and slap the taste out of my mouth. Lord, these people here is something else.

"Anyhow, when the day came, the sky was a pretty blue and that yellow-and-white-striped canopy looked like clouds waving above them women's heads. And they was sharp, sharp as a tack, themselves. Big hats, white gloves, high-heeled shoes. And the lake behind them. Whew, I was just proud to be there, even though I had to serve and my ankles was swelling like two inner tubes. Don't you know, everything had been beautiful until Mrs. Hubbard was about to give the farewell and two of the tables near the lake started sinking into the ground. Looked like the earth was just gobbling them up. Then two more tables. People facing her didn't know why all of a sudden she screamed and then fainted. That was until their tables started sliding back."

"I don't believe this, Lily," Mama said. She had her hands over her mouth and she was shaking her head.

"Let me finish, now. Just let me tell my story. Anyhow, I may be on the heavy side, but I can move when I want to. I ran over and grabbed the ends of that canopy, yanked it down, and gave everybody a handful. Then I ran over to Buster and John Morgan, who was cleaning that bird shit off the rocks, down the way. We was pulling them women one by one. Mrs. Kennedy, Mrs. King, Miss Barbara Jordan. Oh, it was a mess.

"But that wasn't the only mess," Miss Lily said, leaning forward even farther as she flipped her braid over her shoulder. "There was a flood once, bigger than Noah's. A pipeline in the basement of the Five twenty-five building burst and water ran for forty days and forty nights."

"Shut up," Mama said, rolling her eyes. I rolled mine, too, just to do something.

"Well, okay, I added a little yeast to that one. But not much.

And then there was the time when incinerator chutes in the Five fifteen building caught on fire. Look like that movie *The Towering Inferno*. God said fire would follow the Flood. Well, what really happened was they built this place too damn fast. They wanted Lakeland to shine, and in a hurry, and they didn't get stuff right. I tell you, these people here is something else. Let them tell it, Lakeland has always been Chicago's perfect jewel."

My mother was shaking her head and her shoulders were trembling. My father had his paper in front of him, and when my mother hit the back of it, he adjusted it and turned the page. "What do you think of Lakeland now?" she said, bursting into laughter.

"Felicia," he said, raising his voice a bit and lowering his newspaper. "It's easy to find fault, and I don't see one thing that's funny." He looked over at Miss Lily, "And shouldn't you be swishing around in somebody's toilets instead of wasting time here?"

"Thomas!" Mama said, standing. "That was totally uncalled for."

Miss Lily stood. "Don't have to slap me in the face to tell me I'm not welcome."

She folded her newspaper under her arm and walked out of the kitchen, completely oblivious to me sitting at the door. Initially, I thought by the way she plodded down the hall, she had been insulted enough to leave the apartment. But she stopped just shy of the back door, turning into the sewing room, where I could hear her click on the little black-and-white television set Mama had loaned Miss Lily for her stories.

As I left the apartment, I didn't say a word to either of my parents. They wouldn't have heard me anyway. They were yelling at one another, but in this pitch that would never have sounded like yelling to a regular passerby. It was a fast-talking, muffled monotone they'd developed in Lakeland so that neither I nor the neighbors could hear them argue.

By the time I crossed Thirty-fifth Street, I was tired of running. But I didn't stop at the store. Still formulating my plan, I ran far enough away from the store's window so Miss Jonetta couldn't see me. Despite her warnings, I was determined that day to explore the rest of Thirty-fifth Street. Truth is, I didn't feel much like sitting still. I had on my traveling shoes—the name I had heard Miss Jonetta call her pair of peach-and-purple slingbacks.

Next door to the store was a vacant lot where a bunch of men and boys huddled around burning garbage cans. I didn't stop to look, though I wanted to. I kept running, my All Stars sliding through the mud, until I crossed a side street. In front of me stood a storefront church, the Church of the New Saveds. The women in white were holding court beneath a crucifix painted in red on the side of the building. Their mumblings grated like sandpaper as they snatched pages back and forth in their Bibles.

Next door to the church was the ribs house. Some days, I could smell the smoke as soon as I crossed Thirty-fifth Street. That day, in front of the store, I could almost taste it. It was so strong, it moved through me as I stood looking into the window. Three juicy slabs hung from hooks dripping grease and sauce into white buckets lining a short counter. My mouth watered, and before I knew it, I was pressing my face against the glass.

All around me, people were in a bustle, moving in and out of the store, down the street. People constantly moved, shifted along Thirty-fifth Street. There was motion everywhere except this brown brick building next door to the ribs house. A porch wrapped around the front of the brownstone, and when the mailman rang the bell, a woman in a red lace robe answered, pulling her garment close to her body. After she closed the door, the building once again was dead, completely still and quiet. That was probably why I heard his voice.

I made my way down the street, following a booming voice that wove in and out of a chorus of amens. I had forgotten to swallow and remembered only when I crossed another street and was standing in a vacant lot, sandwiched between the currency exchange and the pool hall. So many people surrounded the platform that I couldn't see him at first. One woman was stretched out amid broken glass and old pop bottles. A man kneeled over her fanning with white gloves. Another woman was jumping up and down, shaking her skirt, the mud suddenly transformed into hot, searing coals.

"No more heartaches or disappointments," Alfred Mayes cried. "Just peace. All you need is a little faith. God said, a faith even the size of a tiny mustard seed. And he'd give you peace."

The crowd began to open. Women and men, most walking like the wounded, limped off in both directions down the street. When the crowd cleared, I saw Alfred Mayes sitting on the edge of the platform.

He was pouring money from his Crown Royal bag into his chest pocket. Behind him, a woman with a microphone continued to pace along the platform, singing, "Jesus is the light, the light of the world." She paused from beating her tambourine every now and then to bow before a cherry candle that sat on an altar made of two stacked milk crates. I stood there wondering if he'd remembered me.

I assumed he had, because when he looked up, he waved me toward him. I stepped across the Bible lying next to him. Peered for a second at that fedora with the feather, whose scarlet tip I suddenly wanted to touch.

"Don't be afraid, little sister," he said, pulling a deck of cards from one of his many pockets. "The Lord don't want you to be afraid. Come sit down next to the reverend."

"I'm not afraid," I said. I leaned forward, resting my chin in my hands and forcing the smile off my face by pinching my cheeks.

One by one, he began removing the rings from his fingers and lowering them into his breast pocket. "How come I don't see you and your parents at my church?" he asked.

"I don't know," I said, shrugging.

"On Sunday, I want to see y'all, you hear?"

I nodded, knowing I was lying. Patience not being one of my strong suits, I thought about my parents. I asked, "Do you have some of that peace you had a few weeks ago?"

"Peace?"

"Uh-huh," I said. "You know. That peace you gave that woman?"

"What a little girl like yourself worrying 'bout peace for?" he said.

"I'm just asking," I said. "You never know when you might need it."

He smiled as he shuffled his cards, his hands suddenly moving like magic, moving in ways I'd never seen before. So I stopped talking to watch. I was mesmerized at the way he made the cards do all kinds of fancy tricks, flipping them one over the other like acrobats in a circus.

"They say these cards is the devil's cards," he said. "They say that's why some men can't find no peace. But it ain't the cards that make people do wrong, like gambling. It's the man. What the cards do depends on who's got 'em in his hands. You take 'em," he said. He pulled my hand from my face. "You shuffle your way; then I'm gone show you mine. There's a trick to it, little girl."

"A trick?" I asked.

"A trick," he said.

The woman behind us began to sing louder and she began to stomp harder and harder, until specks of dirt shot up from between the platform planks and the microphone cord wiggled around her heels. "Jesus is the light, the light of the world, forever burning in our souls!" She screamed it to the people walking along the sidewalk. They stopped to look at her, then hurried past her canister without dropping in a contribution. I held the deck, wondering what to do with it. I simply held the cards until one high-pitched note from the woman combined with the wails of a passing ambulance, scaring me so badly that I released the cards into a flurry all over the ground.

"Don't worry none about that," the reverend said. "One thing about the Master is that he'll give you a second chance. Remember that. He gave me a second chance. Saved me from the pit."

"What pit?" I asked.

"You and your folks come on Sunday and I'll explain it all."

He looked over his shoulder at the woman. Without him saying a word to her, she lowered her voice and refrained from stomping. Then he walked over to each card, scooped it up into his hands, and reshuffled the deck.

When he sat back down, I looked up and Judd was rushing over from the sidewalk. I started to pull my hood over my head, but he had already seen me, was looking dead at me. I met him halfway, head bowed a bit so he could see I was sorry.

"Brother Judd," Alfred Mayes said, following a few steps behind me. "The Lord is whispering a message to me." He looked up to the sky, nodding. "Said he wants to lay an everlasting blessing on your soul."

"I ain't your brother, Scooter," Judd said. "I told you that a long time ago. And I got a message for you and your God. You just wait here until I come back."

Judd took my hand as we retraced my steps back to the store.

"You won't tell Miss Jonetta, will you?" I asked, using the sorriest face I could conjure and jogging to keep up with him.

At first, he didn't say anything, just kept walking into that cool wind, our coats flying behind us.

"Please don't tell," I begged. This time, I was serious. "I won't do it again. I promise."

When we got to the store, he kneeled, staring into my eyes and clutching both of my shoulders. "If I ever, ever see you over there next to that man again, I'll bolt that gate myself. You understand what I say?"

I swallowed, nodding.

He waited on the top step until I pushed open O'Cala's door. Then he began walking back down the street in the direction of Alfred Mayes.

Hi, Child," Miss Jonetta said as I entered. She stood behind her counter, counting back change to a customer.

Mr. Chittey and Fat Daddy were sitting at the table, and they looked up only because the rush of wind from the door opening rattled the checkerboard. Fat Daddy tipped his red felt hat. "Well, if it ain't Lucky Cool Breeze," he said.

"That's not my name." I blushed.

"Is now," he said.

Mr. Chittey lifted a frail, uninterested hand, focusing mostly on his next move.

When the customer left, Hump began sweeping the entire store and Miss Jonetta waved me over to the counter. "Child," she said, pointing to an open magazine next to her jug. "What you think of these hip-huggers here?" Smoothing her hand along her hips and looking over her shoulder, she said. "Think my hips too wide?"

I looked down at the page, then her butt, and shrugged.

"Lord, when most girls ain't had nothing but imaginations to slip into a panty girdle, I've always had me some hips, and a thin waist."

She turned the page, commenting on hot pants, leg warmers, halter tops, and when my eyes wandered up to the window, then over to the liquor cabinet and around to the Victrola because I was still thinking about Judd and Alfred Mayes, she said, "Child, what's the matter with you? Don't you know us girls is supposed to be stirred up about stuff like this?"

"I don't have time for stuff like that, Miss Jonetta."

She looked at me, pursing her lips. "You got a job or something?"

"No," I said. I peered down slyly at the magazine, reaching out to curl the tip of the page. "I'd rather you tell me more about that street preacher."

She rolled her eyes at me and snatched the magazine off the counter. "Oh, I know now," she said after several seconds of letting her eyes do the talking—words I can't repeat. "Mr. Red ain't visited you yet. That's why you still hooked on fighting and fishing and nonsense like that."

"Who's Mr. Red?"

"Your monthly, Child," she said. She perched her hands on her hips.

I rushed over and put my hand over her mouth, turning my gaze toward the table.

Lowering her voice and jerking her head toward the pyramid of Kotex, which Hump was now dusting, she said, "All of us girls is kind of unconcerned about pretty clothes and hair bows and lipstick at first. That is, until Mr. Red comes a-knocking. Then all of a suddenlike, your insides commence to bubbling. And wham! The notions department becomes your second home."

I giggled and she lowered her voice some more. "The men wanted to die, just die, when I brought them Kotexes in here.

Chitlin stayed away for two days, and he still frowns sometimes when he looks on them. But I told them, us girls have to keep ourselves clean. Yes sir. Ain't nothing worse than a woman with some stink on her. Well, maybe a woman with a gorilla under her arms. When it's time, your mama'll teach you about shaving your underarms and them little hairy legs of yours."

"I'm not shaving. I'm not ever shaving."

She looked at me, shaking her head. "Oh, you'll shave if your eyes ever come across what I saw a few summers ago." She threw her cloth over her shoulder and licked her thumb so she could reopen the magazine. "It was hotter than hot. And one of them New Saved women had on a sleeveless shirt. Had the nerve to get the Holy Ghost and lift her arms. I said to myself, Honey, you should get happy at home, in your bathroom, in front of your mirror, with a razor before that patch of tar under your shoulders. Lord, she had enough hair to make Fat Daddy over there a toupee for that bald spot he tries to hide under them hats of his."

"Mama has Daddy pluck hairs from her chin sometimes," I added. "She said if she didn't, she'd have a full beard."

"Uh-huh, see there," Miss Jonetta said, nodding. "You come by being hairy honest. That's okay, though, as long as you stay ahead of it." She brushed my bangs back, looking at my eyebrows. "And when it's time, we'll take some tweezers to those brows so they won't come together. You got a pretty face, Child. Such a pretty face."

By the time Judd returned, Miss Jonetta had convinced me that a little lip gloss would go a long way. And Alfred Mayes was about to begin another sermon. We could hear the crowd gathering, cars stopping. Judd offered to take me to the fence. Outside, he led me into the middle of the street, skirting the onlookers. All the while, he held my hand, barely looking over at Alfred, now a massive shadow looming over the crowd.

"I didn't mean to raise my voice at you earlier," Judd mumbled when we got to the fence. He didn't look directly at me. "I apologize."

"It's okay," I said. "I won't go near that preacher again. I promise." Then I smiled, licking my sticky lips before slipping through the vines.

CHAPTER 14

Miss Jonetta:
"That child, Judd said, would grow up to be Alfred Mayes."

Judd once told me that when he was a little boy, growing up down there on Collins and Thirty-fifth Street, it would rain and rain. And them pigeons would fly from the window ledges to the street and back, tracking so much garbage that mud would stick to their wings. Soon they wouldn't be able to fly no more. He said the women in his brownstone would get so tired of seeing all them birds out in the middle of the street making a fuss, flinging mud all over Creation and going nowhere. So they'd tell Judd and the other boys to go chase after them birds and help set them free.

Judd's parents came up from Louisiana with another family in 1904. They came up when colored folks was coming up like flies during the packinghouse strike. The two families settled on Thirty-fifth Street, which, by the turn of the century, all the white folks had left behind. According to the deeds, many still owned the buildings, but you wouldn't know it to look at it. Because whoever was standing in front of a building when the real owner left, that person stepped in and took over. And when the white folks didn't come back, even city hall didn't look our way. Nobody cared about what went on on Thirty-fifth Street even back then. Like when they turned the crazy house into that whorehouse. Folks used to say nobody was sure sometimes whether the moaning and groaning stuck under that wallpaper was from people who'd done got happy or from the trapped souls of the crazy folks that used to live there. I hear told they used to live there in a horrible, filthy shame. But that was how Thirty-fifth Street had always been: this dumping ground for kin—crazy or otherwise—that nobody wanted.

Anyway, both of them families that came up in 1904 had boys about six or seven years later. One was an ordinary-looking child who didn't cause no particular stir or nothing. You know, the type of child women look at and want to hold, coo at. Well, that baby was Judd.

But the other baby was different: a dark brown baby so pretty, all the women in the neighborhood—from Collins across the trolley tracks to what was then Butlers Drive down by the lake—came to see him. And they didn't just want to hold him. They wanted him. They say women whose insides had done dried up cussed themselves when he wrapped his soft brown hand around their wrinkled, cracked fingers. Their whole bodies began to shudder and ache with want. Women who'd already done had their share of children, some so many that they could hardly remember all their names, decided while staring into that little boy's eyes that if the moon was right and the good Lord willing, they'd bring forth another. It's a sin, old folks often said, for God to waste so much pretty on a boy. His hair, a headful, was silky black, the type of hair people run their fingers through before touching their own prickles, hoping to pass on some of the luck. His eyes opened up like the sky just before twilight and when a drop of water spilled onto his cheeks, women scrambled trying to figure out how to ease his pain. That child, Judd said, would grow up to be Alfred Mayes.

Now, Judd told me all this one afternoon when it was just me and him sitting around in the store and it was raining so hard, I was sure Child wouldn't be stopping by. He was at the table, spreading preserves on crackers one after the other. I was leaning on my counter, reading the newspaper, when I heard old Alfred Mayes about to start a sermon, even in all that rain. Like I always did when I heard him outside my window, I ran to my transom and pushed and pushed until it sounded like two trains colliding when it finally came to.

I walked back over to my counter and picked up where I left off on the newspaper. When I turned the page, lo and behold, I saw a story that made my eyes jump back. It said Alfred Mayes was going into an agreement with some Lakeland senator to help close down Thirty-fifth Street. Don't this just beat all, I said to myself. That old dog up there had caused so much hurt and pain along that street and now he was hanging out with the big time, passing himself off as a respectable preacher, when even the howling dogs knowed he was no good.

Reading the story, I kept saying over and over how somebody should just hog-tie him, slit his throat, and be done with it—before he could spread his hurt and wickedness to the people in Lakeland. I musta went on and on, because Judd asked to see the article.

I handed it to him and he stared at it for a spell, reading the lines like they was written in a foreign language or code, and he was trying to make sense out of that voice moving through his head.

Finally, Judd said in a hoarse voice, hoarse because he ain't talked for a while, "He wasn't always that way." He stopped, like he was searching his memory, rummaging through it the way you do a old drawer full of broken jewelry and stale smells. "I know he done you wrong, Johnie, and that don't excuse nothing. Don't excuse his whole life. But I want you to know he wasn't always that way. So maybe he *has* changed."

"What?" I said, walking from behind the counter. "Can a snake stop slithering around on his belly and walk upright? A man like that can't change. Can't never change. He was born no good. And that's the way he'll leave this earth."

Judd breathed out real loud and pushed the jar of preserves to the other side of the table. Suddenly, he was too full. "I knowed Alfred since he was this high." He held his hand to his knee. "The grown folks used to call him Scooter because for the longest the boy wouldn't walk. Just scooted from place to place. Women would hardly let him scoot, though, for picking him up so fast. He used to be a good boy, Johnie. A fine, fine boy. Not everybody come into this world evil—capable of selling their own soul and somebody else's to boot. Alfred didn't come here that way."

I sat down next to Judd, not wanting to hear the story at first. But then, I must admit, curiosity got the better of me. So I settled into my chair, cracked open my mind a piece, and listened.

> Scooter's father, Ernest, worked alongside mine packing meat for International Harvester. Folks used to shuck Ernest because when he wasn't at work, he worked just as hard trying to get his wife, Marjorie, in the family way. They tried and tried and nothing happened until they decided to visit some old root woman here from Coopers Parish, in Louisiana. Miss Sadey gave Marjorie something to stir around in her tea, and people say in the fall of 1911, Marjorie was in her apartment, playing that piano Ernest had found and put back together, when she fainted. Slid right off the stool.

Well not long after, here come Scooter. Ernest was so proud. He still had long days in the stockyards, but he hurried home to be with that boy. Sit with him on the porch, throw him high in the air. Just smiling as people passed and told him what a fine, fine son he had.

Now, Marjorie treated Scooter like he was gone break. And that happens sometimes when your firstborn takes so long in coming. Every time Ernest threw Scooter up in the air, they say, she sat on the edge of her chair, tapping the leather off the tip of her shoe. That boy's nose didn't run good before she was taking her skirt tail to wipe it. He couldn't stew long in a bad diaper. Other kids couldn't cough a croup on him or come too close, neither.

Normally, a child like that could get spoiled. But not Scooter. As he grew, wasn't one mother that didn't call him the sweetest little boy you'd ever want to meet. Wasn't one mother that didn't tell her son, "Go play with him for a while." All the women watched as Scooter fawned over his mother, bringing her sweaters on cool nights before she even asked for one. They say all she had to do was shiver a little and he was heading up them stairs. It wasn't just his mother. He was the only boy that helped old ladies up the porch stairs and carried their groceries. The rest of us didn't care much for Scooter because we got tired of him trying to show us up.

I thought he was a sissie boy, under his mama all the time. Even played the piano. After school, my friends and me would lift ourselves on the garbage cans under his window and peep in, watching the two of them sitting at that piano, seem like sometimes all afternoon.

My mother took such a liking to Scooter that she told me time and time again that he was the type of boy I should be hanging around. Now, I wasn't a bad boy, didn't have bad friends. It was just that the church choir and the teachers' switch hadn't whipped all the mannish out of me good. And I was getting into my share of mischief. Mama kept giving me nickels so I could take Scooter for some ice cream, take him to the five-and-dime for a sucker. Truth was, I didn't want nothing to do with a boy that didn't have one callus to his name or at least one or two holes in his knees he'd carry for the rest of his days. So I'd take that money my mother gave me and get me two ice cream cones. Sit outside the store and lick 'em both, until the ice cream ran down to my elbows and my sleeves stuck to my arms.

Then when Scooter was going on twelve years old, in the summer of 1922, Ernest died. Say it was a heart attack or something. And I ain't never seen no two sadder people than that boy and Marjorie. Scooter'd sit on the porch all by himself most days after school. Just lonely. Marjorie would be gone for hours, working like a dog. She was never at home. Didn't have time no more for that piano or anything else. It seemed to die with Ernest.

One day, I was feeling a little sorry for Scooter, so I invited him to come play stickball with me and the rest of the boys. We played after school in this clearing on the east side of the trolley tracks.

"Can you hit, boy?" I said, not sure yet if I wanted a mama's boy on my team.

"I guess so," he said, hunching his shoulders.

"Well c'mon then, boy," I told him, "we ain't got all day."

By then, Scooter was almost a head taller than all of us and when he walked, everybody had to run to catch up. When we got to the clearing, I gave him a stick and tossed him a ball to see what was what. And that boy reared his head back and knocked that ball so far Rayman and T.C. had to go looking for it in a thicket of weeds and brush in an area where we used to go smashing turtles and small frogs. They came back with their legs bloody from the thorns and their hair knotted with sticky bugs, but they was smiling wide. That day, we won our first game against them rug rats from Twenty-third Street.

After winning game after game, I decided Scooter wasn't that bad for a mama's boy. I started to take a liking to him. He was big and quiet, didn't say much, so he couldn't say the wrong things. And that made him ready for the ice cream my mother thought he'd had a long time ago. After that, I showed him a couple of the places the boys and me hid out. Not all of them in the beginning, just a few. The first being the gambling house, where we peeped in the window in the back and his eyes popped wide open at all the money on them tables.

Then I took him to the ribs house. Back then, it was nothing but a shack—four walls and a tin roof barely held together, sitting on the ashes of the post office that had burned down in its place. Smoke never stopped rising from that lot.

The ribs was cooked in the alley behind the shack on this metal grate built up on two barrel drums. I made Scooter walk behind me so I could peep into the back door of Miss Shirley's kitchen. That's where she cooked her barbecue sauce. In the summer, she cooked in nothing but a brassiere, shorts, and high heels, sipping bathtub gin. And it was worth going back there just to watch her hips as she stirred the sauce and her shorts rise up when she stretched to reach the can of Colman's mustard on the top shelf. Nobody could stir sauce like Miss Shirley. Had two big dimples behind her knees that looked like she was smiling at you from behind.

I whispered to Scooter, "I popped her brassiere once."

"Her brassiere?" he said. His eyes grew wide as two mud pies.

"She slapped the hell out of me for it," I told him. "Heard bells for two weeks."

"It wasn't worth getting hit," he said.

"The hell you say, boy," I said, winking at him. "The hell you say."

After I schooled Scooter on the pleasures of ribs, a few weeks later I took him to my other secret place, where we ate them. Right next door to the whorehouse, there was this little underpass nobody used. We sat under the stairs, eating until our bellies ached, watching all the white aldermen with freshly pressed tweeds and shiny wing tips meeting their fancy cars in the alley. Tracking mud back to Hyde Park, Englewood, respectable neighborhoods.

Well, the music was always loud around that place, but there was this one cove in the basement where you could find peace. More peace there than in the entire neighborhood, seem like. That was where I took him next, to this room in the basement. I figured he'd really like this place because there was an old upright piano in the middle of the room. When the boys wasn't around, I used to pick at it on days after we watched Scooter and Marjorie.

Scooter sat down at that piano and I could almost see Marjorie sitting right next to him. He started playing "Nearer My God to Thee." I let him play a few bars. Figured it couldn't hurt none when you considered we was in the basement of a whorehouse. Then I moved Marjorie on out the way and sat down beside him. I tapped a little ragtime into the bass keys. And soon God moved over and Scooter was following me up and down those keys, our fingers falling, stumbling, chasing one another all over that ivory. From heaven to you know where and back again. Lord, we was moving. Making that piano scat and holler.

That's when I decided Scooter was ready for the next place. We went outside, climbing the fire escape around the back. All year round, since I'd been peeping in them windows, they always stayed open—wide open in the summer; raised a little in the winter to let fresher stale air through.

We went from window to window, watching women lying alone, filing, polishing their fingernails, smoking cigarettes, waiting on their next customer.

Then we came to the next window, one I'll regret going to for the rest of my life. Scooter looked inside and I was snickering the whole time. Waiting for my look. Then I saw Scooter's face turn gray. I swear I was sure I could feel him turning cold. He leaned against that window ledge. Blinking. Blinking. Barely catching his breath. The fire escape had been shaky since we stepped on it, but I knew the rumbling underneath now had little to do with the girders pulling away from the bricks.

Scooter wiped through the film of dust on the window.

"Mama?" he said. He said it so low that only somebody standing over his shoulder could of heard it. It and that moaning, a belly-low whimpering coming from that boy that sounded like a wounded dog about to be put to sleep. Marjorie was laughing and giggling, staring at the man on top of her. The music from the radio over in the corner was too loud and the man too busy for her to hear or see anything that wasn't right in her face.

"Mama?" he said again.

Even at twelve years old, one boy can look at another and see him breathe in air and know he'll never let that breath out again. 'Cause it'll get stuck somewhere so deep, nobody'll ever find it. There it'll sit for years in the pit of his stomach, under a heart that'll never beat right again.

"Mama, you a whore?"

When the man finished, he and Marjorie just lay there, his elbow pressing against her throat and his other hand hanging off the side of the bed.

By then, Scooter done took to running down the fire escape, jumping the steps two, three at a time. He hit the ground and started running down the alley, tripping and sliding through the mud. Bouncing from building to building like a caged animal, trying to get free.

I'll live to be a hundred years old and I'll never forget the look in that boy's eyes. Years later, every time I saw him, he wouldn't say much to me. Didn't have time. Somebody was always on his tail—the police, some gambler, some girl he done wrong. Even at Adeline's and the girls' burial, I looked up as they lowered their coffin into the ground and I saw Scooter standing behind a tree. Two seconds later, it seemed, I looked up again and he was nearly out of sight. Just running away.

I can't help but think that if I'd never taken Scooter to that whorehouse, maybe he'd have grown up to be a man. Maybe he would have learned how to stand up straight, look people in the eye, and we could see the front of him for a while instead of always having to see the back of him, doing little more with his life than tracking mud.

By the time Judd finished talking, the rain had stopped and Alfred's sermon had ended. Judd got up and put on his army jacket, lifting the collar around his neck to protect against the chill. I just sat there staring into that news article, reading them words about Alfred trying to do some good, wondering why after forty years Judd chose that day to tell me what he knowed.

Then, after Judd left and I locked up and washed down the counter and swept every corner of the floor and folded my towels and wiped off the table, the Victrola, the piano, it hit me. Judd wasn't telling that story for me. He was telling it for himself. After all them years, he still had hope for Alfred. That day, he wanted to believe Alfred had truly changed. There was something about seeing it in black and white that made it seem real and official-like. There was something about seeing it in the newspaper that made Judd believe even a little boy that was hurt worst than hurt, all them years ago, could go in and remake himself. Gut out all that mess and start brand-new. Well, I try not to doubt the power of the good Lord, but it seemed to me that that was work even he woulda had a whale of a time helping somebody do, especially if that somebody was Alfred Mayes.

Tempestt:
"Take me to the water . . ."

After missing an entire week of school, Valerie returned the day before the debutante ball. That afternoon, she was sitting on the rocks with her back toward me when I ran over. I cupped my hands over her eyes, getting ready to say "Guess who?" when I could feel moisture on my palms. Unlike with Gerald, I couldn't pretend I didn't notice. Her face glistened against the sun. Her eyes, blood red, made her face look misshapen and old.

"Valerie," I said, kneeling beside her. "Is something wrong? Where've you been?"

Wiping her face on her sleeve, she then found a loose thread on her jumper to tug on before looking out into the water. "Ain't nothing wrong," she said dryly.

After a few seconds, she pulled her knees up toward her chest and wiped her entire face with her hem. Her two braids flopped forward and she didn't say anything more, just kept staring out across the water.

I sat there with her, though I didn't look at her long. It didn't seem right to watch her face like this, so I fiddled with the moss between the rocks. I listened to the gulls squawking, gathering at our feet, waiting for food that wasn't coming.

When class resumed, I sent her a note, once again asking why she was crying.

"I'll tell you later," is what she whispered over her shoulder. But she never did.

I watched Valerie that entire afternoon. She seemed as though habit more than anything dragged her up to the blackboard to do a simple math problem, which she got wrong. And when she walked back to her desk, the suction noises from her shoe boots and the class's snickers were deafening. Even when Mrs. Jackson asked the class to settle down, the sound seemed to echo throughout the afternoon.

Then, just before the three o'clock bell rang, my friend began to slump, almost rooting herself in her chair. Her limbs looped and stiffened around the wood and metal of the desk. And she became so quiet that I wanted to shake her to make sure she was still real. Silence gripped her like a straitjacket. Something unnatural for a little girl whose body normally held back nothing, especially while in the middle of sharing her secrets. That day ended the way each had when Valerie came to school: with the yellow Nova idling at the curb.

My parents had decided to let Valerie sleep over the night of the debutante ball. Because of this, there was no yellow Nova. All the girls had been giddy and talking about Chicago's, Lakeland's, most important black-tie event of the year. Everyone was talking about it, but no one looked forward to it more than Valerie. It was as though this were her very own private party for which she had waited a lifetime.

That day, Valerie flitted about the rocks, chasing the gulls and flopping down beside me several times, out of breath. We chased each other and laughed at the children behind us.

In class, we watched a slide show about the Underground Railroad and Valerie laughed harder than anyone when I folded my hands and made a silhouetted rabbit dance and hop across the screen. At the end of the day, we lined up to leave and Valerie jumped down each stair, taking some two at a time. Miss Jackson didn't bother to stop her. Once out the door, Valerie pulled me—half-skipping, book bag slamming into her back—to her apartment building so we could gather her things.

Two men in their sixties, dressed in navy blue overcoats and pressed slacks, sat on a bench outside the Five thirty-five building. One leaned forward, resting his chin on his cane, while the other sat upright, with his legs crossed. They laughed and chatted, watching squirrels play a game of hide-and-seek, winding in and out of willows and lilac bushes.

"See those men?" Valerie whispered as we approached them.

"Uh-huh," I said.

"They call themselves brothers. But John say they funny mens. You know what that mean?"

Embarrassed, I shook my head.

"It means they kiss and do it."

"Two men?" I asked, frowning.

"Uh-huh," Valerie nodded. "One day, they forgot to send down their laundry and John took his master key and went up to their apartment. He said he knew Mr. Richards needed his suits cleaned for a big meeting. So John had to go up there. I heard John telling Miss White, one of the laundry ladies, that under the mattress they had stacks of funny books with naked people. And they only had one bed. You ever saw a funny book?"

"Once," I said. I really hadn't, but I didn't want Valerie to know.

"Remind me to show you one," she said. "John keeps a couple in his pillowcase."

Valerie's eyes were wild and greedy as she locked her arm in mine and we walked stiffly past the two men, swallowing back an explosive store of giggles. We didn't breathe until we made it to the lobby door. When the doorman nodded, we laughed out loud at him, then tore past the bronze elevators to a side elevator that whined as it lowered us to her basement apartment.

It was hot and humid down there, and so dark, it took several seconds for my eyes to adjust. Valerie's adjusted almost instantly. We followed yellow track lights along a hallway that smelled of standing water and rotten eggs. By the time we got to her door, it was so muggy, I'd undone the first button on my blouse and rolled up my sleeves.

"We're here," Valerie said, throwing down her book bag. Though paint blistered on the cinder blocks and the furniture was a menagerie of old worn pieces and hand-me-down newish ones, she panned her arms over the living room as if we'd just entered a palace. "This is it," she said. Then, pointing to a man lying belly-down on the floor between the sofa and a coffee table, she said, "And that's John."

John was dressed in a khaki custodian's uniform. His pants were soiled and frayed around the edges. On one foot was a work boot and on the other was a faded blue sock that was wearing thin at the heel and ball of his foot.

"Watch this," Valerie said, winking. She pulled her leg back and with all her strength kicked John's boot. He let out a deep, muffled breath but didn't wake up.

"What'd you do that for?" I asked. "If I did that to my father, I'd better have a good excuse."

"Not John," she said, bellowing out an exaggerated laugh to prove her point. "Mama say Jesus would have an easier time waking Lazarus again than he would trying to wake John. He sleeps so hard because the people in the building works him hard. John say like a Hebrew slave." She sat down on the sofa and propped her feet up on the table." He was up all last night pressing the cuffs in Mr. Taylor's pants. Mr. Taylor likes the cuffs military-style, and if John don't get it right, he got to keep doing it. A whole hundred times if he has to, until Mr. Taylor say it's okay. Night before that, John found Miss Jacob's grandfather's teeth in his suit pocket. Wrapped in a handkerchief. You know what he did?"

"No," I said.

"He stayed up real late trying to figure out how to return them the proper way." She saw the puzzled look on my face. "Well, it ain't that easy. What would you do?" She walked up to me, her hands forming a sphere. "'Scuse me, sir," she said, extending her hands. "You forgot your chops and I wanted to get them back to you before you had a notion to smack on something."

She leaned against me, laughing, rubbing her stomach.

"So why does John do all that?" I asked.

"He don't want us to have to leave Lakeland. He say he'll do whatever he has to to not get fired. He wants me to have a chance, he say, and for us to stay here forever."

"All that to stay here?"

"Uh-huh," she said. She reached over to a rotary telephone that sat on an end table. The table was missing a leg and was supported by a sawed-off two-by-four. She "accidentally" knocked the receiver off the hook. Then she straddled John's back, bent down, and cupped her hands over his ear. "John, wake up," she yelled. His leg twitched. "John, can I spend the night over at Temmy's house?"

"Sugar Babe, that you?" he asked, jumping up—eyes tightly shut—nearly knocking Valerie off his back. She held on as though he were a bucking horse she was trying to tame.

"Yeah, John," she screamed. "Can I spend the night with Temmy, pleease?" She closed her eyes, hunched her shoulders, and crossed her fingers, then her arms for extra luck. I, too, crossed my fingers. I held them up so she could see.

"I don't care, Sugar Babe," he said, snorting and plunging his nose with the heel of his hand. He still hadn't opened his eyes.

"So it's okay?" she asked. When he didn't say anything, she asked again, "It's okay?"

"Yeah, yeah, yeah," he growled. "Now go'n so I can get me some rest."

"Thanks, John," she said, smiling up at me, uncrossing her fingers. "Thanks a bunch!"

The entire apartment was rather small and Valerie's bedroom alone was only about half the size of Miss Lily's sewing room. Her pallet, neatly tucked and folded, lay over in a corner under a rusting pipe, next to a shoe box–size opaque window. A dressmaker's dummy with straight pins and slivers of colorful textured swatches stood behind her deb dress, which hung on a metal pipe coming out of the ceiling. Passing by the pale blue dress, Valerie stood on tiptoes to brush dust off the lace bodice and the velvety rose belt. After smoothing the slightly furled hem, she slipped her dress off its hanger.

"That's the pipe I hear things from," she said. She walked over to a curtain that hid a cardboard closet, then reached behind a stack of canned foods to a pile of folded underwear. She grabbed two pairs of panties, a pair of ankle socks, and a towel with hooks. As she placed the items into a brown paper bag, I walked over and grabbed the towel.

"What is this?" I asked.

"Can you keep a secret?" she said.

I nodded.

Unbottoning her blouse, she showed me how she'd transformed another towel into a makeshift girdle. Then she unhooked the bindings, displaying two pinkish nobules on her chest.

"Valerie!" I said. She shushed me, covering my mouth. So I whispered, "Where'd you get those?"

"You'll have some soon," she said, putting her clothes back together. "I'm older than you. I'll be thirteen in January. John told me not to tell."

"Thirteen?"

"Uh-huh. Nobody else knows. So it's our secret." As she continued gathering her things, I watched her, unsure of the next step. When it had been quiet for too long, she said, "Did I tell you about the old lady who lives on the third floor?"

"She's the one who harks and moans all night long and wets her bedsheets, right?" I said.

"Uh-huh. John say even a grown man ain't stronger than old lady pee. Smell like pneumonia. Want to see my earrings?"

"Okay," I said, shrugging.

She pulled a coffee can from the back of her closet and as she reached in, a spider jumped down her arm. She quickly swept it out of her way, then wiped her hand on her uniform. "When Mrs. Hubbard left the day I saw her and John doing it behind the elevator shaft, I went back to look around. And I found these. Ain't they pretty?" She spun the gold hoop earrings around her fingers. "Mama pierced my ears just so I can wear them. John still don't know. I don't let him get close enough. Anyway, Mrs. Hubbard came down to the shaft twice looking for the earrings. John asked me if I saw them and I said no. I crossed my fingers because it's okay to lie if you remember to cross your fingers. I bet they're pure gold."

She put one of the earrings on herself, then the other on me. I grimaced, but I didn't stop her. She led me over to a mirror that was hanging on the wall next to her closet. Placing her arm around my shoulder, she said, "Now we're twins."

We stood side by side, her head leaning against mine as we looked into the mirror. Valerie was shorter than I was, probably by about three or four inches, which, after a while, I didn't think about, because sitting on the rocks, her stories had made her seem ten feet tall. Now her breasts made her seem even taller. As she and I stood there staring, I brushed down my bangs and stooped a bit so we'd be closer to the same height, and her sandy braid looked funny falling onto my shoulder.

Valerie went back to packing and I lay flat on her pallet, weary from the heat. Folding my arms behind my head, I stared up at the ceiling. When Valerie was ready, she wiped sweat from her forehead and lay beside me on the pallet. Pointing to the patchwork of flecked and dangling paint chips, she told me if I squinted and concentrated long enough, I could see faces.

"It's like looking at faces in clouds," she said.

She pointed to one spot that resembled Joel Russell with his fat lip and another that looked like Natalie Hubbard. Two circles allowed for her profile, including the big nose. We lay there for a few moments looking up at what had suddenly become a skylight, zillions of times bigger than the window beside her bed, with so many possibilities, it was hard to believe they could all fit into such a tiny room.

I was so excited, I could hardly open our front door. I dropped the keys twice and fumbled with them until Mama finally opened the door for me.

"Mama," I said proudly. "This is Valerie."

"Well, nice to meet you, Valerie," Mama said, wiping her hands on her dish towel.

"I've been trying to call your father. Is he at home?"

"Yes, ma'am," Valerie said coyly.

"We went over there after school, Mama," I said, pulling Valerie over the threshold. "He said it was okay for Valerie to spend the night. He's sleeping now."

"I still need to call him myself, Tem."

"But I heard him say it was okay," I said.

Valerie walked into the foyer behind me, her body slowly following her large eyes. "Wow," she whispered to me. "Your mother's pretty."

In the middle of the foyer, Mama had placed a small round table with a bowl of fruit. Valerie stared at it until Mama told her she could help herself. Valerie grabbed two apples, a pear, and a banana and stuffed them into her paper sack.

We walked into the living room and Daddy looked at us over his reading glasses. Taking them off and standing, he said to Valerie, "You must be Miss Nicholae."

"Uh-huh," Valerie said, sheepishly peeping around me.

"Well, make yourself at home. You need anything, feel free to get it. No strangers here."

Valerie nodded and scratched her head. "He's too tall," she said to me under her breath as we walked away. I was sure Daddy had heard her, and I confirmed it when I turned around and he was smiling at us.

I pulled Valerie to my bedroom the way she'd pulled me to hers. We passed the kitchen, where Miss Lily was sitting at the table, waiting for my mother to return so she could finish polishing my mother's nails. I peeped in.

"Hey, Miss Lily," I said, holding on to Valerie's hand.

"Hi, Red," Miss Lily said, looking down at her own nails. To Valerie, she said, "Hey there, Sugar Babe."

"Hi, Miss Lily," Valerie said as I pulled her away from the door.

"Y'all be good, now," Miss Lily said, smiling. "I don't want to have to come back there with my belt."

In my bedroom, Valerie draped her dress over my bed, placed her bag beside it, and went over to the stack of stuffed animals. After the first week, I'd almost forgotten it was there. I showed her my model airplane, but she wasn't at all interested, especially when she saw the ornate comb and brush set Grandma had given me. Valerie stood over it, transfixed for a few seconds, before combing and brushing the loose strands around her braids.

Not long after, Mama walked into my bedroom.

"I want you girls to start getting ready," she said. "Temmy, you let Valerie take her bath in your room; you come on back to mine."

Valerie smoothed her hair and her jumper dress. "You're very pretty," she said to my mother. "Not prettier than my mother, but really pretty."

"And I can say the same about you, ma'am," Mama said. "Okay, girls, we should probably start getting ready if we expect to be on time. Tem, I'll do your hair first."

When I walked into the kitchen, Miss Lily was leaving, huffing and puffing, as usual, to stand, then to walk down the hall. Daddy came in right after her and curtseyed. "My little girl is going to be the prettiest belle at the ball tonight," he said, kissing my hand. I blushed and Mama rolled her eyes, trying not to smile.

"Now, now, Felicia," he said, stooping for a closer look. "This is my child. Look at her. Girl, you're fine. Look just like your daddy."

"She looks like me, Thomas," Mama said, hands on her hips. "She just happens to have your hair. But she's all me."

Daddy walked over to the closet outside the kitchen. My dress was hanging on the door. It was tea-length, cream-colored, with accordion pleats. He held the dress up to me, then picked me up and swung me around until my legs felt like they would stretch to the ground. It seemed so long since I'd been in his arms. Suddenly, I was as giddy as Valerie, and this night, as I hoped it would, was turning into something incredibly special.

He took my hand and led me back to the chair where my mother was standing. Kneeling on one knee, he begin singing something awful he was composing as he went along. Mama was laughing now. And she snorted even harder when he crawled over to her feet and began serenading her, as well.

When he flung his arm up to hit a high note, we noticed Valerie standing in the kitchen doorway, staring grimly. Her hair, unbraided, was wild and fell to the middle of her back. And although she was beautiful in her dress, the pink velvet bow fitting her waist perfectly, her dirty shoe boots destroyed the look and hid the lace trim of her ankle socks.

"I look ugly," Valerie said, nearly in tears.

"No you don't," I said, walking over to her. We both looked down at her shoes.

"You know what, Valerie?" Mama asked. "I think we can find some of Temmy's patent leathers that'll fit you. Come on in, dear. If you want, I'll give you two pretty braids and I'll put some bows on the end. Don't let me forget to give you both perfume."

"Bows and perfume?" Valerie smiled and quickly sat down in the chair.

"Don't worry, dear," Mama said. "When I'm done, you and Temmy will be the prettiest girls at the ball."

Mama clinked the hot curlers on the stove. Though Valerie's hair curled naturally, Mama cooled the curlers, then pressed them against Valerie's edges to smooth flyaways.

"Temmy says you and your dad have only been in Lakeland for a year?" Mama asked.

"Yes, ma'am," Valerie said, making a face as my mother untangled her hair. Valerie reached over to smell the Queen Bergamot hair dressing on the table and smiled at its minty fragrance.

"Your mother's still across the street?"

Valerie nodded. "She's doing good work saving lost souls in the projects."

"Lost souls?"

"My mama, John, and me have fun like you all just had," Valerie said, mushing her palms. "But Mama is one of the New Saved people and she can't have fun all the time because she and the others go from apartment to apartment taking care of kids, teaching them how to live right, and helping shut-ins."

"Shut-ins?" Mama said.

"Yes, ma'am. Last year? Mama helped Miss Grace when she became a shut-in. That was after Junior died. Junior jumped over the twelfth-floor fence."

Mama stopped braiding, and before she knew it, the three long columns of hair were slipping through her fingers. She caught them before they completely untwisted.

"I didn't see him," Valerie continued, "but I heard about it. They say he ran out of his apartment on the eleventh floor like he was on fire. Mama said Holy Ghost fire, all up in his bones. He ran up one flight to our floor, shaking his arms and hands, shaking his head and spitting his tongue out like a snake. He was screaming so loud, he woke up everybody. I ain't never liked Junior much before because he was always trying to boss somebody. But I like him now. Mama said it's only right.

"Mama was there when he jumped. She said she saw him glide down into the playground below, leaving a trail of ashes. It was like he was on a long sliding board. She said he didn't really hurt himself because God took Junior in his arms like the baby he was, and God rocked him until he landed light and feathery into his hands. The next morning, Mama said there was so many flowers in the playground that it looked like a garden. She and the other New Saveds went down there to give Junior a proper homegoing. They snipped that yellow ribbon and lined up holding hands and singing." Valerie began tapping her foot, nodding her head, " 'Take me to the water, take me to the water. Take me to the water, to be baptized.'

"And every day, even now, Miss Grace keep coming up to our floor with her lawn chair and she sits there all day. Mama gives her a blanket and some soup. She combs her matty hair. And Miss Grace just shakes her head a lot and says, over and over"— Valerie's voice deepened—" 'Ain't got no more tears. Ain't got no more tears.' " Valerie turned to show my mother how the woman shook her head and a blank stare came over Valerie's face. Mama sat down at the table. I got a lump in my throat.

"Miss Grace looks out over the porch fence like something's there. But ain't nothing to look at but sky, sometimes rain or lightning bolts, the lake, and the big white birds. Mama tells her every day that Junior is better off. The Good Book say God'll let you climb the rough side for just so long, and when you can't stand no more, he'll lift you. Every single day, Mama tells Miss Grace that's why God gave Junior wings. Mama say everybody got wings. Ain't nothing to be sad about because Junior's better off. But Miss Grace don't listen."

My mother was in a daze until she realized that the hot curlers had caught on fire. She turned the flame off, set the hot curlers on a hot plate, then sat in the chair next to Valerie. She brushed Valerie's hair back and took her in her arms.

CHAPTER 16

Tempestt:
"When I think back on it, I suppose the kiss didn't last very long."

The Newhouse Country Club sat on a partial cliff, in the center of Lakeland's shore, about one hundred yards north
of the academy. It was the only rise on the shoreline and the high-
est piece of land behind the fence. The structure itself, a Frank
Lloyd Wright–inspired building with cantilevers, stone walls, and
stained-glass windows, was one of Lakeland's jewels. At night, soft
blue lights gave it height and turned it into something of a
national monument. All of the black-tie to-dos were held there,
award ceremonies, the senior prom, political fund-raisers. Once a
year for the July Fourth extravaganza, the newspapers captured it
in a blaze of glory as fireworks sent red, white, and blue sparkles
around its crest. And on Memorial Day, there were similar pho-
tographs taken, this time with the gulls soaring overhead. Every
Memorial Day, legend had it, about ten gulls were gathered into a
pen, dipped in blue and red food coloring, and released into the
sky while the boys' choir belted out "America the Beautiful" followed by a fifteen-gun salute.

That night, as my parents, Valerie, and I neared the country
club, Valerie pointed to the two white beams twirling against the

clouds. Mama and Daddy walked in front of us, holding hands, and every now and then Valerie would stop to listen intently. "You hear it?" she whispered. "I bet it's the biggest orchestra in the whole world." She bent down to refold her socks so that the lace trim of each was the same when she put her legs together to measure. Then she smiled, snapping her fingers and bouncing to the beat. "I can't wait to dance."

In the courtyard, we walked in behind a group of feathered and chiffoned ladies waiting to enter the hall. The snapping blue lights from the cameras threaded through all the beads and sequins, brocades and diamonds, causing a fury of light so bright, they made me dizzy. Mama tugged on Daddy's coat sleeve. "There's so much fluff and puffery beyond those doors," she said, "I hope you remembered your shovel."

But my father didn't hear her. I'm sure of this, because he was too busy looking over the shoulders and heads of the people in front of us, trying to see what lay beyond the doors. Valerie was just as eager, stepping out of line several times to see around the crowd.

After checking our coats, my parents stopped to talk to some neighbors. Valerie, too excited to wait, grabbed my hand and pulled me down a long, mirrored corridor. She slowed once to smooth her hem again and to make sure her braids hung properly so that the bows were in clear view when she stepped through the doors of the grand room. I, on the other hand, looked at my hair, that bright red hair, and thought about what Natalie Hubbard had said about me finding a dress that didn't clash. A part of me wondered if it did. Then, once again, I decided I didn't care.

The hall led to a huge room with velour high-back chairs that lined a red-carpeted center aisle. At the front of the room, a group of men and women gathered around a black lacquered grand piano, sipping champagne and pinching canapes off the tray of the waiter who weaved through the crowd. When he came to Valerie and me, I took one, tasting it with the tip of my tongue, afraid to take a whole bite. Valerie, as usual, took as many as her hands could hold.

People were gathered in little patches throughout the country club. Camera crews from television stations were setting up to broadcast portions of the night live on the news. Reporters from Chicago's two newspapers interviewed the dignitaries for the annual story that would run in all editions of both newspapers and on the front page. In a back room, the debs themselves were putting the final touches on makeup and hairdos and speeches, which to a fault included how they planned to bring about world peace and a cure for cancer. And fathers lined up down a long corridor, smoking cigar after cigar as they waited to introduce their little girls into society.

Just before the ceremony was to begin, Valerie and I found a set of French doors that led to a balcony overlooking the lake.

I folded my arms against the cold air. Valerie folded her arms as well, forgetting for a moment how careful she'd been not to rumple her dress. We bent over the railing. Behind us, there was light everywhere. But in front of us, there was a wall so black that the water flowed into the sky and a heavy fog swallowed everything, from the light on the lighthouse to the gulls flying out beyond the shore.

"What do you think is on the other side?" Valerie said.

"I don't know," I said, opening my eyes wide, trying to see.

"I wonder where them birds fly to. When we was in the projects, I would stand on our porch, watching them go. But we only lived on the twelfth floor, so we couldn't see much. You got a much better view on the twenty-second floor."

"We'll take a trip," I said. "In the spring, when it's warm, we'll pack a lunch. You got a bike?"

"John found me a bike. But he say we got to let it sit for a while until it cools off."

"Did he steal it?" I asked.

"Heck no," she said. "Nancy Walker got a brand-new one because her old one was only a three-speed. When she threw it out, John got it for me."

"Well, by next summer it should be cool enough. We'll find out how to get over there and we'll take a trip."

"You'd do that for me?" Valerie said.

I crossed my heart, then took her little finger in mine, cementing the promise with an around-the-world circle.

"I'd like to see what's over there," Valerie said, staring into the dark night. "I think it's heaven, because last year, when the birds was dying, that's where they was going. I would sit on the rocks and they'd be flying, flapping their wings until I couldn't see them no more. John said somebody had slipped packages of rat poisoning down between the rocks. He said whoever did it knew them birds is nasty and will eat anything.

"John said somebody wanted to get rid of them because of the mess they makes. That's why every day I give them a little something. So they won't eat no more poison. So they can stay over here instead of flying across the water."

When a drumroll began, we left the balcony for the grand room. Mama waved at us to hurry to take our seats. A red curtain was swept up into the ceiling, revealing a shiny wooden floor and the orchestra, which formed a crescent around the stage. Following an introduction, each young miss danced out on her father's arm to the microphone in the center of the stage. The men handed the girls large bouquets of flowers awaiting them in an urn beside the microphone, then stood back with their hands folded as their daughters spoke eloquently, exuding grace and charm. Then the white spotlight bubble slid from under them, their cue to disappear back behind the curtain.

After the last girl and her father crossed the stage, the mayor made his comments at a podium near the piano. To mass applause, he praised the poise and elegance of the girls and hailed them as future leaders of Lakeland, credits to their community.

He stepped away from the podium. The lights dimmed slowly and the stage began to fill with dancers. First the debutantes, then everyone was allowed to join in. I looked over at my father. He extended his hand, looped my arm through his, and led me out to the dance floor.

In the old house, when my father and I danced, he would hold me close to his heart and I would bury my head in his chest as we clumped off-beat around the kitchen, always to some old, warped Muddy Waters record that Daddy had to constantly jab to stop the needle on the player from scratching. My father had long been a closet dancer. And rarely did he dance in public, no matter how much my mother pleaded. But in the house, with the blues under his feet, my father would grab both my mother and me and the three of us would be swaying and dipping together, bumping into the kitchen table and stove, stumbling all over ourselves.

That night, we didn't have the benefit of the blues. We danced to some staid number I'll never remember. Our steps were delicate, measured, and at times rather polite. The music moving through us in terse, refined strokes. Everybody moving the same way. Barely moving. Everybody swaying the same way. Barely swaying. Hardly touching. It was like dancing in a box. I hated it.

I saw Valerie sitting on the sidelines watching us. She was sitting with my mother. "Daddy," I said, "would you dance with Valerie?"

"Sure, princess," he said. "Are we done?"

I nodded and went to get Valerie.

At dinner, I was supposed to sit between my mother and father, but Valerie scooted into my mother's seat. Mama looked at Valerie, smiled, and pulled out the chair to Valerie's left.

The man seated next to my father was Illinois senator Bruce Johnson. He was campaigning to be Chicago's first black mayor. History books would cast him as one of the greatest legislators in the state—a political pragmatist—and one of the founding fathers of Lakeland.

I didn't know him and was quite content listening to Valerie and my mother chat until I overheard him saying something about getting rid of Thirty-fifth Street.

"We need your support on this, Thomas," he said. "I think we'd all agree that it's time to clean up Thirty-fifth Street. A couple of sticks of dynamite should suffice." He laughed out loud, rode back in his chair. "First we get rid of those projects. Then one by one, we start clearing out those dilapidated stores and vacant lots."

Daddy took a sip of water and the senator followed.

"President Ford himself wanted to stomp here," the senator said. "He's promising a Lakeland in every pot. But with the recent assassination attempt and all, there's no way he's coming. And mainly it's because of what's outside our fence. We've stressed how safe Lakeland is, but the Secret Service isn't buying. It's like being a swan in the middle of a pigsty.

"The common thinking right now is that we be proactive, Thomas. Paul Jacobs over there is an architect. Lives in the Five thirty-five building. He's agreed to draw up preliminary sketches of what we have in mind. The idea is to expand Lakeland for a second phase. I want you to be a part of this, son. I've heard nothing but good things about you."

Finally, Daddy interrupted. "What do you do with the people there now?"

"Oh, we'll be fair," the senator said.

"Fair?"

"There's a Reverend Alfred Mayes over there. He and his congregation have been trying to clean up Thirty-fifth Street for years. There's a complex of vacant or nearly vacant projects that begin at Forty-seventh Street and goes on south for a couple of miles. Mayes has agreed to work with us in convincing the city to rehab those buildings and offer public housing that way."

Daddy looked over at me, then back at the senator.

The senator continued: "It'll be imperative that we're all on one accord on this issue, Thomas. So far, there hasn't been anything we can't do if we put our minds to it. The city listens to us. We may not be but a fraction of the voting bloc, but we are strong."

"Let me ask you this," Daddy said. He brushed his hair back. "Since what we're doing is expanding Lakeland, expanding opportunities, will some of the people be able to move over here? That is, if they're willing to live by different rules?"

"That's hard to do, Thomas," Senator Johnson said, shaking his head. "When you have people coming from subsidized housing—"

"Oh but, Senator," my father said, "Lakeland is subsidized housing."

"Lakeland?"

"We have everything over here. And we pay next to nothing in rents. The application makes it clear that our contribution to Lakeland . . . Let's see, what was it exactly? 'Your contribution to Lakeland will not be a monetary one, but one in which you add to its aesthetic, academic, and social achievements.' I suppose when you look right at it, Lakeland is a project. The city's little science project."

The senator sat perfectly straight. Appalled that my father would use the word *project* and the name Lakeland in the same breath.

"Besides," my father continued, "my family didn't come from lavish means. We had a little house on the far South Side. True, we've been here a little over a month, but we're doing fine."

"I know where you came from, Thomas. It was nothing like Thirty-fifth Street. Now, I know their circumstances have been unfortunate, but people are creatures of habit. I'd like to think that all we'd have to do is give them a decent place to live and they'd respond accordingly. But life's not that simple and neat."

"Depends on how simple and neat you're willing to make it, Senator," Daddy said.

"Well, this is called survival of the fittest, my boy. You'd better get used to it. It's time for Thirty-fifth Street to change into something respectable, and we can't hope it'll just happen. We've got to make it happen."

My father took a long sip of water, then leaned forward on his elbows. All I could think about was Miss Jonetta, Hump, Judd, Mr. Chittey, and Fat Daddy. What would happen to them if Thirty-fifth Street was destroyed? How would I get to see them?

I tugged on my father's sleeve. "Daddy," I said, rubbing my stomach, "I don't feel so good."

"What do you think is wrong, Tem?" he said, bending over to me.

"I think I might throw up."

"Me, too," he whispered, smiling. He excused himself from the senator, grabbed my hand, and whispered into Mama's ear.

"Where're you going, Temmy?" Valerie asked.

"She's going home," Mama said. "She doesn't feel good."

"But you're going to miss the young debs' picture," Valerie said.

I nodded solemnly, then turned and walked away with my father. Behind me, I could hear Valerie lament, "And I may not get to dance again."

"You'll dance again," Daddy said to her. "I'm coming back."

During our walk over to the apartment, Daddy didn't say much. A few times, he forgot he was walking with me and his gait became too large for me to compete with, so he apologized, slowing down.

At the apartment, he took my coat. "If I were a betting man," he said as we walked back to my bedroom, "I'd bet your recovery time is a short one."

Touching my forehead, he said, "You don't feel like you have a fever. I'd guess you got a bunch of butterflies in your stomach. The thought of having to stand in front of all those people, smiling and everything all night, would make me a little sick, too. We'll be about another hour; then we'll be back. Okay?"

"Okay, Daddy," I said.

He spread a blanket out over me and kissed me on the forehead. I listened for him to close the front door, lock it. Then I grabbed my key and headed down the back elevator to the fence.

Once outside the fence, I stood behind the tree for a second looking up at the twelfth floor, Valerie's mother's floor. At night, Thirty-fifth Street was dark, full of shadows and barely lighted vestibules. People were crowded around the steps. I had to squint to see them. But I could hear them talking, yelling, and their loud music.

On the corner, Li'l Beaver sat hunched over and shivering a few feet away from what remained of that day's pile of U.S. mail. Even in the semidarkness, I could see his face was bruised and swollen so badly that both eyelids were puffed, caked-together slits. A glass of water was positioned next to one of his gym shoes. And one of Miss Jonetta's white cloths was tucked in the collar of his wool coat like a bib. It was stained with splatterings of blood from two gashes on his bottom lip where his teeth had plowed in.

I walked closer. He slowly lifted his head. "Come back for some more?" he said, trying to stand. He tried and tried, kicking his legs, like a child trying to walk for the first time. "Ain't had enough?" he drawled. "You come back for some more?"

I stood there nearly frozen, my legs shaking as I backed away from him and ran around to the store. Jumping down the steps, I could hear him still yelling, "Come back for some more?"

In O'Cala's, the men were gathered around the radio, listening to Muhammad Ali talk about his fight with Joe Frazier, the "Thrilla in Manila." Mr. Chittey had been generous enough to unplug his earpiece and position the radio in the center of the table. Judd was the first to look up as I entered the store. Then Hump looked up and frowned. They both stood.

I settled myself and walked over to Miss Jonetta, who was sitting on my stool, face down on the counter. Her jug, nearly empty, with only a corner of cough syrup left, sat next to the cash register.

"Hi, Miss Jonetta," I said, poking her in her shoulder. She didn't move.

"What you doing out so late?" Judd asked, placing his hand on my shoulder. "Let me take you back home."

Hump bent down so that he could stare directly into my eyes.

"You know you ain't suppose to be coming over here by yourself," Judd said.

"I had to tell Miss Jonetta something," I said to both of them. "I just had to."

Then Fat Daddy started pounding the table and everybody jumped. "Well, shut my mouth wide open," he yelled, responding to something Ali was saying or bragging about. "That dude is bad, ain't he? That motherfucker is wicked, I tell you! A whole five hundred I won off his ass! I'm so happy, I could lay me a golden turd."

Judd walked back over to the table and jerked his head in my direction.

Fat Daddy looked down at his expensive-looking gold watch. "Man, what she doing out here so late?" he said to Judd. Turning back to me, he said, "Didn't Miss Johnie tell you it wasn't safe to be over here after dark?" He was waiting on an answer when Miss Jonetta finally lifted her head.

"Why, don't you look pretty tonight," she said. Her eyes were red-rimmed and watery, and pink fingernail polish streaked across her fuzzy white sweater. The teardrop-shaped bottle sat on the counter, but the brush had fallen into her lap.

"Miss Jonetta, I've got something important to tell you," I said, patting her shoulder.

She looked up at the Pepsi-Cola clock, then outside the window up to the sidewalk. She opened her mouth but didn't speak. A stretch of saliva created a bridge between her parted lips.

"Miss Jonetta," I said again. "I got something to tell you."

Mr. Chittey turned off the radio.

Miss Jonetta lowered her head onto the counter and when I shook her, her black bun unraveled down to her waist. I thought I'd touched something I shouldn't have, so I jerked my hand back and looked up to see if anyone had noticed. Hump and Judd had, but they didn't say anything.

"Miss Jonetta," I said again, "I was at the deb ball tonight and—"

"Child," she said, lifting her head again, "ain't you something pretty? Take that old coat off so I can see you."

I didn't care about being pretty, but I knew I wouldn't be able to go on if I didn't show off my dress.

As I slowly turned, Miss Jonetta swirled the remaining contents of her jug, tossed her head back, and took a hard swallow. "You're prettier than Miss Ann."

"But Miss Jonetta," I said, "I was at the deb party tonight and they were talking about getting rid of Thirty-fifth Street. The projects. Getting rid of all the stores, including O'Cala's."

She waved her hand, nearly falling off the stool. I rushed to help her keep her balance. "Honey, people been talking about shutting us down for years, especially them preachers. Truth be told, one of them tornadoes could rip through here and we'd be the lone survivors."

"But this man said there were papers and that street preacher was helping. . . ."

"Ah," Judd said, walking up to the counter to greet a customer entering the store. "They ain't got nothing nobody else ain't had at one time or another." He lifted Miss Jonetta by her arm, replacing the stool with his chair. Then he rang up two bottles of Thunderbird and a can of Old Style. When the customer kept staring at the bottles, his hands trembling on the counter, without moving to retrieve money from his coat pockets or a rolled-down sock, Judd simply handed over the brown paper sack. "No need in getting yourself worked up over nothing," he said to me as he reached into his own wallet. "Believe me when I tell you we gone be here forever."

"Forever?"

"Forever," Judd said, mussing my hair.

Once again, Miss Jonetta's head did a sort of slow drag against the counter. That final time, she couldn't lift it again. I reached out to touch the tip of her hair. It was fine and covered with heavy oil. After brushing several strands away from her wet face, I wiped her lightly freckled cheeks slowly with the back of my hand. She looked so unlike herself—haggard and frail. I moved her hair back again, looking for the Miss Jonetta I knew, but she wasn't there.

Judd walked from behind the counter to the aisle with the taffy candy and beckoned for me to follow.

"Miss Johnie done had herself a hard day," he said in a low voice. "She tired now, that's all. You have any sisters or brothers?"

"No."

"Well, Miss Johnie had herself a sister, Essie, and today is the anniversary of her passing. So Miss Johnie is feeling kind of low."

"Can I do something to help her?"

"No," he said. He was quiet for a moment. "Why don't we not worry our minds about all that right now. Miss Johnie knows your heart is in the right place," he said. "Why don't I get Hump to walk you on over to the fence, and I promise when you come back tomorrow, she'll be a lot better."

Although I believed Judd, it didn't feel right leaving Miss Jonetta. After staring at her for a long time, Hump handed me a note. "She'll be okay" is what it said. I folded it, placing it in my pocket as he led me out the door and up the stairs. When we got to the corner, I looked for Li'l Beaver. But he was gone. Only Miss Jonetta's bloodstained cloths remained, along with droplets of blood that left a trail on into the alley.

I sneaked back into the apartment through the back door, slowly looking around, rehearsing the lie I'd prepared in case Mama and Daddy had returned before me. But as soon as I made it to my bedroom, I could hear the keys unlocking the front door. I hopped into the same spot I was in before my father left and pretended to be asleep.

Mama, Daddy, and Valerie came into the room. Mama felt my cheek with the back of her hand. "Will the little sick child in the house please step forward?"

I opened my eyes, stretched my body out. "I feel better now, Mama," I said.

"I just bet you do," she said, kissing my face. Daddy bent down to kiss me, too. He said good night to Valerie and me, then left the room.

"Valerie, I'll try your father one last time," Mama said, unbuttoning the back of my dress. "You think he's home?"

"Nope," Valerie said, staring into the mirror, watching her two braids sweep from side to side as she shook her head. "He doing his rounds."

"Are you sure he said it was okay?"

"I heard him, Mama," I said.

"Are you sure?" Mama asked again, tapping her chin. "I suppose as late as it is, he would have called out the cavalry a long time ago if he hadn't approved."

"Uh-huh," I said.

Valerie didn't say anything because she was still staring at herself in the mirror.

Mama told us to get ready for bed. Realizing that Valerie wasn't going to undress until she left the room, Mama kissed me again and kissed Valerie on her forehead. "Now leave this bathroom light on so Valerie can find her way if she has to," she said, pulling the bedroom door nearly shut. "And no giggling, hear? Go straight to sleep."

When all the other lights were out and Valerie and I were in bed, Valerie began chattering like a windup toy. She whispered now and then, getting louder as she talked about dancing with my father. "He's too tall," she said. "But he's a good dancer. A real good dancer. He danced all night. With your mother, and with me. I think some people thought I was his daughter."

"But you aren't," I said, my words tinged with jealousy.

"I know that," she said. Then sitting up suddenly, she added,

"The picture. You missed the young debs' picture. Mr. Mann said I was so pretty that he took one of me alone." She got out of the bed and felt her way to her dress, now draped over the chair. Handing the picture to me, she made me lean into the light. "See, I can't wait to show Mama. It's too bad you got sick."

I glanced down at the picture. I knew I was looking too quickly, but I was hurt that she'd danced so much with my father.

"Oh, and another thing," she said, jumping back out of bed, reaching into her coat pocket. "I got you one of these. I took two when they was handing them out."

She grabbed my hand and slipped a bracelet around my wrist. It was silver with a band that read: "The 1975 Lakeland Cotillion."

"Do you think I can sleep over again?" she asked, her voice fading off.

"I think so," I said flatly.

"You think we'll be friends for a long time?"

"Uh-huh," I said.

Valerie grabbed my hand and held it tightly—so tightly, it hurt. She held on to it the way Gerald had one day when we climbed the willow in his yard and he was about to fall. I reached out to him, holding his hand until he steadied himself on a bottom branch. I remember my hand throbbing, turning red, the blood rushing straight to my fingertips. That was how Valerie was holding on.

She continued to talk until her words didn't make sense anymore and she fell off to sleep, loosening her grip and folding her other hand over her chest so that the bows on the tips of her braids lay perfectly flat.

In the middle of the night, I awoke to Valerie making whimpering noises, sharp staccato rants mixed with muffled breaths that sounded as though she was in pain. It was as if she'd hurt herself and was afraid to release the true noise out of fear of waking me or my parents.

I sat straight up in bed.

"Valerie," I said, bending over her. "You okay?"

The light from the bathroom created a slanting triangle along the floor, and it stretched across the bed. Valerie, still asleep, had kicked off the top sheet. The bottom one bunched between us as her legs thrashed above the covers. Her twisted nightgown was pulled up over her panties and a thin film of sweat covered her forehead, connecting a streak of tears that ran from her tightly closed eyelids down to her earlobes and hung like crystal earrings.

"Valerie, are you okay?"

She moaned slightly.

Her head was no longer on the pillow and I noticed that in all the moving her hair bows had fallen to the floor. Her braids had begun to unravel into her face and I could smell the Queen Bergamot hair oil.

"Valerie?"

I watched her chest heave, her back arch into strained, unnatural curves. She curled herself into a ball, jerked her body back out into a straight line as if she were standing at attention, then curled up again with her back toward me. Again she moaned out, louder this time.

Jumping out of bed and running over to her, I slid down on the floor. "Valerie, wake up."

Her eyes fluttered, but they never opened. She smiled, and then as quickly and unexpectedly as the smile had come, it vanished, and her entire face became long and sullen. Her lips were moving, forming words I couldn't hear. Only her breath, in and out, slow. I moved closer to listen and I tried not to notice her hands—one in between her legs, the other reaching out to me. I moved even closer. "Valerie?"

Then—in a million years, I still don't know where it came from—Valerie put her arm around my waist and her lips against mine. When I think back on it, I suppose the kiss didn't last very long. But at the time, it seemed to go on forever. It wasn't the tight-lipped kiss Gerald had given me one day after school when he lost his mind and declared me his girlfriend. It was a grown-up kiss that kept me up the rest of the night, pressed against the far side of that full-sized bed. With Gerald, I'd drawn back to hit him. With Valerie, I swallowed hard, her taste mingling with mine. I swallowed again, keeping my eyes gawk-wide, searching every inch of the room that the bathroom light had failed to illuminate. The entire room folded into the darkness around Valerie. But I refused to look in her direction, to turn my head the slightest amount, until about 2:00 A.M., when someone knocked on the door.

CHAPTER 17

Tempestt:
"Valerie turned around to half-smile at me
and I could see the tears in her eyes."

Valerie was deep asleep, snoring. But my eyes were wide open when I heard someone banging on the door. I could hear my father's heavy footsteps dragging from his bedroom down the hall. I jumped out of bed and ran toward the living room, crouching down against the wall so I could peer around the corner.

"Who is it?" Daddy asked, looking through the peephole. He adjusted his pajama bottoms so the fly lay on a diagonal.

"Sorry to bother you, Mr. Saville, sir," the man said. "I'm John Nicholae and I'm looking for my girl."

When Daddy opened the door, John was wiping sweat from his top lip with a handkerchief he quickly shoved into his shirt pocket. He took off his baseball cap and, lowering his head a bit, said, "I don't mean no harm, sir, but Mr. Mann said he saw Valerie with your family tonight. I been looking all over for her. She here?"

"Yes, sure," my father said, still a bit disoriented. "Come on in."

I ran back to my bedroom. Shaking Valerie, I whispered, "John's here and it looks like you're in trouble."

At first, Valerie looked at me as though she didn't understand.

Then she bolted up straight in the bed, looking to the left, to the right.

"Want me to hide you?" I asked, thinking she was looking for an escape route. "We can go down the back elevator?"

"No," she said, and she closed her eyes tightly and crossed her fingers, her arms, and finally her legs.

"What'd you wish for?" I asked.

"For John to go home and leave me alone."

At first, we just sat there, listening to the muffled voices—my mother's, my father's, and John's. Unsure of what was being said, I ran to my bedroom door, peeped out, then started down the hall.

Mama was walking hurriedly toward me, tying the belt in her robe. "Did you know Valerie lied to her father in order to spend the night?"

"Valerie didn't lie, Mama," I said as she passed me and I tried to catch up. "John's got it all wrong."

"That's Mr. Nicholae to you, ma'am."

I followed Mama back to my bedroom. Valerie was still sitting up in the bed.

"Valerie," my mother said. "Dear, your father is here in a state. We've got to get you ready to go home. I've enjoyed having you, honey. You're a sweet child, but lying wasn't the way to go about this."

Valerie didn't say anything, just kept staring down at her palms.

"She didn't lie, Mama," I said for her. "John is the one lying."

"Tempestt Rosa, take your fanny into your bathroom right now and wash something. You hear me? I don't care what. Wash something, and now!"

"But I'm not dirty, Mama. . . ."

"Now, I said."

I pulled the bathroom door behind me and turned the water to a trickle. Then I listened at the door.

"Valerie," my mother said, "is everything okay?"

Valerie lowered her eyes and nodded.

"You sure?" Mama asked, kneeling beside her.

Valerie nodded again.

"Well, let's get your things ready."

Valerie rolled out of bed and walked over to her paper sack, which was sitting next to the chair. She reached in for her jumper dress, pulled it over her gown. Then she put on her shoe boots. She draped her deb dress over her arm.

"You know you're welcome anytime," Mama said, slipping several pairs of my new underwear into Valerie's paper sack. Valerie nodded and shortly afterward they left the room. I followed behind them far enough so Mama wouldn't make me turn back around.

In the living room, John was sitting across from my father. When he saw Valerie, head down, walking toward the door, he stood.

"Sugar Babe," he said, walking over to her and grabbing the paper sack, "I was looking all over for you."

"But you said I could stay, John," she said in a gruff voice, one normally reserved for school. "I asked you this afternoon when you was taking your nap."

"Sugar Babe, you know I don't know nothing from nothing when I'm resting. You know I'd agree to have my head chopped off if somebody asked me. I tells you over and over to wait till my eyes is wide open. Now come on, let's go."

He put his arm around Valerie's shoulder.

"So can I stay now, John?" she asked with eyes pleading up to him. "Can I stay now? Please?"

He didn't say anything to her. "Sorry to bother you folks," he said, steering Valerie out the door. "But Valerie'll be grounded for a few days."

"She's not a bad child," Mama said to John. "I don't approve of what she did, but I know she didn't mean any harm."

Valerie turned around to half-smile at me and I could see the tears in her eyes. She told me once that she could cry on command. She said all it took was blinking really hard and thinking about something that made you feel sad. But this time, I could tell even from across the room that these tears were real.

The next morning, I slinked past Mama, who was in the kitchen having breakfast with Miss Lily. Mama said she was sure I had been a coconspirator with Valerie in her attempt to spend the night but that she wasn't yet certain to what extent. So she decided not to punish me until she had more evidence. Besides, she and Miss Lily had planned to go downtown that day to do some early Christmas shopping and she didn't want anything to spoil her plans.

"But be forewarned," she said, allowing me to go outside, "as soon as I find out the whole story, I'll give you what-for."

I nodded and closed the door.

On the way down the elevator, I considered going to visit Valerie. I wanted to see her. Partly, I suppose, because I wanted to find out what happened after she and John left. But more important, I wanted to know why she had kissed me. Each time I thought about the kiss, it made me uneasy. Still, I decided to let it wait a while and visit Miss Jonetta instead.

The scratchy, whiny blues coming from the store was loud, but not loud enough to drown out the preachers. Saturday was the day for laying hands and people were waiting in the cold for Alfred Mayes to heal them. He stood on the platform with his arms stretched out over a line that snaked past O'Cala's door and continued for blocks. Most of the people in line were superstitious about me breaking it, so I had to wait until there was a sufficient gap. Then, to their horror, I crossed the line. One woman tried to grab me to make me retrace my steps, but I dodged her grasp, jumping down the stairs to O'Cala's.

When I opened the door, Miss Jonetta and Fat Daddy were doing a side step to a nearly warped record that moaned as it spun on the Victrola. In preparation for Hump and Retha Mae's wedding, two days off, the aisles of food and the display of Kotex had been pushed against the back wall. The piano had been moved closer to the front window, next to the checker table, which was now covered with a white paper tablecloth. Judd was hanging streamers and balloons on the walls, covering paint chips and this one large hole in the plaster that Miss Jonetta said was created one day when Li'l Beaver came in trying to rob the place. In the struggle, Judd threw him against the wall. Miss Jonetta said she forgave Li'l Beaver but left the hole in case the lump on his head healed too completely and he needed another reminder about why what he did was wrong.

Mr. Chittey was sitting in his chair with a bowl on his lap, tapping his foot to the music but complaining about having to peel potatoes for Miss Jonetta's salad.

"This is a shame," he growled. "What I look like—Betty Crocker?"

"Want an apron, Chitlin?" Miss Jonetta laughed. She was twisting her hips, making the tassels on her go-go boots jiggle. "Honey, don't you know, this salad's gone be the best ever 'cause you cut the potatoes." When she saw me just standing by the door, she waved. "Come on in, Child. I got a surprise for you today."

Judd turned the music down before going behind the curtain and returning with an A&P shopping bag that held a brand-new fishing rod.

"Wow," I said, sitting down on my stool, caressing the reel and the leader. It was similar to, if not exactly like, one I'd seen in a

Sears catalog. I knew I'd have to sneak it into the house, hide it under my bed.

"You know folks come in here all the time trying to sell me things," she said, dancing over to Mr. Chittey. She wiped a few potato peelings off his hand and pulled him over to the center of the floor. "Just last week, I bought fifteen dollars' worth of lipstick from them Avon ladies I been trying to get rid of for the past five years. Child, I can't pass up a sale. And I remember you telling me how much you and your papa liked fishing. So when that old dude came in yesterday with this rod, I took a look. Judd said it was a good one. Didn't you, Judd?"

Looking over his shoulder while hanging a balloon, he said, "Best one I seen in a long time. They don't make them that way no more. Guides and fittings there are rustproof," he said, pointing, "and the handgrip is guaranteed not to blister your palm."

"Somebody was selling fishing rods like this?" I said. "On the street?"

"That's right," Miss Jonetta said. "Honey, you can buy anything on Thirty-fifth Street. You might even find Calvary for sale."

Laughing out loud, she was the total opposite of the way I'd seen her the night before. And boy, could she dance. The entire floor rumbled with her moves. She did a showgirl kick over Mr. Chittey's little head. He hunched his shoulders and started rolling his stomach like a belly dancer as his cane slid right off his arm and his pants started to ease down his waist. She did a shimmy, rotating her shoulders, and Mr. Chittey started clapping his hands and stomping off-beat. Too cool. Miss Jonetta said, "Go, sweet feet, go!" And he kept moving. Pointing, bending, dipping east and west, then north and south.

The song, "Stormy Monday," faded to an end and all you could hear was the grinding and sweep-swishing of the record against the turntable. Miss Jonetta walked over to the counter. "I was born to do a jig, honey. Came into this world, my papa said, feet moving like a tap dancer." She took out her compact and blotted her face. "Came into this world moving and moving."

Fat Daddy bebopped over, snapping his fingers and clicking his heels against the planks. "You ever heard T-Bone Walker before?" he asked.

"Them people from across the street don't know nothing about the blues," Mr. Chittey offered, smiling.

"I know the blues," I said, haughtily flopping backward onto the stool.

Everybody laughed, even Miss Jonetta. Placing her hands on my shoulders to settle me, she said, "Now, what do you know about the blues?"

"My father likes Muddy Waters and B. B. King," I said proudly. "Mama likes B. B. King, too." I thought for a minute. "Oh, but her favorite is Billie Holiday."

Fat Daddy nodded, impressed. "They good, real good," he said. "But they don't beat my T-Bone. Bless his soul." He shook his head and tipped his hat, a purple wide-brimmed number with a thick rose-colored band. "T-Bone passed away earlier this year. March. March seventeenth. Boy, that thing hurt my soul. Nobody'll ever be able to pull some loving, some sho 'nuff squealing and hollering, from a guitar like T-Bone. You could say me and him was old friends."

At Fat Daddy's references to loving and squealing, Miss Jonetta looked at him and made him follow her eyes over to Judd. Without saying a word more, Fat Daddy walked over, meeting Judd's arm and a streamer midway up the wall.

"Fat Daddy thinks he met T-Bone when he came to Thirty-fifth Street in '44," Miss Jonetta whispered. "But that wasn't him.

Fat Daddy was playing cards with some fool Negro who was calling himself T-Bone Walker. But I knowed me some T-Bone. T-Bone had great big pop eyes, a heavy conk in his head, and a pencil mustache. This fool Fat Daddy met was just another fool gambler, telling lies. I done told Fat Daddy over and over that it wasn't him, but he don't listen. So I leave him alone. Can't help a man who want to cozy himself up to a daydream. Just got to let him wake up on his own terms."

She pointed over to Judd's and Fat Daddy's decorations.

"Hump and Retha Mae is the luckiest people around," she said. "It's countdown time to their hitching. I sent Hump home, though. The decorations and all was enough to send him into a spell, and none of us felt much like scooping him up today. I just love weddings. You?"

"Not really," I said, frowning. "You have to dress up in frilly stuff and smile a lot and people pinch your cheeks when you don't want them pinched."

"Oh, honey," she said, "weddings is beautiful. They make you feel like you can start all over and be brand new. My favorite part is when they say, 'Kiss the bride.' And everybody puckers up, bride or not, and eyes get hot and watery."

"Kiss the bride?" I asked.

"Yep," Miss Jonetta said.

"Miss Jonetta, have you ever been a bride?"

"Heavens no," she said, brushing loose strands back up into her bun. "All my life, I been moving too fast. But I'll tell you one thing, remaining footloose was always my decision. Wasn't never a spinster, mind you—them is women so homely that if you dressed a hog up in a pair of pants and propped him next to an altar, even he wouldn't sit for the ceremony. But that wasn't me, Child. I was pretty in my day. A stone fox."

"Miss Jonetta, I think you're still pretty."

"Ah, you're just saying that because it's true," she said, winking. "But anyway, as far as marriage goes, I didn't ever want to be tied down. Wanted to be able to come and go as I pleased. Wanted to be free as a little bird."

I hesitated, looking up out the window, around the store. "Have you ever been kissed?"

Miss Jonetta normally didn't smoke in front of me, but she pulled her pink cigarette case and gold lighter from her purse. She took out a long cigarette holder.

"Sure I have," she said out the corner of her mouth. "I only said I ain't never been married. Don't get me wrong, Child, you too young to be keeping company with boys. When you get older, a lot older, you'll learn there ain't nothing wrong with a little peck every now and then with the right young man. And at the right time. Why, it's only natural."

"Well, you remember my friend Valerie?" I paused because I knew I was about to tell something I probably shouldn't.

"Sure I do," Miss Jonetta said.

"She spent the night over at my house last night? And when it was time to go to bed? Well, after that. When she was asleep, she kissed me."

"That's okay, Child. She's your friend, ain't she?"

"But she kissed me funny," I said, curling my bottom lip with my finger.

"What you mean by 'funny'?"

I made her face the liquor cabinet so the men couldn't see. "Like this," I said, closing my eyes and moving my tongue around my lips. Opening one eye, I could see Miss Jonetta had lowered her cigarette to the counter.

"Now tell me again what she did," Miss Jonetta said. By then, her eyebrows had furled and deep lines creased her forehead.

Once again, I ran my tongue around my lips and this time I pulled at my waist, the way Valerie had.

"You sure, Child?" Miss Jonetta said.

I knew I shouldn't have said anything about the kiss, and I definitely wasn't about to tell that Valerie touched herself.

Miss Jonetta said again, "You sure that's what she did?"

"Uh-huh," I said.

"She put her lips on yours?"

I nodded.

"And she opened her mouth?"

Miss Jonetta turned back around to the counter. "This ain't right," she said to herself. She took a deep breath and told me, "You remember when I said it wasn't a good idea to bring Valerie by the store?"

I nodded.

"Well, I want to see her. When the next time you see her?"

"I'm not sure," I said. "Valerie doesn't come to school every day. She's not in trouble, is she?"

"No, Child. I just want to meet her is all. Doesn't come to school, huh? What about after school? You see her then?"

"She's with her mother after school," I said. "Over in the projects, saving lost souls."

"In the projects? A Lakeland girl?"

"Her mother stayed behind to save souls," I said again. "Valerie says she got the prettiest soprano voice you've ever heard. And she helps her mother."

"Well, this is what I want you to do: On Monday, if she comes to school, bring her by here. Understand? The wedding'll be going on and I can give you both some cake and ice cream. Okay, Child? Bring her by after school. Now don't forget."

As I was about to leave with Judd, I turned once again to look at Miss Jonetta. Mr. Chittey had placed another record on the

Victrola and he was hobbling over to the counter to grab her hand. The way she followed was almost as though he could have led her out into the middle of the street and she wouldn't have noticed. This time when she danced, she swayed slowly and without rhythm, shifting from one side to the other. This time, it didn't look as though she was dancing at all. It was more like she was marching in place, marking time.

CHAPTER 18

Miss Jonetta:
"Besides, old folks'll tell you, if you don't want wrinkles, you better learn to let
them worries run off you like a steady stream."

The more I thought about Valerie's kiss, the more something just didn't set right. Ain't nothing new about little girls kissing one another. Hell, when I was young, you couldn't stop me from planting my lips on my sister, Essie. My first girlfriend, Lydia, she and me hugged and kissed all the time. Kissed hello; kissed good-bye. But Valerie's kiss was different. The more I thought about it, the less I was able to find innocence running through it. I knowed what it often meant when little girls learned too much about stuff like that too soon. I have to say, that thing scared me like nothing had in a long time. In them days, I didn't scare easily because so many seasons, fifty-nine to be sure, had showed me so much. Besides, old folks'll tell you, if you don't want wrinkles, you better learn to let them worries run off you like a steady stream. Well, nothing was running nowhere anytime soon. So bright and early the next morning, I asked Fat Daddy and Judd to go over to the projects to find out more about that child. Fat Daddy had all kinds of contacts, old boys from way back—some respectable, some not so. Child had only told me Valerie's first name and I hoped that that was enough to go by.

By the time they came back later that night, I'd done sent everybody home and was heading through the curtain upstairs to my apartment. Lord, was I tired. The preachers normally kept up a fuss during the week, but on Sundays, they really knew how to raise hell. All that screaming and yelling, bad singing, they could wear even a good Christian down. Anyway, Fat Daddy banged and banged on my door till my latches shook and seemed like they was gone pop off. At first, I thought it was just some old dude needing something from my cabinet, acting like he couldn't see that big GET HERE BEFORE MIDNIGHT sign on my knob.

But then Judd yelled out, "Johnie, let us in." And something told me right off that the news wasn't gone be too pleasing to the ears.

Well, I let them in, all right. Fat Daddy took off his hat and wrung it like it was wet. He laid it on the counter. And I said, Oh Lord, to myself.

"You won't believe this shit," he said, shaking his head. He pulled two paper cups from my cabinet, got my jug, and fixed us a couple of shots of Johnnie Walker. Fixed it from the get-right bottle I kept under my counter. It was the only hard piece of booze in that store not watered down.

Fat Daddy walked over to the table, Judd pulled back a chair for me, and I sat down between them.

"You sent us over there, right?" Fat Daddy said, hands trembling.

"That's right, honey," I said. I grabbed his hand. "I asked y'all to go over there."

"You sho you want to hear what we got to say?" Judd said.

Slowly, my stomach started balling up like it'd been dipped in hot grease, and I was twisting that towel I had in my hand nearly into shreds. "Yeah, go ahead."

"I hear told . . ." Fat Daddy paused to take a swig from the cup. "I hear told there's a young woman. Her name is Ruth."

"Ruth, you say?"

Fat Daddy shook his head.

"She used to be part of the New Saveds with Scooter," Judd said. "But she keep getting let go because she got a jones that's out of this world. Some days, it's enough for her to get a sniff off some glue or take a hit off a joint." He paused, took a deep breath. "But other days, it's so bad, Johnie, that she selling her own child."

Judd stopped and I turned to Fat Daddy. "She dresses the little girl up like one of them loose women in frilly things. Let men, certain men, come by in the afternoon and mess with theyself while the girl sits there on the sofa. Just so she can get enough money for some smack. We got it out of Lenny Watkins. He told me where she lived and everything." Fat Daddy unfolded a squat piece of paper and pushed it across the table. "Me and Len go back a long way, Johnie. He was my first customer when I took over the pool hall. I knew Len was low, but I didn't know he was that damn low. When he smiled telling the story, I took out my razor and Judd had to hold me back. I swear, Johnie, I wanted real bad to slice him from here to kingdom come. Then I wanted to go get old Ruth's ass. What kind of mother would do shit like that, huh?"

Fat Daddy lifted the cup to his mouth again. His hands was shaking worser than the first day I met him, standing in that breezeway. This close from slicing up this old dude for not paying his losses from a game of pool.

"Little girl's been at it for almost a year now," Judd said. "I don't know if this is what you was looking for, Johnie. But it sure ain't what I went over there expecting to hear."

I couldn't say a word to them. I just stared down at the table, at the smudges, the cracks, and the splinters. All I could see over and over in my head was what that little baby had to go through. Ruth? Ruth was the mother?

Lord, all that sickness. I remember sitting for nasty men myself when I was pregnant. Bea knocking on my bedroom door, three raps with her black stick, her "nigger-beater," she called it. Then her leading me by the hand to the back room down by the cellar. No bed. Just two chairs facing each other, two wooden chairs. I would try not to look at them men as they walked in and sat down. As they began their business. I would try instead to fix my eyes on the wall, stare a hole in it, creating myself a nice little pass through to the other side. I can still remember how I felt having to raise my skirt to show some thigh when asked; having to slide my shirt up or lick my lips or say things I didn't want to say. Just so they could hurry. Please, sir, let them hurry up and zip themselves so I can go wash them off me. Wash them off Chloe. You see, Alfred told me I was lucky, because I wasn't being touched. But I had to get him straight. Just because they don't touch you don't make them no less thieves, I told him. No, they may not be the kind that run through you, snatching up your prized possessions, leaving little behind. But these old dudes was sometimes even worse: slick-handed pickpockets of the spirit.

"You know, Johnie," Fat Daddy said, pulling me back. "I ain't led no saintly life. I know I got some out there that belongs to me that I ain't done right by. But I done my best, sending some of my winnings when I could. And, I can't lie, there been times when I been in some shit so deep, I don't even want to think back on it. But I ain't never heard of nothing like this, especially a mother doing it."

"I know, honey," I said, patting his hand. "But you go on home now. And put it out your mind. I'm gone take care of it."

"What you going to do, Johnie?" Judd said.

"Now, that ain't your concern. You both just go on home for the night and rest your minds, knowing I'll take care the whole thing."

"You'll take care of what?" Judd said. "You know they crazy as hell in them projects."

Fat Daddy said, "I know you ain't planning on going over there tonight."

"Oh no, honey," I said. "Now I appreciate what you both done did. And you know I wouldn't put myself in nothing I couldn't get myself out of. But you all just go home and let me worry about this thing."

The projects wasn't safe in daylight, so I knowed what to expect after dark. First Fat Daddy left, and I watched his car pull off down the street; then I eased Judd out by promising him I wasn't going near the projects. Said that I was going upstairs to take a long, hot bath before going to bed.

I got my coat, my hat, and exchanged my heels for some flats in case I had to run. Looked at the pistol Chitlin gave me when I took over the store. It had a sight so crooked, I'da had to aim left to hit right, so I left it right there. Lord knowed, I couldn't pull the trigger anyway. I did take my old knife from under the counter. The blade was so dull and so rusty that the only thing it was truly good for was giving somebody a heavy dose of blood poisoning. That is, if I was lucky enough to pierce their skin.

I walked over there humming me a tune I made up on the way. The meaner the young boys looked, the louder I hummed. And I held my back straight, walking with my hands in my pockets like I meant business.

On one side of the street, Lakeland's fence stood high with all the ivy. Looked like green satin growing out of the ground, curling in and out on itself. But on the other side, everything was dark and filthy, squat-ugly—that building, the faces. Young boys was sitting on the steps, smoking reefers and pitching quarters in the dark, talking loud over their blasting radios about a whole lot of nothing.

"Hey, mama, you got two quarters?" shouted one boy. He was young enough to be my grandson.

"Sho don't, daddy," I said. I didn't want to look at him the wrong way, so I caught the breath that was slipping from me. And walked on by, daring him or anybody else to try to test me. I won't lie, I was scared. Scared. But I kept thinking about how scared that baby musta been each time Ruth made her prop herself up in front of them nasty men. At the time, I didn't know that child from any other. But to me, she was yet another baby along Thirty-fifth Street that needed somebody to hold on to. Knowing that is what kept me going, past the stairwell—a stack of newspaper turned toilet paper—to the elevator, which was just as bad.

Honey, the ride like to drove me crazy. The stank was so sickening, I had to hold my breath. How anybody can let themselves go in an elevator, I don't know. And when I reached out to punch number 12, I had to take out my hankie to wipe a whole wad of spit off the button. It was a dirty shame. But that old elevator crept and bumped till it got to the twelfth floor. It then bounced real hard, and when the doors opened, I had to step down because the elevator wasn't flush with the floor.

I got off and I was on this long porch, like a hallway. But one side was open to the outside, with a ugly fence for people to look over; the other side had windows—some bricked in, others with shades pulled down—and doors where people came in and out their apartments. It was so dark on the porch, I nearly broke my neck, tripping over a old dude laying in the middle of the floor. Didn't see him till the last minute. But he wasn't feeling no pain.

I took me out a match so I could see where I was going better. Fat Daddy's piece of paper said apartment 1210. All the way at the end of the porch. When I got there, my little match couldn't hold up against the wind, so I throwed it over the fence. I pulled out one more, my last, and it blew out just as fast. I knocked and knocked on Ruth's door till my knuckles hurt. Hadn't even fixed the right words in my mouth yet. Had no idea what I was going to say to her. But I knocked anyway. She didn't answer. I banged on the window. I opened the screen door so I could get to the steel one, and I banged on it, and still she didn't come. I even tried turning the knob. I waited for a few minutes more, and don't you know, that wind up there was whipping my snuggies good. Pressing all kinds of nasty odors against my breath.

As I pulled my coat to and started walking back to the elevator, I thought about the Ruth I'd knowed and loved all those years ago. And I hoped to God that she wasn't the same one, the one with the pretty big voice. She used to stand on the sidewalk outside my store next to them other New Saved singers, belting a tune till heaven got the news. Her voice was too big and too strong to belong to such a little girl. A whole hundred pounds, it was, heavier than her little body. Each time I heard it, I would peek around my curtain just to see her swell her chest and throw her head back. The Ruth I knowed loved being pushed to the center of the circle to sing. Loved watching the crowd get happy. Loved clapping her hands harder as she watched her mother's tears flow down her cheeks from birthing such a gift. I didn't want to believe that the same child that could make you feel light could now invite up old dogs to mess over her little girl.

That night, I promised Valerie that I was coming back the next day to see what this Ruth had done. I promised her I wouldn't let up till we all got some kind of understanding. Those was the promises I made.

The metal wash bucket sitting on the platform wasn't there when I left out for the projects. Neither was the line of about twenty people, New Saved members waiting in that weather for Alfred Mayes to baptize them, sprinkle a little water on their foreheads. But they was there when I got back.

Alfred was standing on the platform with his arms stretched out over everybody. Bowing and grunting out Scriptures.

"God don't care it's after midnight," he yelled. "And he don't care none about the cold. If you have faith, a faith even the size of a tiny mustard seed, I can give you peace."

So he sprinkled head after head, cleansing their souls, he said. Making everybody new and saved. Just looking at those fools, especially Alfred, made me so mad that I cussed them all. Cussed them right in their damn shoes as I passed by. Wanted to cuss God, too, for letting Valerie have to go through all that mess. Still not sure what stopped me as I walked down my steps, unlocked my door. Once inside, I put a hammerlock around Johnnie Walker's neck, sat right down at the piano, and swallowed me a few tastes until I fell asleep. That night, I had me a dream about my sister, Essie. Reason I remember it so good is because even to this day she don't come to me too often.

I dreamed it was real quiet. No preachers. And Essie walked in my store. She was wearing her navy blue suit dress and she had on the prettiest Sunday flop hat. That blue suit dress was what she had on in '50 when I looked down on her in her casket. She was only thirty-seven years old, poor thing. I was thirty-four.

When Essie came to me in the dream that night, I knowed I was dreaming, because in life, Essie never came down to see me. Once Aunt Ethel learned I was in O'Cala's, selling *Satan's juice,* she, Essie, Ruth, and all them used to stand out front, preaching and singing to me. Calling on "those who shall be named only by God,

who committed great sins such as having babies without the benefit of matrimony and selling their bodies to devil men. Come out
and be forever changed." Once she even slipped my birth certifi-
cate under the door to the store, because to them I didn't exist.

I came out a few times early on to try to talk to my sister.

"How are you, Essie?" I'd yell at her over her singing and the
beautiful singing of the child standing next to her. Lord knows, I
wanted to just throw my arms around her. "You got a husband,
yet, honey? Is this little girl here my niece?" She'd grab the child
and walk away from me and I'd follow like a little lackey dog.
"Remember we said we was gone get married on the same day and
live next door to each other in gingerbread houses with frosted
windows and chocolate trim?"

Essie'd just stand there, singing down into the pages of her
black hymnbook. And Aunt Ethel would run over and push me
away with her white gloves. "First, to God," she'd say, "then come
back to us."

One day, I looked at her and let her know I wasn't that sad little
slip of nothing she threw away all them months before. I warned
her that I would push her right over into glory if she shoved me
again. And she looked into my eyes, my pale old face and froze
right in her white boots. Well, never mind all my big talk. Chitlin
was sitting at the table, watching me after I came back down into
the store.

"You asked me for this job, didn't you?" he said in that heavy
voice that scared me at first, until I learned it didn't mean nothing.

"I did," I said, flinging the cloth over my shoulder, placing my
hands on my hips.

"Well, I don't pay you to keep looking up at that window
sorry-assed. And I don't pay you to keep running outta here, spe-
cially when there's a customer at my counter."

"Sorry what?" I said.

"Sorry-assed," he said, "and won't take it back. If you ain't got enough sense to know them fools up there is fools, then maybe you a fool, too, and need to find yourself employment elsewhere."

I started untying my apron strings, getting ready to reach for my pocketbook, my hat, and my coat. As part of my new me, I told myself wasn't no Negro ever gone talk to me sideways again.

Then he said, "If you ain't got enough sense to know that nobody on this earth can make you feel like a no-count and no-good but yourself, that they just doing all the shouting but you the one taking it all in, then maybe you too dumb to work for me."

Chitlin got up and walked right over and stood his little short self right in my face. Now, Chitlin ain't never been no beauty spot. Truth be told, that close up, he looked a might homely and was likely to scare somebody. But what he said next made a whole heap of sense.

"A good friend of mine once told me"—he pointed to his chest; he pointed hard so I could hear the thumping—"you can get by with a hole in your heart. Ain't easy, but people do it all the time. But you don't last through the night when one starts to eat into your soul. Don't let them New Saveds in, you hear me? Don't let 'em in."

I walked right back behind the counter and it didn't happen that day. It took a spell. Some cold, lonely winters; some springs without flowers or dew. But finally, I did like Chitlin said: I stopped letting them in. Whenever I heard their singing, and even that little girl's singing, or their calls outside my door, I drowned them out, either with my good friend Johnnie or Chitlin's radio. Got real close to both. . . . A few times, Chitlin, bless his heart, dragged a bucket of water to the roof of the building and let it go right on the New Saveds' heads. He'd come back down and we'd laugh and laugh, watching them soggy white boots really get the Holy Ghost.

Then one day, in my head, my kin stopped coming altogether. So for years, I hadn't seen my sister until she died.

I remember how nobody hardly even wanted to tell me my own blood had passed on. Died of female cancer, poor thing. Aunt Ethel sent a message by way of one of her flunkies, telling me not to come to the services. Think of somebody else for a change, she told them to tell me. Well, Aunt Ethel's message was the last message she shoulda sent.

That morning of the funeral? I got up early, real early. It was the time of morning when the sun begins to peep over the bottom edge of the sky, waiting to shine bright as gold lamé. I used two soup spoons and some tea bags on my eyes to hold back the puffiness from all the crying I did. I put on me a *move something* dress, the tightest, reddest little number I could find. And I got out my ten-dollar red satin slingbacks with the rhinestones. I got Sarah Ann to swoop my hair up high, tie in red bows and ribbons. She didn't want to do it at first, but I told her my green would spend just fine somewhere else, so she came around. Then I brushed off my fox shawl I wore for special occasions.

As I was coming down the aisle of the church, the ceremony was near over and the minister was dripping water— "holy water," he called it, over the casket, getting ready to close it down.

"Wait," I said. "Don't you close that box till I sees my sister."

Aunt Ethel, sitting in the front pew, whipped her head around, then stood up. She started toward me, but Aunt Mae Bell whispered something to her and she sat back down.

The minister stopped covering Essie's face with the white satin cloth and folded the cloth back over her hands. He stepped away, giving me room, like I was one of them lepers from the Bible. People was whispering. I heard them, but I didn't care. That was my big sister in that box. What I did care about as I walked toward her was something I couldn't do a damn thing about: the years. All those years we wasted. All the memories we coulda made. Like rocking our babies together. Complaining about dirty diapers and no sleep. Complaining about husbands who didn't want to act right or bread that didn't want to rise when it was time. I looked down on Essie and for the first time, I could see my face in hers. Oh hell, it wasn't no secret that she and me didn't have the same papa. We'd tell people we was sisters and they'd look at us right crazy. But as the years flowed, Mama's face took over both of ours. The nose spread out a little more, making them cheekbones sit up like good custard. I wondered if when she looked in her mirror she had saw me. If my face in hers had made her remember how we was before Aunt Ethel poisoned her mind against me. I wondered if seeing my face made her smile.

"Essie, honey, you need some color," I said to her. So I bent down and kissed her right on the lips. Ruby red. I kissed her on her cheeks and smeared it for blush.

When I was done, I bent down into the casket, placing my forehead on top of my sister's. "Now go 'n, girl," I whispered in her ear. "You looking mighty good now. Old Gabriel'll be a fool not to let you in."

The congregation didn't know what it took for me to be there that day. For me to walk down that aisle, having not seen my sister for so many years, only to see her up there as stiff and waxy as a candle. They didn't know, because if they knowed, them good Christians would not've stared at me the way they did when I turned to walk back down that aisle. They looked at me like I'd done stole something. All them black faces searching me. My cleavage and up around my hemline, for the goods. Heads shaking, handkerchiefs flying so fast over their noses like they couldn't stand to breathe the same air I was breathing. Like I had done introduced them to hell and all its fire.

Well, since they thought I was some freak in a sideshow, I

decided to give them something to really turn their noses up at. So I dug in my heels. For all those people sitting there judging me, I shot my head straight up to the rafters. I threw my shoulders back. And I began to walk. (It was a walk Sarah Ann said, one night when she forgot her religion and got a little taste from my cabinet, was a sho 'nuff kiss-my-ass walk.) It started in the tip of my toes and rose slow and easylike all through my body. First I threw my big round hips to the east. Then I threw them to the west. Back to the east, to the west. Got the rhythm going so tough, you could hear a whistling underfoot. Up-tempo.

Don't you know I got halfway down that aisle when the minister had the nerve to call me out.

"You see that woman there?" he said, that deep voice cutting through what little peace I had left.

I stopped in my tracks but didn't turn around. Took a look over my left shoulder the way you do when you looking for a run in your stockings. Then I watched as the congregation started fidgeting in their seats.

One woman stood and said, "Yes, brother." She pointed her finger at me. "We see her!"

"This is a sister that's caught in a life of sin." He musta moved closer to a microphone, because his voice got louder, clearer. And the whole congregation leaned forward like they was listening to some good gossip.

"Let us all pray that the Lord deliver her from sin the way he done delivered us. Let us pray that she can live the life her sister led. Holy and pure. Let us pray that instead of walking out this here church, she falls on her knees and gets herself new and saved. Pray, y'all! Pray!"

The organist's hands caught a electric shock and started moving all over that thing. And music was coming from every hole it could find. New Saveds, one after the other, started hopping up and down, pointing at me with the Holy Ghost dripping from their fingertips. Oh, you shoulda heard the mumblings and the shoutings and the "Please, Lord, Deliver her, Lord . . ." coming from the pews. Still, I refused to turn around.

"Pray, y'all," the minister said again, clapping to the music. "Pray! Pray! Pray!"

As I slammed the door of the church behind me, I said to myself and to that sun perched high and tall in the sky, Humph, gone take more than a prayer to get me to bow down before you bastards. Gone take the Lord himself. Then I pulled my fox over my shoulders, made sure my hemline was situated somewhere below midthigh and near respectable. I took myself a deep breath. Seem like it was the first one I'd took since I learned Essie was dead. Seem like the first one I took in a long, long time.

In life, Essie never came down those stairs to see me. But in my dream that night, she did. She and her daughter, Ruth, walked in. She sat right beside me at the table in her pretty blue suit dress. Ruth stood scarylike by the door. Essie started stroking my hair. Her face was calm, without age, like when we was young and running through the fields. She had all kinds of color in her cheeks.

"Now, Johnie," she said, pulling me toward her, rocking me. "I don't have to tell you this, but a storm is coming. Circling right around Valerie and that other little girl. Child."

I buried my head in her bosom and I hugged her so tight, I could feel her flesh and her bones. I could smell the lemon mint and lilac soap we used to wash our hair with, for special occasions. I felt so safe for just those few seconds that she was with me again. Old folks'll tell you that you shouldn't cuddle up too close to the dead in your dreams. They say you should keep your distance because they might snatch you along. But I tell you, if it wasn't for Child and Valerie, I surely woulda gone.

"Listen to me, Johnie," Essie said. "This storm? You gone have to stand in it, honey. Right in its core. It's gone try to suck you in. But you tell it, it's a lie. You gone toss and turn for a while. But you just keep right on telling it, it's a lie."

"I'm not worried," I told her. "In a few hours, I'm going back to see about that child."

"I know, honey," she said, turning to look at Ruth. "I know."

The next morning, Chitlin woke me up, tapping on the window with his cane. He was always the first to come, the last to leave. But that morning, he was extra early because of Hump's wedding. Without my face on, I looked right sickly. And Johnnie Walker was doing a gallop across my brains like nobody's business. I got up anyway. And when I passed the window, there was a little bluebird perched on one of the bars. Now, honey, any fool could tell you bluebirds didn't take a notion to flock along Thirty-fifth Street just every day. So that one was special. I opened the door for Chitlin; then I sat down on the concrete step. And, don't you know, that little bluebird just chirped and sang. I dared one of them old white pigeons to come near.

I said to the bird, "How do, Essie girl? You looking mighty fine. Just sit yourself on down and make yourself feel at home, honey. You can lift your voice so high till heaven get the news, for all I care. Just as long as you stay for a while."

Miss Jonetta:
"So much dirt ain't right on little babies."

R uth came to me in 1955, five years after my sister died. One day I'm looking out that window and I see some shoes up on the sidewalk, just pacing back and forth. They'd leave. Come back the next day, pacing and pacing. This went on for about three days. Wasn't the pacing, mind you, that caught my attention. It was them shoes. That child had done took her white shoes and dyed them red. Dye didn't take right, but you couldn't tell that to a little girl who wanted herself some red shoes. When you want something that bad, you color in the light spots, in your mind. So when you look at them, all the colors even out into belonging.

Well, I saw them shoes and started to go up there to see what was what. Next thing I know, Ruth marching her little self down them steps, opening my door.

She walked in real slow, with her hat leaning too far off the back of her head and her hands gripping that pocketbook like it was gone grow legs and run away.

"Aunt Johnie?" she said, low and scary. When she said it, my cloth slid right out my hand. She looked so much like Essie when she was sixteen years old that I thought I'd took one sip too many from my jug. I couldn't help but stare at her. Her black hair, down to her shoulders. Big wide eyes, puny lips, and her grandmother's healthy heap of nose. "You don't know me," she said. "My name is Ruth. I'm your sister Essie's daughter."

I didn't open my mouth. I remember it feeling like it was loaded with a ton of bricks. A pretty brown child. Looking just like Essie. When I still didn't say nothing, she opened her pocketbook, pulling out a picture, a old picture of Essie and me in our Sunday hats, gingham dresses.

"Essie Goodings?" she said. "Your sister?"

I nodded. I was so full. In one breath, I wanted to hug her close to my heart, but in the next, I was afraid, wondering why she was coming to see me. If she knowed about me, surely old Aunt Ethel had done poisoned her mind against me.

"I'm here," she said, holding her head stiff and high. "I'm here because I'm in the family way and I ain't got no place else to go." She even said it kind of meanlike.

"Some man done planted his seed in you, child?" I said, looking at her belly.

"Yes, ma'am," she said. "Aunt Ethel put me out, but I'm going to get married. My fiancé was called down south on some church business."

"Called down south?" I said.

"Yes, ma'am," she said. "He's a junior deacon, on the way to leading the church one day. Doing all kinds of fine, fine work, saving lost souls. But he been south for quite a while and I want to go see if he's okay."

"He's okay," I mumbled, picking up where I left off with my cloth, cussing that bitch Aunt Ethel in my head. "He just ain't coming back is all."

"What?"

"Honey, they was calling boys off down south when I was your age. And this one just like all the others: His mama done sent him away so he ain't got to worry about no responsibilities."

"Beg your pardon," she said, standing up tall.

"You can beg all you want," I told her. "But you gone have to find something to do with yourself and that baby, because that boy ain't coming back." I looked at her over my eyeglasses. Wasn't all that sure about the words that was jumping up on the edge of my tongue, getting happy. "You can stay here with me if you like." I said it real fast—before I lost my nerve.

When she started to look a little light-headed, I helped her over to the table. I locked the door to the store; then we slipped through the curtain in the back to the door behind the panels. I took her upstairs to my apartment. She held on to my hand all the way.

I lifted her heavy coat off and I could see the little pooch in her tummy. Her navel was already starting to poke out. And my heart got so happy. I said to myself, I can take care of you both. We about to have ourselves a baby. I started to reach out to touch her stomach, but I stopped my hand. Oh, I was so happy. She looked so much like Essie. "Babies are a way to start over," I said to her while helping her into the bed. I made her lay down and I got a cold cloth for her head. The next thing I know, the child was sleeping.

For hours, I stayed up just looking at her. I pulled a chair next to the bed and I just stared at her sleeping. In the morning, I said to myself, smiling, I'll fix you a hot country breakfast. And we'll talk. We'll plan. You'll tell me about Essie. Had she talked about me? If she had, what'd she say? Surely, there was something that made you believe you could come to me. Come to me in all that darkness.

Well, I don't know when it happened, but I fell asleep, too. Had a good old sleep that night. Best one I had in years.

But by the time I woke up the next morning, don't you know, Ruth was gone. So was all the money in my pocketbook and the money in the cash register down in the store. The door was wide open, slapping against the frame.

I hurried out to Aunt Ethel's house. That was the first place I thought to look. Lord knows, I had vowed never to cross that old heifer's doorstep again. But I had to for Ruth. I got over there and the house was the only one left on the block. It was sliding into itself—windows broke out, door flapping on its hinges. Aunt Ethel was sitting on the front porch with a blanket wrapped around her old humpbacked shoulders, rocking to "Precious Lord" playing on the phonograph.

Seeing me, she struggled to stand, looking frailer than frail. Her hair was uncombed and her white dress was gray and fraying. I said to myself, If you got to look like that, you should go on inside.

"Ain't no whores allowed in God's presence!" she yelled, wheezing and coughing in between. "Get outta my sight, you no-good!"

"I come for Ruth," I said. Didn't lower my head one bit. "Is she here?"

"All of you no-goods can just go right back to the devil, where you belong."

"Do you know where she is?" I said.

"I know exactly," she said. She was coughing so bad, I thought she would die right then. "But I ain't gone tell you. She could be right under my little fingernail and I wouldn't tell the likes of a whore."

Well, I stared at her for a few minutes, watching her body wrench as she spit up black phlegm into a coffee can at her feet. One spell got so bad, it sounded like somebody was twisting her throat inside out, twisting with both their hands. That was when I began walking away. All the way down the street, I could hear her

heaving, struggling to breathe. I could hear her over children playing out on the curb and over cars blowing their tired horns. But I
kept on back to the store.

I looked for Ruth for a long time, mind you. I can't tell you
how much I looked for her. Thirty-fifth Street was just ten blocks
long, but people could hide for years, tucked away in some corner
or crevice. I went over to that storefront church. Seemed like I was
always just one step behind her. I asked Fat Daddy to help me find
her. He said she spent some time at his pool hall with some man.
She'd done backup singing for a group at Club Giovanni. She'd
been a numbers runner for the gambling house. Then it hurt my
heart when somebody said she'd even spent time in the whorehouse. Hurt me even more to learn she'd spent her share of nights
in that alley, shooting blues in her veins. Then rumor had it that
she'd left town when the police come after her for giving the clap
to some high-ranking detective.

Years passed, and I told myself I probably would never see my
niece again. That was until ten years later, the night Malcolm
X was shot down like a dog. That night, fools everywhere was
looting and setting buildings on fire. Across the street, Lakeland
was just about to open. Normally, firemen wouldn't come to
Thirty-fifth Street, and we'd have to put the fires out ourselves.
But they came to control things that night so everything would be
peaceful for Lakeland.

I don't know where Chitlin was. But Judd and me was the only
ones in the store. We heard the bells going off and I locked the
store so we could go help out at the biggest fire, down on Davis.
We got there and was standing in the crowd watching the firemen
and their hoses. People from the building was getting oxygen,
coughing. I shook my head because this was the same building the

men and me had done cleaned out, room by room. Took us two whole months of cleaning, just so people could have a place to stay. I shook my head because now it was all gone up in flames.

Judd and me was about to leave when I noticed a little boy sitting on the edge of the curb, holding a little girl. He had been crying, his nose was sooty, and he was rocking that child. She was no more than two or three years old. He himself couldn't of been no more than ten. But the way he was rocking that child made him seem older, like a grown man, even with a face full of tears.

Me and Judd walked over to him. He was fair-skinned, with a keen nose and curly sandy hair. The girl in his arms looked a lot like the boy, but she had one long sandy braid that hadn't been combed in days. And you could tell that even before the fire they both was far dirtier than what was right.

"Child," I said to the boy, "where is your mama?"

He looked up at me, then swerved his head back around to the baby when she started coughing. He put her up to his chest and patted her back.

"She down at Club Giovanni singing," he said, meaner than mean.

Offering the boy his coat, Judd knelt down, "You got someplace to go until she come for you, son?" he said. "We just want to make sure you got somebody to look over you."

"I don't need nobody to look over me," the boy snapped. He barely looked at Judd's coat.

"I know you don't," I said. "But I won't let you sit out here in this cold with that baby all by yourself."

Well, we waited and waited that night, and it became clear that that boy thought as much about moving as a tree planted by the water. The fire trucks had left and so had the people who was standing around. All that remained was a scraggle of smoke rising from the building. And that boy kept rocking that baby. He used his shirt to cover her at first from the chill. Then when his sister's teeth started to chatter, he didn't even look at Judd when he grabbed for his coat. It was almost a reflex, because that boy woulda grabbed anything in sight to protect that child.

We was sitting there watching cars go by, not saying nothing, when Judd said, "How long you gone let being stubborn stop you from doing right by this here baby?"

"I'm doing all right," the boy said.

"Yeah," Judd said. "But you could be doing better. Either tell us where your mama is or let us take you someplace where it's warm."

The boy thought about it for a minute. The little girl had closed her eyes as soon as Judd's coat touched her body and now she was fast asleep.

We had finally convinced that boy to come with us, for the little girl's sake, when, lo and behold, a car pulls up and Ruth come falling out of it. I heard her before I saw her good. She was singing some song with the words running into one another. But even with all that liquor soaking up her vocal chords, her voice was still like an angel's.

"Ruth?" I said. The shadows sometimes is forgiving of our transgressions, because when Ruth stepped out of that car, leaning into the glare of the headlights passing by, she looked old as me. Dark circles around her eyes. Face puffy. Skin bad. Looked nothing like her mother or herself.

"Do I know you, Miss Lady?" she said. She tried to step forward to look into my face. Then looking down at the children, she said, "John, what you and Sugar Babe doing out here so late?"

The boy didn't say nothing to her. Just kept staring at his sister.

I walked up to Ruth and this old dude who was holding her up by her arm. He was a dumb-looking son of a gun with crooked legs. If she woulda let go, she woulda fell right on her face. She was so drunk, she hadn't even noticed that the building behind her was burnt near to a crisp.

"Ruthie," I said to her. I could smell the alcohol, but I knowed that wasn't the only high she was on. "I'm your aunt Johnie. You remember me?"

She looked right in my face and shook her head yes, and to this day I don't think she knowed me from Tuesday.

"You see your building here done burnt down. Why don't you let me take these babies until you find yourself another place to stay."

She looked over her shoulder to the building, and her man nodded and helped her back into the car. This time, she slid into the backseat, where she passed out. She still hadn't saw a thing. Probably couldn'ta saw the hand in front of her face.

I reckon that wasn't no surprise, because during the whole time she was standing there, she couldn't see the hurt on her boy's face. Lord knowed, if she could miss that, she coulda missed anything.

The children stayed with Judd and me for one night. Just one night, mind you. But it was one of the best nights of my life. Now, Judd and me had took people in before. Sometimes kids. Li'l Beaver had been one. We'd kept many a Thirty-fifth Street child, bringing them in out the cold.

But John wasn't just any little boy. The last time I knowed about my great-nephew, he was in his mama's belly. It made me sick to think what he'd been through them last ten years, what his eyes had witnessed. But any fool could tell that there was something in that boy deep down that wouldn't allow his mother to ruin him or his sister—at least not without a fight. You could see that in the way he walked into my store: determined to open the door for himself, even though his arms was full. And the way he almost didn't want to let his sister go, even when I pointed to her filthy heels and knees, telling him I had to wake her so I could give her a bath. "The only way she can get a good night's sleep, honey, is if you let me wash some of this dirt off her."

He looked at her ankles, then back at her knees, like he was trying to decide if the dirt wasn't that bad after all. But he handed her over. And he even let Judd help him toward a washup.

When the children was clean, they looked like two different people. So much dirt ain't right on little babies. They don't come into this world that way. It just ain't right.

Judd was sitting in my easy chair, reading a newspaper, when I came out the bathroom with that baby in my arms. He had washed both kids' clothes and gave John a soaking in the laundry tub in the basement. With a little water on him, that poor boy couldn't stay awake no longer and he was on the couch falling in and out of sleep. When he saw his sister was fine, he fell all the way, like something hit him.

And then, don't you know, that little girl climbed down out of my arms and walked right over to Judd. With her two fingers in her mouth, she crawled up into his lap, leaned her little head on his chest, and fell asleep.

I watched Judd lift his hands to rock her, then put them back down like he was afraid to touch her. Wrap your arms around her, I said to myself, it's okay. But it wasn't. I knowed that baby musta reminded him of his own little girls he lost in that fire. He couldn't help but think of them; I know because I couldn't help but think of Chloe. Loss like that is like lowering your hands into a red-hot flame; afterward, you don't never want to touch anything again. Never want to feel that kind of hurt again.

That could be why when Ruth came the next morning, half-sober and unable to look me in the eye, Judd and me had to give them children back. We had to. It was the hardest thing watching that little girl walk away holding her brother's hand.

Every bone in my body wanted to say, "Ruth, let me keep them. I can raise them for you." But out of all the good I thought it would do, I couldn't bring myself to say the words. Neither could Judd.

"I can take him fishing some days if you want," was what Judd said. "I can take that boy fishing." Ruth didn't turn around.

Judd didn't say nothing else; I didn't open my mouth. We knowed what it felt like to have our children ripped from our arms, never to see them again. So I let them poor, poor babies get in that car with Ruth. I let John and Sugar Babe drive off, leaving behind nothing but the memory of them sad faces staring out that back window.

Tempestt:
"But there was no sound except the music."

On Monday, Valerie didn't come to school. So afterward I went to her building, down to her apartment, and knocked on the door. When nobody answered, I waited for a second, listening with my ear pressed against the door. The only thing I could hear was the steam whistling from clanking pipes in the corridor and a crunching sound from the incinerator chute a few steps away. So I left, heading for Hump's wedding.

It didn't hit me until I slid through the gate and stood right there in front of that redbrick building. Staring at the twelfth floor. The wind was colder than it had been in months. So cold that you could see your breath and so wild, it lifted fallen leaves into swirls around the rainwater drains and the steps leading up to the building. Without children swinging on the banisters, jumping rope on the sidewalk, the broken windows and graffitied walls made the building look abandoned, as abandoned as the soap factory in the old neighborhood. Gerald and I had spent many afternoons scrounging through it for treasures, smearing mud across NO TRESPASSING stickers, and kicking holes through the plaster. It was the one place we'd been warned time and time again to stay away from.

Now this stunted redbrick building in front of me had an all-too-familiar cast. As I stood there, I decided right then that, after the wedding, I was going to try to find Valerie at her mother's house.

When I opened the door to O'Cala's, the wind pushed back the velveteen curtain and Miss Jonetta looked out from behind it.

"Oh, I'm so glad you could come, Child," Miss Jonetta said, waving me toward her. "Come on back here with us. And while you're at it, say hi to Rev. Miller."

The Reverend Miller was a short, stocky man. He was standing next to the checkout counter, waiting to begin the ceremony and sniffing at Miss Jewel's rum cake. Miss Jonetta's hors d'oeuvres and tea cakes were strategically placed around it in silver bowls.

Six pewter folding chairs, which Miss Jonetta had borrowed from the funeral parlor, sat in the aisles. Fat Daddy, Miss Jewel, and Mr. Chittey were seated. Judd stood at the front of the store, tying Hump's bow tie. When I passed by Fat Daddy, he handed me a tea cake.

"You still think you're lucky?" he whispered.

"Yes," I said.

Looking up at the minister, then back at the curtain, he eased a horse-racing booklet from the inside of his coat pocket. He turned several pages and pointed to a list of horses' names. I'd found similar books in my grandfather's coat pocket and knew immediately what it was.

"Pick one," he said, smiling.

I studied all the names several times: Baby Blue, Lucky Charmaine, Pistol Pete.

"You always this slow?" he said impatiently.

"You want the right one, don't you?" I said, looking over the names again. After careful deliberation, I said, "Tickled Pink."

"You got to be kidding," he said. He flipped to the back of the book to look at the horses' profiles and odds. "You sure nothing else hit you better than some Tickled Pink?"

"Tickled Pink," I said again.

And Fat Daddy shook his head.

Miss Jonetta peeped from behind the curtain. "You coming back, Child?"

"Yes," I said, leaving Fat Daddy.

"So I reckon you couldn't find Valerie, today, huh?" she asked.

"She wasn't at school," I said, admiring her yellow dress. It was the first time I'd ever seen her in a dress that hit her midcalf.

Miss Jonetta was busy smearing rouge into the face of a woman I'd guessed was Retha Mae. The woman was staring into a hand mirror that hung unsteadily from a rusting nail on the wall.

"I look like Foo-Foo the Clown," she said, adjusting the mirror so she could see clearly.

Miss Jonetta rolled her eyes up to the ceiling.

"Retha Mae," she said, looking more at me than the woman, "this is Child."

Retha Mae was about Miss Jonetta's age, brown-skinned, with a short, tapered salt-and-pepper Afro. When she didn't say hi to me, just kept staring into the mirror, Miss Jonetta said, "I told you, it was starting to get heavy. Didn't I say that's enough rouge, enough lipstick, enough eye shadow? Didn't I? But you kept saying, 'I want some more. Gimme a little more.' And look at how you sweating."

Moisture had begun to gather around Retha Mae's forehead and the space above her top lip. She looked up at Miss Jonetta with tears welling in her eyes. Miss Jonetta rolled her eyes up to the ceiling again.

"Okay, honey," Miss Jonetta said, placing her hands on Retha Mae's shoulder. "Just take a deep breath. Everything's gone be okay."

"I must be going through the change," Retha Mae said, fanning herself as Miss Jonetta reached over to the ironing board for a box of Kleenex.

"She must mean the change in her pocketbook," Miss Jonetta said to me under her breath. She pulled Retha Mae's chin up and patted it with a folded Kleenex. Then she took out her pick comb, steadied Retha Mae's head, and began plucking tightly curled strands. "There," she said.

Retha Mae looked into the mirror and started to smile, but she stopped when she realized she didn't have her teeth in. She reached into her purse, pulling out a ribbed plastic container. Clicking its contents into her mouth, she said, "Now we cooking with gas, girl."

Miss Jonetta said, "You ready?" and Retha Mae nodded, grabbing her bridal wreath.

"Y'all close to ready?" Miss Jonetta yelled out to Hump.

Judd said, "Yeah," and sat down at the piano and began playing "Here Comes the Bride." Miss Jonetta told me to sit down in front of Fat Daddy.

After the first refrain, Retha Mae marched out bouncing. The store was so small that she took her time so everybody could enjoy her off-white dress and her fishnet headpiece, which she flipped over her shoulders.

Hump reached out for her hand, and the minister took his place in front of them as Judd wound down the tune.

"We're gathered here today," the minister started, "to join in holy matrimony Herbert Fastile Porter and Aretha Maebell Richardson."

Miss Jonetta rocked forward in her chair, smiling, nodding, twisting a handkerchief tied around her wrist.

The minister wasn't from Thirty-fifth Street, so he didn't dally much with a lot of words. Getting right to the matter at hand, he said, "Aretha, do you take Herbert to be your lawful wedded husband? Will you love, cherish, and obey him till death do you both part?"

Retha Mae sung out, "I do." I laughed and Miss Jonetta elbowed me.

I looked over my shoulder at the clock, and behind us, Fat Daddy was still looking at his horse-racing book. He'd placed it inconspicuously between his thighs so that Miss Jonetta couldn't see him. Mr. Chittey was leaning forward on his cane, listening to the vows as though he'd be the one asked to answer. The Pepsi-Cola clock showed it was five and I knew that if I was going to stop by the projects, I'd have to leave soon.

"Miss Jonetta," I whispered, "I've got to go now."

Miss Jonetta was about to say something when the minister said to Hump, "You may kiss your bride."

Everybody stood and clapped. Retha Mae kissed Hump hard and lifted her leg.

"You want to take some food home with you, Child?" Miss Jonetta asked.

"No, thanks," I said.

"Well, before you go," she said, "don't forget to say bye to Hump and Retha Mae. And I'm gone get Fat Daddy to walk you to that fence."

When we got to the fence, I opened the gate and closed it behind me as I waited for Fat Daddy to leave. Certain he was gone, I opened the door slightly, just enough to see him nearing the corner with his racing book folded and stuffed into his back pocket. I ran across the street, up the stairs of the building, and entered a breezeway with two elevators on one side, an open stairwell on the other. An old woman with shopping bags was waiting, holding the elevator door open with a bag of groceries while reaching for her other bags.

My heart raced at the thought of meeting Valerie's mother, the thought of seeing Valerie.

"Don't just stand there staring," the woman said. "Grab one of them bags and come on."

The woman pressed the ninth-floor button. The lights blinked on and off with the passing of each floor and the elevator wobbled as though someone was hand-cranking it up each level. I opened my eyes wider to see through the darkness. I was happy for the company, unkind as it was. The truth is, I don't know if the woman said another word, kind or otherwise, because as we approached the ninth floor, a piercing bass beat that sounded like bomb blasts was getting louder and louder.

The elevator door opened and the woman was met by two young boys who looked as though they had just awakened from a deep sleep—hair uncombed, eyes bloodshot, lips swollen. I slipped past them and walked the remaining three flights up the stairs.

The music made my ears ache. I could feel the thumping in my chest and in my head. It was the loudest on the eleventh floor, so loud that I had to cover my ears until I made it to the twelfth-floor landing, where, as soon as I walked up, a rat was scurrying into an opening in a drainage pipe.

The porch was barren that evening or I would have asked somebody to tell me which apartment belonged to Valerie's mother. I waited for a few seconds for someone to exit one of the apart-

ments. When no one did, I began walking down the porch, looking into the windows and picking at the peeling green paint on the
fence that stretched the length of the porch.

In one apartment, an old woman sat on a sofa, cracking open
peanuts and throwing the shells into a wastebasket between her
legs. She squinted, leaning toward her television set, trying to hear
it over the noise.

The shades of the next two apartments were pulled down, so I
couldn't see inside them, but in the following one, a girl sat near a
kitchen, getting her hair braided.

"Excuse me," I yelled into the window. "Could you tell me
where Valerie lives?"

"Who?" the girl yelled back.

"Could you tell me where Valerie lives?"

"Valerie?" the girl mouthed. "Oh, you talking about Sugar
Babe," she yelled. "She two doors down."

Two apartments down from where I was standing, white sheets
were blowing back and forth onto the porch through an open
window. I suppose they had been blowing the entire time. Only, I
hadn't noticed. On the fence in front of the apartment, a tattered
white towel was drying. Water dripped from it, forming a puddle
on the concrete.

I cupped my hands to look inside the window. The first thing I
saw was a yellowish bulb hanging from wires in the middle of the
ceiling, casting a dim light on a small living room. Heat from the
apartment made my eyes water. And then on a gray sofa in front
of me, I saw Valerie's jumper dress, identical to my own and lying
on the sofa as though some invisible person were still pristinely
sitting up in it, watching me watch the dress. Valerie's shoe boots
were directly under it, side by side, laces hanging off the rims.

I knocked lightly on the door. But there was no answer.
"Valerie, it's Temmy," I whispered, knowing no one could ever

have heard me over the music. I tried the knob. It turned and the door opened.

Walking into that apartment was like walking into a steam bath. The walls sweated. And your breath was taken by the heat and the vomit smell of the moldy carpeting. To my left was a tiny kitchen, a few feet away. To my right was the living room, with Valerie's clothes, and straight ahead was a short hall with a bathroom at the end. That hall bent into an even longer one.

I walked slowly to the back. I wanted to call out to Valerie, but I couldn't say anything for staring, watching where I stepped—around a pile of clothes, around a stack of crumbled newspapers with roaches darting in and out of the pages.

And then there was a loud creaking sound, louder than the music, and a woman's voice climbed out of a hole in the wall. "Ain't no touching," she yelled. "Ain't no touching, you hear?"

The woman's voice came from the room in the center of the hall. When I looked in, she was sitting on the edge of her bed, her head slumped as she watched the cigarette between her fingers burn and the ashes pile on the floor. "No touching," she muttered.

My heart pounded as a tenor screeched into a bass beat, skipping along, getting louder and louder. It would stop, then start again, each time growing larger, fuller, heavier. I remember thinking I should turn around, that I should leave. A curtain of yellow light framed the door at the end of the hall. Shadows danced out onto the cinder-block wall. When the music stopped for a second, I could hear the door creak as the wind blew it open, then shut. I felt myself lifting up onto tiptoes, looking over my shoulders, inching forward. When I was close enough, I stopped. The door opened wide and I could see inside. A candle burned in the corner. Valerie sat in a chair. She was dressed in a gown and was sitting as though she'd been squeezed into a tiny space and asked to sit for a portrait: still and straight. Her hair was unbraided and flowing down her back, her eyes pasty white and dimmed, staring straight ahead.

"Hi, Valerie," I whispered. I eased open the door some more, entering.

The rings are what I remember clearly. In the dark of that room, I could still see his rings, a spangling array lined up along the edges of his open raincoat. All those rings. And him sliding down into the sofa cushion with his large bare hands erupting in his lap.

Valerie didn't see me at first—until I passed through the candle's light. Then she blinked, her eyelids dropping as though a heavy blanket had been lowered over her head. And suddenly, there was so much darkness. She started tugging at her gown, gasping for air. I didn't know what to say or do or think. Her mouth hung wide open. But there was no sound except the music. She started to stand, then stumbled over the chair. All I could hear was the bass drums when she pushed past me. All I could feel was the music exploding out of my chest when she started running down that hall.

I followed her, past her mother's room. She turned at the corner, the gown trailing her. I followed, calling her name.

She opened the door to the apartment; the screen door slammed against the brick wall. When I got outside, I saw her perched on that fence, her lace nightgown fishtailing on the breeze, her hair beating wildly as she looked down twelve flights. I reached out for her. And she reached out for the sky, rocking back and forth on steel spikes. Then, on that cool autumn evening, beneath a crisp navy blue sky, I saw Valerie fly away.

Miss Jonetta:
"That night, two little girls thought they could fly."

I promised little Valerie that I wouldn't just leave her out there in that wilderness. I promised her that I would go back over to see what Ruth had done. She was all I thought about after Child left and Hump and Retha Mae sat for a while longer eating cake, nibbling off them horsederves. My nerves started to get bad, real bad. I could hardly sit still. Felt like the whole room was starting to spin around and I got this funny feeling in the pit of my stomach, like when the sky suddenly turns pitch-black and the wind gets real still. As much as I loved Hump and wanted to see him off, I had to go check on Valerie.

On the way over, I wondered if she was the same child I'd spent them hours with years ago, the little girl who had cuddled up in Judd's lap, patting his neck, almost like she knowed, for just them few seconds, he needed her as much as she needed him.

I couldn't help but to think about Ruth. Was this Ruth my niece? Never mind if she was or wasn't. How could any Ruth stoop so low? Sell her own child.

Well, I musta wrung my hands silly all the way over there. I musta been so far away, because I didn't hear the music—loud, crazy-making music—until the elevator door opened and the music stopped. Just stopped. The way it blurps when you lift the phonograph needle right off the record.

When I stepped out onto that porch, the first thing I saw was Child, standing all the way down the porch, holding on to the links in the fence. A strip of white cloth was snagged on a spiked tip of the fence, waving up and down. Alfred Mayes burst through the door a few seconds later. I started running toward them, my coat sliding down my shoulders.

"Did he hurt you, Child?" I asked her. "Did he touch you? Did this old dog touch you?" She just kept staring into the fence at that piece of cloth. Maybe staring through it, over at all them old houses across the way. The sky maybe. The water maybe.

Then that's when a woman down below screamed. She let out a shrill so loud, it was like she was in pain. Like something had done ripped her apart. I looked over the fence, down into the playground. Lord, twelve whole flights down. Alfred looked over the fence with me. His hands started shaking. First he looked through the links; then he lifted himself onto a little step so he could see over the spikes without the metal lattice in his way. So he could see clearly.

People heard that woman down below and started running out their apartments. And more and more people started walking up to the fence, first looking down, then at the waving cloth, then back down, then back at the cloth, and screaming and shouting. It was like the bricks cried out and the concrete got hot and mortar started to crumble and paint began to peel away. And people didn't know what to do or where to go. I grabbed Child away from the crowd because people started gathering around Alfred Mayes. Standing around in a half circle. Some afraid to look down.

I pulled Child into a shadow next to the apartment, behind the screen door. I could feel her whole body just trembling. Trembling and trembling. I made her face me, and I started patting her on her back the way you pat a baby to make sure she breathing right. "It's gone be okay," I told her, rubbing her back, holding her hand. "It's gone be okay, Child. You hear me? Child?"

After so many people had gathered on the porch, fingers started pointing like hot pokers. People kept looking down, then at that cloth Alfred Mayes had planted himself next to. Down again, then back at that cloth.

"He did it," one woman said finally.

Alfred didn't say nothing. Probably didn't hear her. He was still holding on to the fence.

"Killed that baby like that," she yelled. "Pushed her to her death. I saw him."

One young boy, around Li'l Beaver's age, walked right up to Alfred, and other men did, too. A couple grabbed his arms while the others started punching him in his face and in his stomach, kicking him, spitting on him. At first, he didn't seem to know he was down on that cold concrete. Then all of a sudden, he started trying to break loose and cover his face.

The crowd had gone stone-crazy. People was yelling and crying, cussing one another.

Then when everything seemed more confused and mixed-up than it could ever be, Ruth stumbled through her apartment door. At first, her back was to me and I couldn't see her face. But she spun around and I knowed who she was right off, even though she bore only a faint likeness to the little girl I remembered. It was like looking through a dark veil of age and sickness. All that mess in her veins made her old and tired. She could hardly lift her eyes. All them years of looking down, into nothing. But I knowed who she was.

She pushed her way through the crowd, past Child and me, mumbling a tune into the collar of a dingy white blouse. She was

cussing everyone for making so much noise in front of her door
and for not inviting her to the party. Then she finally made it to
that fence, her bare feet tracking scarlet footprints through Alfred
Mayes's blood. Rocking off balance on unsteady tiptoes, she
started calling out for her daughter.

"Sugar Babe," she moaned in between coughing and wiping her
nose. "Sugar Babe, where my dinner?" Her voice traveled down to
the playground, down twelve whole flights. But of course there
was no answer. So as Ruth waited, she decided that old crowd was
for her. And she laughed and danced with the people standing
around. Moving slowly like hot vent steam, she curtseyed in and
out of that crowd, until some teary-eyed young woman grabbed
her by the hand and led her back into her apartment. After that
night, we'd never have to see my niece again.

No sooner than the screen door to Ruth's apartment slammed,
a flashlight started bobbing toward us, and when we saw it was the
cops, the young boys ran down the porch. The crowd opened up
the circle, as they had for Ruth, so the cops could see Alfred
Mayes, who was curled up on the ground, still bleeding bad.

"He did it!" that same woman yelled out. "Pushed that baby!
He the one!"

The two cops knelt down beside Alfred and I scooted Child
away from all that mess. I scooted her on down the porch and
down the stairs. I was moving too fast to be careful, too fast to
care about the swimming I got in my head. Just moving. Until we
got to the bottom floor.

I took her face in my hands and made her look into my eyes.
Right now, she was the one who was important. Not Alfred, not
Ruth, not Valerie. "Child," I said.

At first, she just looked at me like I wasn't even there "Child," I
said again, this time shaking her. "Listen to me good, Child.

Everything is gone be okay. You hear what I say? Everything is gone be okay. Now, when we walk out of here, you got to show me that part in the fence where Hump and them say you slides through. You hear me? You got to show me because you got to run home."

I grabbed her close to me and I could hear the sirens coming, the wailing, swirling like the wind around the walls in that open hallway.

"Can you run home, Child? Can you make them little legs move like fire?"

Outside, police cars was everywhere. Lined up along Thirty-fifth Street. Child and me hurried past the cars, walking fast in the opposite direction. They didn't mess with a old lady and a little girl. But they was stopping all the young boys, lining them up face-down on the sidewalk.

Child led me to the fence. She started feeling her way along the ivy. There had been only darkness—on the porch, in the stairway. But when we crossed Thirty-fifth Street, Lakeland had a great big light that shined on the street.

In the glow of the light, I could see Child's face. And don't you know, I wanted to cry out. I was numb. There was nothing there. Her eyes, her whole face, was completely drained of life, of color. I used to imagine Chloe wrapped up in that newspaper. I used to wonder what it musta felt like to come into this world wanting to finally stretch out and just be. Then all of a sudden, somebody wrapping you up, stopping your breath. That's what I saw in Child's face. Somebody had stopped her breath.

That night, two little girls thought they could fly. They locked steps, joined hands, and hitched themselves onto a clear blue sky, and in a matter of seconds, it dropped them both. Just let them poor little girls tumble to the ground.

I watched Child feeling through the leaves, running her little fingers around all that ivy. "It's gone be okay, Child," I told her again. "I want you run straight home. Can you make it?"

She turned and nodded her head real slow.

"Straight home," I said again. "As fast as you can." Then she slipped her little self through all them tangles in the vines.

When I got to the store, I locked the door behind me. I started wondering if I'd done the right thing by letting Child run home by herself. The men was at the table. I walked straight to my counter and sat on that stool. All the while, I was thinking, how did I make it back to the store? So how could that baby make it home by herself?

Fat Daddy walked up to get a slice of wedding cake from the counter. Seeing me, he said, "Well, Hump and Retha Mae on they way to honeymoon land. And them fools in the projects must be barbecuing in their bathtubs again. Listen to all them sirens."

Then he musta took a good look at my face.

"Johnie," he said. "What's the matter? You okay?"

I kept holding my hands folded in front of me and I whispered to Fat Daddy, hoping Judd couldn't hear me. "Honey, go around and get your car." I wasn't ready to tell Judd the whole story yet about Valerie.

"What happened?" Fat Daddy asked, hurrying to put on his hat. "What's wrong?"

"The little girl I asked y'all to see about the other night just died," I said. "And I got to go see about Child."

"Who just died?" Chitlin said to Fat Daddy. "Who just died?"

From the corner of my eye, I could see Judd standing up, then sitting back down, like somebody had done hit him in his belly.

"I'll tell you later," I said.

"To hell with later," Chitlin said, taking his earplug out. "I wants to know now."

I walked over and rested my hand on Judd's shoulder. I stared Chitlin right in his eyes. "I'll tell you the whole thing later," I said.

Fat Daddy came around with the car, honked twice, and we drove down to Lakeland's main gate. He didn't say nothing. I suppose he, too, was bone tired of the same old story. Some baby, somewhere along that old street, gone on and never coming back. To keep hearing that same news over and over made you feel like somebody was opening old wounds. Made you feel like poison was running through you from head to toe, finding places it'd done missed from the last time.

Fat Daddy pulled up to the gate and got out the car to talk to the guard. I couldn't hear what they was saying, but as they was talking, Fat Daddy took his wallet out, trying to offer the man some change. The man shook his head and took out his billy club. Fat Daddy was trying everything in his power to get to Child. He knowed how much I loved her. Truth is, he loved her, too. All them men thought as much of Child as I did.

Standing up there like that, Fat Daddy reminded me of my papa down south. One black man was talking to another black man the way Papa used to have to talk to white men—hat in hand, held down by his side; head bowed; standing back a proper distance. Any other day, I woulda told Fat Daddy to stand up there like a man, but seeing I didn't just goes to show how much I wanted to get in there to see about that baby. Oh, why did I let her run home by herself? I was praying that that guard would let us in. Help us find her so I could make sure she was gone be okay.

Well, that guard didn't care about us none and wasn't bit more about to let us in than we was about to make the moon our next stop. Fat Daddy came back to the car leaning in the window. "He want us to get off the property," he said. "But we ain't got to. I can keep pressing him."

I thought about it for a minute. Then I held my hand up and said, "Everything's gone be all right, honey. Everything's gone be all right."

"You sure, Johnie?" he said.

He got in the car, mumbling cuss words under his breath as he backed it away from that black gate. I noticed how white the pavement was behind the fence and how the bright lights made it look like diamonds had been sprinkled into the concrete. The street stretched out for a spell, then curved into a place I couldn't see no more, no matter how I tried. Lord, there was so many trees. And the wind shook them so hard, making them peep out over the fence, blowing sugar kisses down onto that pretty street.

Fat Daddy and me drove around for about an hour. Just driving and thinking. When we got back to the store, Judd was still sitting where we'd left him. Chitlin was pacing up and down the aisle. He stopped when we walked in. The radio was blasting early snippets of the news, so they already knowed most of what Chitlin had wanted me to tell him.

"You was there when it happened, Johnie?" Judd said.

"Right after," I said.

"And that little girl, Child, was there, too?" Chitlin said.

"They was little friends," I said, nodding.

"She seen it?" Chitlin said.

I unscrewed Johnnie Walker, and took me a sip as I walked over to the table and sat next to Judd. "Everything," I said.

"The news say a street preacher did it," Judd said. "A street preacher with a long rap sheet. That true?"

I didn't say nothing.

Chitlin said, "They ain't releasing names because no formal charges been made. They just calling him a suspect."

"Is it Scooter?" Judd said, impatientlike. "Was it Scooter?"

I looked up at Judd and tears was running down his face.

"He was there," I said.

Fat Daddy had been standing in the doorway the whole time and he walked over to the table, placing his hand on Judd's shoulder. Chitlin stopped pacing. Stopped right in front of the window and leaned forward, looking up out onto the sidewalk. He was standing exactly where hours earlier Hump and Retha Mae had exchanged vows.

CHAPTER 22

Tempestt:
"I had run that night solely because Miss Jonetta told me to."

It would take years to piece together the run home that night. The memory of it—primarily accounts from people who saw me and later told my mother—would never seem all mine. Even today, it continues to set off this rumbling in my head—a fever capable of engulfing my entire body and making me feel once again that I'm running blindfolded through tangles of time and space.

I had run that night solely because Miss Jonetta told me to. On my own, I could never have found the strength to move my legs. Miss Taylor said I ran right in front of her car as she was driving down Medgar Evers Avenue. The avenue's short S curve, about fifty yards from the fence, forced cars to maneuver slowly. Miss Taylor said if she'd been driving more than the required 10 mph when she hit me, I might have been seriously hurt. Seeing that I was so visibly shaken by the accident, she drove me to the apartment building. She waited with me in the lobby as the doorman called upstairs for my parents. But because they had gone out for the evening, Miss Lily was the one who came for me.

In my bedroom, Miss Lily helped me undress, removing my overcoat, then my cardigan. She said after the coat was off, she noticed I had wet myself. She cleaned me up and helped me into my pajamas. The entire time, I hadn't spoken one word.

Believing the accident was more serious than she'd originally thought, Miss Lily called my parents home. She made me stretch out on the bed and she began feeling along my arms and legs for fractures and sprains; searching for bruises and tears in my skin. But she couldn't find a thing. Five doctors lived in the Five forty-five building, and she went through the list after each said he couldn't find anything wrong, either. Even when my temperature started to rise and I began to sweat and tremble, no one could figure out what was the matter.

When my parents came home, my mother sat in my room, watching me all night. She said there was a point during which I started to murmur and run in my sleep, the covers twisting and folding around me. Settling me, she said, she didn't think much of it because I'd always been a busy sleeper.

Only, I didn't sleep that night. I doubt if I even closed my eyes. I was afraid that if I did, I'd see Valerie falling. Once again I'd see her running through that apartment, the hem of her lace night-gown twisting on the wind. I'd see her scaling that fence, then perching for a second atop steel spikes before finally letting go. And me? All the while, I'd just be standing there, hopelessly hoping she'd land with little more than hot, stinging feet—the way she did after jumping from the monkey bars in the playground. She'd hit bottom hard, giggling away the pain, then climb back up to do it all over again.

My grandfather died about a year and a half before my family moved to Lakeland. That morning, my mother and father found Gerald and me in the backyard, lying belly-up on the grass. We had just run three blocks from a dog we'd taunted and were trying to catch our breath when Mama and Daddy came out the back door. We didn't see either of them until they were standing directly over us. Mama knelt beside Gerald and told him she had something important to discuss with me alone.

"Gerald, dear," she said, offering her hand, "can you come back later?"

Gerald often wore a perplexed look and he wasn't one for asking questions, so he simply nodded. He shoved his hands into his pants pockets and headed out the back gate, down the alley.

Then slowly, very slowly, Mama began explaining death to me. I heard most of what she said—about death being a part of life and how those who die plant seeds while living so they live on in our hearts and our minds as brightly layered flowers.

But, when she spoke, I was only half-listening, because what I was really concentrating on was that dog. How Gerald and I had cleared two upended garbage cans in the middle of the alley, and how we'd sailed through the Jenkinses' backyard, almost getting tripped up in line-drying purple boxers, but sailing nonetheless.

At first, my father stood silently, with the sun framing him, and I couldn't see his face. Behind him, the burnt orange shutters in the guest bedroom clapped against the windowpane and the screen door creaked on its hinges. When my father moved into the sun's light, I saw he'd begun to cry. I'd never seen my father cry before. My mother, but not my father. I watched the tears moving down his face, across tiny moles and light brown freckles, then gathering under his chin. The tip of his nose was turning apple red. I remember him removing his only monogrammed handkerchief from his pants pocket, blowing his nose but wiping his eyes on his sleeve. When he knelt beside my mother, he looked as though he was sinking, as if the ground was softening under his weight and within moments he would disappear.

I still hadn't heard or truly understood much about my grandfather's death. But when I saw my father cry, I cried. It was a reflex that at first had nothing to do with my grandfather, only with my father's pain.

The next morning, for the second time in my life, my mother and father came to me with the news of a death. This time, I understood immediately. I felt it as sharply and as thoroughly as the time I'd slammed into the side of the house, my skateboard sliding from under me. Mama sat on the edge of my bed. Her lashes were wet and everything in my room seemed to collect into one large mass, then disappear into her eyes.

My father stood next to her at first. But then Mama took my hand in hers and he sat on the opposite side of my bed, his body slightly turned from me, facing the window. For the longest, nothing was said—not one word spoken. All that could be heard in my bedroom came from what seeped in through the French doors; what reached up twenty-two flights: the clanking of hammers and the buzzing of power drills along the south fence that had begun almost before dawn.

"Tem," my father said. Mama squeezed me in her arms and I could see only my father. "Your little friend Valerie . . . Well, she's . . . she's passed on."

I didn't say anything. My throat began to shrink. It seemed barely capable of allowing air to pass through, let alone the faintest sound. It was my father speaking those words that had made Valerie's death more permanent than anything I'd seen or felt the night before. It was his words that made the room burst into this blinding white light, and my eyes begin to burn and ache. Once again I could feel my entire body shaking. But I couldn't stop it. Even holding on to my mother couldn't stop everything from feeling so cold.

"She died last night, dear," Daddy said. He took a long, deep breath and put his arms around me. "I'm so sorry about Valerie. I'm so sorry you've got to feel this."

"We're going to get through this together," Mama said, her voice trembling.

The three of us sat in a huddle on the bed for what seemed like hours as the seconds stretched between us and the morning sun strung a rivulet of white beads from the edge of the balcony across my bedroom floor.

In my mother's arms, I was overcome with sleep, but I awakened when Miss Lily's passkey rattled against the lock on the back door. She entered, heading straight for the kitchen.

Mama left my room, following Miss Lily. I got out of bed and followed them.

"I'm old as dirt," Miss Lily said, removing a newspaper from the laundry basket she braced on her hip, "and I ain't never felt this way before. How's that baby handling it?"

"I don't think it's really sunk in yet, Lily," Mama said. "Everything's happening so fast. But her fever is coming down."

"It just makes me sick," Miss Lily said. "And for it to be the Reverend Mayes, too. Was just charged this morning. First-degree murder. I got a friend that's been trying to get me to that church for the longest. But I knew something wasn't right. Just knew it."

"I can't believe this is happening, Lily. That child was just over here. Right here in this house. Did the man say why, how he could have—"

"They say he's in shock. Ain't said a word since he been there. No better for his crazy ass is what I say. He can fry, for all I care."

I was sitting by the kitchen door when my father turned the corner from the living room. He was so distracted that he hardly noticed me.

"What's all that noise going on down by the fence, Lily?"

"You ain't heard?" Miss Lily said. She handed him the newspaper. "Look at page three."

"Heard what?" Daddy said impatiently.

"They putting bob wire around the fence. All the way around. That's just one of the things they doing. Senator Johnson is on his way back from Springfield. People is up in arms. You heard all the mayor's doing?"

"I know he's beefed up the police."

"Not just the police," Miss Lily said. "He's asking the governor to send out the National Guard to protect the crews he's finally sending over there to clean the place up."

"They're asking for the National Guard?" Mama said.

"National Guard. State police. You heard right. The people been up to their asses in garbage for months. Been begging for some relief 'cause the kids have turned to playing on the piles and there's rats and roaches everywhere." She pointed to a picture in the newspaper. "Now the mayor got the city scrubbing down the walls, fixing the broken lights, taking the boards down out the windows and fixing them, fixing the elevators. I can't tell you how many babies done fell down those shafts. And they tell me that's just the beginning."

"The beginning of what?" Mama said.

"Sounds like they cleaning the place up to tear it down. Sounds like they won't be needing that fence no more because all that talk they been doing for years about cleaning up Thirty-fifth Street is about to happen. Because a Lakeland child died. That's part of why the Guard is coming."

"But a child has died," Daddy said, folding the newspaper and slamming it down on the table. "Not a Lakeland child. A child."

"I hate to be the one to tell you, Thomas," Miss Lily said. "Children die over there maybe every day. We ain't shed many tears for them. We just happened to know this baby."

Miss Jonetta:
"Well, word spread and spread."

The next morning, word of that child's death traveled like wildfire throughout Thirty-fifth Street. Oh, children had lost their lives along that street many times before. But this child was different, folks said, because she was from behind the fence.

People seemed to pass by my window in twos, talking and talking. Even Jimmy Rae, who'd been talking to himself for years, found somebody or something to talk to—the sky, a rock, them white pigeons. Even Jimmy Rae, who'd always been crazier than two loons, was trying to make sense out of this whole thing. But you can't make sense out of a baby dying. No matter what side of the fence that baby come from.

Out of all the feet I saw passing by my window and the mumblings I heard, none belonged to Child. I kept looking for her to come back. Wondering how she was getting along. I wanted more than anything to see her and hold her if I had to.

Fat Daddy and me drove back over to the gate as soon as the sun came up good. Guards from shift after shift kept telling him the same thing: "You don't belong here. Don't you see that NO TRESPASSING sign? We don't want your kind." When I couldn't bring myself to go over there again, Fat Daddy kept going, poor thing. Then coming back each time with his head held low like a little boy who'd lost something important and was afraid to tell.

Chitlin kept seeing me look up at the window, staring at every little rusty leg that walked by. He came over to my counter a few times, placing his hand on my shoulder. "That little girl gone be okay," he said, nodding. "You just rest your mind."

"I know," I said, lying. "I know."

Normally, around the end of October, customers who ain't said a word the rest of the year outside of ordering would come in and talk about the falling temperatures or about Christmas being just around the corner. Everybody promising everybody gifts. Nobody never getting nothing more than those nicely wrapped empty promises.

But that year, all the talk was about little Valerie and Alfred Mayes.

My customers was sliding their business deep into their back pockets and standing in the aisles, feeding on the news. Chitlin's radio may as well of been a picture tube. People was staring into it, squinting into it, as if frame by frame they could see the whole thing: Ruth coming to herself the next morning and driving that yellow Nova of hers into a pretty wet sunrise. Police finding a note back in her filthy apartment, scribblings that said this was the only thing for her to do. Her asking God to forgive her. Customers' mouths was wide open when that bit of news came over Chitlin's radio. That and other updates. All the hands hired to scrub and exterminate them projects. Alfred Mayes's rap sheet. A history of selling little girls. And then how he had changed. How he was supposed to help Lakeland get rid of Thirty-fifth Street.

Updates—sometimes on the hour, sometimes up-to-the-minute.

But the talk wasn't just around me. Sarah Ann said women was talking about plea bargains and death penalties in the beauty parlor. She said hair wouldn't curl right because nobody could hardly sit still. Twisting their necks, whispering, some still getting full over why it happened. Why Alfred Mayes had to go and kill a Lakeland child. Us showing our color.

Sarah Ann said the reason the preachers' voices had gone down to a whisper was because most of them was down at the courthouse picketing and holding vigils for Alfred to be set free, saying he was framed. Though, one man, a brother Tyrone, stayed behind, walking up and down that street, screaming mostly in front of the currency exchange line, "The end is near. Lord, the end is near."

At the ribs house, Judd said his cook, Li'l Row, burnt damn near two slabs when a customer came in to tell him that the mayor was sending out troops to start inspecting all the stores. Closing down those that wasn't up to code. Well, nobody had cared about us and violations and codes before.

Li'l Row come bursting into the store right after the news. "Mr. Judd," he said, stammering all over himself. "What about the gas line? You know it's rigged. What about all them wires coming out the back of the stove? And that hole in the wall. How we gone fix all that?"

"We ain't," Judd said. He barely looked up at Li'l Row. Just kept staring like everybody else into that radio. "Ain't gone worry about it at all, you hear?"

Well, word spread and spread.

And all the talk was chatter—heartfelt, mind you, but still chatter nonetheless till word got out that Valerie would be buried over here. Over here because she came from over here and because John wanted the people to see what they had done. Then word got out that Mr. Felix down at the parlor was scrambling because he had ran out of coffins that small. Said it was bad luck to keep more than twenty-five that size on hand.

True, I worried that one wouldn't get to the parlor on time for Friday. But what hurt my heart most was knowing so many children had died along Thirty-fifth Street. Through the years, so many children had gone on that the undertaker man was out of boxes to bury one more in.

For me, that was reason enough why Thirty-fifth Street had to go.

CHAPTER 24

Tempestt:
"The ceremony would be closed casket."

During the two days that followed, it snowed nonstop. Classes were canceled, and many of the stores, save for the hardware and grocery, closed down due to the weather. With work on the fence completed, the noise had quieted and very little could be heard outside my balcony except for snow crystals ricocheting off the windows and the thugging of expensive cars slamming into flower berms and embankments, followed by the whir of spinning tires. Every now and then, the gulls squawked—a low, barely discernible yelp that traveled from the lighthouse back to the rocks. You had to listen carefully to hear them. And you had to listen because you couldn't see them for the thick gray fog that hung over Lakeland and stretched out over the water.

I spent most of the time with my mother in the kitchen, chopping celery and carrots for soup, measuring flour for fresh bread, slicing apples for pies and custards—all for the repast, which Miss Lily was organizing.

Both days, I stayed so close to my mother, trying not to think about Valerie. I soon learned that it would be impossible, especially when the clock over the sink began to tick toward noon and

I would be reminded of lunchtime on the rocks, her secrets, and the final one about how she spent her afternoons. I had wanted to know that particular secret almost from the first day we talked. Now, knowing it made my eyes burn and the thin black numbers and hands on the clock's face turn into this white blur, eventually blending into silk wallpaper underneath.

As I stood in the middle of the floor, my eyes so fixed on the clock, my mother stumbled over me twice while backtracking from the stove to the sink. The second time, she sat me down at the table and pulled her chair close to mine.

"Temmy," Mama said, brushing flour from my cheeks, "you know, you can talk to Valerie whenever you want. She'll always be with you. Remember what we said about Granddaddy?"

I nodded.

"Well, the same applies here. They don't leave us, dear. They never leave us."

I wanted to tell my mother what I'd seen, that I'd known about Valerie long before she and my father entered my bedroom with the news. But every time I searched for the right words in my head, gathering them piece by piece, delicately, like shattered parts of broken glass, the words never seemed to fit right or come together in the proper arrangement.

In between making the food for the repast, my mother made my father an omelette. She told me to take it to his study. Since we'd arrived in Lakeland, the study had been my father's private room, a refuge of sorts. I'd refused to visit him in that room because it was so unlike the pantry-office we shared at the old house. His new study was the neatest room in the apartment because he had total control over it. Most of his books were there, a new desk, a small television, and a leather-covered globe of the world that creaked when spun on its axis.

That morning when I peeked in on my father, he was blasting

the television and the radio. He hadn't shaved yet and both the city's newspapers were strewn across the room. Flipping from station to station, he was waiting for updates on the man who, according to reports, had pushed a Lakeland girl off the twelfth-floor porch of the Thirty-fifth Street projects.

When I walked in with his omelette, his back was toward me and he was standing with his hands braced against the desk. In front of him, snow slapped wide bands of ice against the window and the sky was a wet white mist. I placed the plate on top of the television and left the room.

I didn't see my father again until hours later, when the evening edition of the *Sentinel* hit the streets. He went out, still unshaved, for the newspaper and to take John a large helping of soup and bread. When he returned, Mama met him at the door.

"I don't have to ask how he is," she said as my father removed his coat. "I can't even imagine losing a child."

"I heard him telling somebody that when all this is over, he's leaving Lakeland," my father said. "He said there wasn't any reason for him to stay now." Daddy sat down on the sofa, leaned forward on his elbows. "There were so many people crowded into his place, Felicia. I introduced myself, but I don't even think he remembered who I was. I didn't want to stay long. You should have seen it, such a tiny, tiny place. Reminded me of the basement apartment we moved into right after we got married. Furniture mismatched . . ."

"I didn't know Lakeland had apartments like that, Thomas. Didn't know such a perfect place could allow anybody, even the help, to live cramped like that."

My father looked up at her, but his head was still bowed a bit. She'd begun to pace in front of the coffee table.

"Now isn't the time, Felicia," Daddy said in this monotone I'd never heard before.

"Why not now, Thomas? I swear if I don't say what's on my mind, I'll explode. I'm so angry with you. A part of me knows I shouldn't be, but I am. I can't help but think that if we'd never come here, Temmy wouldn't have to go through this."

"And you think I feel good about it? You think I could have predicted something like this would happen? All I wanted to do was give my daughter a—"

"Don't say it, Thomas. I'm sick and tired of hearing about what you wanted to do for Temmy. This had nothing to do with her. This was always about you. How we could make Thomas feel better about himself." Mama stopped pacing, draping her dish towel over folded arms. "I listened to the lies you told about all the things broken in that house. Let you tell it, the house, the neighborhood, all of it was crumbling right before our faces. It wasn't good enough for us anymore."

"I wanted something better for my family," Daddy said flatly.

"Better? At least there, what was broken could have been fixed easily with a hammer and a nail, Thomas. Here, things are so screwed-up, nobody knows where to begin. A little girl has died, and what are people doing? They're going around putting barbed wire on the fences. Double-locking doors. What's broken in Lakeland can't be fixed, not in any simple way."

Miss Lily had entered through the back door, but I hadn't heard her. By the time she made it to the living room, she cleared her throat and banged against the wall, announcing her arrival. I scooted away from the hall.

"Y'all heard about the service, ain't you?" she said to my mother. Without waiting for an answer, she stalked across the living room to look out the window, down onto the fence, now shrouded in a fog. "They was supposed to have a memorial service for that baby at the church."

"A service? What time?" Daddy asked, standing.

"Well, they was supposed to have one, but they say the weather too bad."

"What? It doesn't normally snow in Lakeland?" Mama snipped.

"Don't normally snow this hard anywhere in October," Miss Lily said. "And everybody been running around trying to clear the streets. But it's coming down faster than it can be shoveled away."

"The funeral is Friday," Daddy said. "Since it's going to be across the street, the least we can do over here is have a memorial service."

"Would be the least we can do," Miss Lily said nonchalantly. She paused. "Since ain't nobody going to the funeral."

"What?" my parents said in unison.

"What are you saying?" Mama asked, walking over to Miss Lily.

Miss Lily could never have been accused of mincing words. But she almost seemed afraid to continue. She took a deep breath. "That's another part of the reason I'm here," she said. "They asking us to collect money for John Nicholae." Miss Lily turned to my father, then back to Mama. "Got nearly a thousand dollars so far. And flowers are lining the lobby."

"They think sending money is going to be enough," Daddy said.

Miss Lily didn't say anything.

"They think that's going to ease their fucking consciences?"

"What possible reason could anybody give for not going to that funeral?" Mama said. She was crying now.

"Leesha," Miss Lily said, putting her arms around my mother. "These people are deadly afraid of what's on the other side of that fence. Sure some of them only worrying about their fine cars getting stolen or somebody walking up to them, mugging them. But some of them are just afraid and they don't know why. They're so afraid, even something like this can keep them away."

My father looked down at his watch, then left the living room and went back to his office. He lifted the receiver and started spinning numbers around on the rotary dial as though he were trying to twist off the lid on a jar that had been closed for years. For two hours, I ran from the kitchen to his study, listening to him dial nearly every name in Lakeland's directory. And each time he hung up, he was getting madder and madder. It reminded me of the calls he'd made during voter-registration drives. Every excuse people gave for not coming out to the polls, for believing Election Day was just another day would send my father shouting into the receiver, pounding on his desk.

The calling finally ended when Daddy reached Senator Johnson. By then, the day had worn on each of us, but it showed most on my father. His razor stubble and uncombed hair made him look like someone who'd been locked in a dark room. I'll never know what was said before I got to his door, but what he said afterward, I'll never forget, because it reminded me so much of the man I'd known before—the man who drove his cab on weekends to some obscure street corner, where he handed out pamphlets about a war he believed to be unfair, about a welfare system he felt was sucking the breath out of black folk.

"At what point did we lose ourselves, Senator?" my father asked, rubbing his forehead. "When did we forget who we are? When did it become more important to be high society than human? All week long, we've been trying to find ways to protect ourselves—from them. Separate ourselves further, from them. Under the guise of keeping Lakeland safe. All week long, we've been reminding the media how different we are.

"But we are them, Senator. Aren't we? We're as intricately woven as the ivy on the very fence that divides us. When did we forget that? Tell me how long does it take before being here turns you into a monster? A coldhearted monster? A month? Two months?

Damn it, a child has died. And now the only real thing separating us is the fence we've constructed in our minds and around our hearts. You've got to be there Friday, Senator. We all have to be there. It's the absolute least we can do."

My father hung up the phone and turned around to face the window. There was nothing I could see but a blanket of white. But somehow I thought surely my father could see much, much more.

The morning of the funeral came too quickly—like thunder following lightning. I sat in the backseat of the car with Miss Lily. Mama kept looking over her shoulder at me, brushing my face with the back of her hand.

"I'm so sick of going to funerals," Miss Lily said under her breath. "Just sick of them."

Nobody said anything. Mama and Daddy stared straight ahead as we turned onto the path by the lake. By morning, the snow had stopped. Mounds were sitting along the roads. By noon, it would look almost as though it hadn't snowed at all. I must admit I'd expected there to be a procession of cars behind us as we crossed Lakeland's main gate. I thought my father's voice alone would stir Lakeland's residents to do what was right, but it hadn't. They hadn't. The streets and the parks were wide open and desolate, and ours was the lone car crunching through the snow.

On the way over, I thought about my parents' talk, which was to prepare me for the funeral. The ceremony would be closed casket. Daddy said I wouldn't be able to see Valerie the way I'd seen Granddaddy. He wouldn't be able to lift me to kiss her good-bye. I remember kissing my grandfather and frowning because his whiskers tickled my nose.

I was nervous when we made it to Thirty-fifth Street; my heart was pounding, once again pulling away from my chest. And I wanted to cry, but I didn't. Instead, I tried to focus on all the peo-

ple heading in the same direction as we were heading. All the people spilling over from the sidewalks, walking in the middle of the
street. All roads leading to Mr. Felix's funeral home, a white frame
building at the end of the block, with a white hearse sitting in its
side driveway.

Daddy parked the car on the street and we joined the end of
the line. It moved slowly up the stairs of the porch, through a
foyer, which held a wicker basket. People were dropping coins,
dollar bills, and gold chains inside. When we passed the wicker
basket, Miss Lily looked at my father, stooped slightly, and slid
Lakeland's monetary contribution from her purse, then dropped it
inside the basket.

I held my mother's hand as we entered the sanctuary. Deep
maroon draperies covered the entire back wall. And a crucifix hung
from the ceiling. Directly below it was the podium and below that,
Valerie's white coffin, surrounded by so many flowers.

John sat in the front row, a few feet from the coffin. He could
have reached out to touch it, had he leaned forward. But he sat in
the pew, keeping his back straight, smiling, nodding at the people
who passed in front of him. One after another, people patted him
on his shoulders, bent down to hug him.

When we made it to the front of the large room, my father said
to John, "If there's anything you need, anything at all, you just
ask." John smiled faintly at Daddy, then at Mama, who bent down
to hug him. I ran my hand along the cold metal top of the coffin.
I could see my reflection in the shine, and suddenly I realized I
hadn't studied Valerie's face, the way I had my parents' faces after
Granddaddy died. After my grandfather died, I was determined
not to have to rely solely on an old photograph to remember their
faces. So every opportunity I got, I examined the contours and
lines; every pockmock, mole, blotch, crease. I tried to file away
every hair, from my father's whiskers to wayward strands on

my mother's chin that Daddy plucked once a month with her tweezers.

But with Valerie, I hadn't studied her face at all, because children our age didn't die. We were supposed to live forever.

Just before the service was to begin, a woman in white gloves stood at the end of the aisle, passing down memorial programs. I immediately recognized the picture on the cover as the same one taken the night of the debutante ball. Valerie's two braids hung past her shoulders, with the bows Mama had tied on the ends lying perfectly flat. Her smile was wide and her eyes were squinty, as though she were staring into the brightest sun either of us had ever seen. The night of the ball, I'd looked at the picture too quickly, almost dismissing it. But that morning, I couldn't stop staring at her. Begging her to tell me another story. Willing her to come back to me. So we could return to the rocks and to the water.

Miss Jonetta:
"In the dark upper room, we all hide from view."

When the day came, I closed down the store. We had decided to meet at O'Cala's and walk over to the parlor together. We being Hump, Retha Mae, Judd, Fat Daddy, Chitlin, and myself. We also decided that on that day, Chitlin was to turn off his radio and keep it off. Wasn't a day for finding out the latest about Alfred Mayes, mind you.

Fat Daddy, Judd, Chitlin, and me arrived early, so we was there watching the clock, waiting on Hump and Retha Mae. I was at my counter, wiping off dust that had settled overnight, when I noticed how quiet it was. It was so quiet that once in a while when my cloth whipped fast across the counter, you could hear the static pop. You could also hear Fat Daddy's chair creaking as he rocked back and forth, and the loose change Judd was fidgeting around with in his pocket. At first, that was the best we could fill the air with that day. Wasn't room for much else.

I stood there thinking about what Judd and me had did the day before. We got on the bus, in bone-chilling snow, and went all the way down to the Cook County jail. Same place I'd bailed Li'l Beaver out time and time again. Each time swearing to God I wouldn't ever come back, that I'd let him stay there. But each time knowing that place was no place for a child.

The whole ride downtown, Judd and me didn't say one word. The way we kept staring straight ahead, people looking at us woulda thought we was scared that the driver couldn't steady his course right in all that snow. People looking at us woulda thought the tired on our faces was from straining to see what was up ahead. You couldn't see anything in front of you until you got right up on it. Until you got close enough to almost pass it. That's when things was the clearest, and even then, like memories sometimes, you almost didn't know what was what.

When we got to the jail, they made us take everything from our pockets and they put my pocketbook and Judd's wallet into this locker. We followed three different guards down three different halls, each guard telling us how Alfred hadn't said a mumbling word the whole time. So they didn't know what we was expecting him to say.

"Not a word?" Judd said to the last guard.

"Hasn't eaten, either," the guard said. "Don't think he's slept."

"Umph," I said.

We came upon a room where you sit down with glass separating you and talk to the prisoner on a phone.

Judd pulled the chair out for me. He stood. We waited and waited. I found myself singing real low, a mess of hymns I used to hear old folks singing while they was working in the fields. They'd stop every now and then to dig prickly thorns from their bloody fingers and stretch out weary, nearly broken backs.

I was still singing when the door in front of us opened like wild horses was busting through it. A guard pushed Alfred out in a wheelchair. His face was swollen and bruised, cut up. His eyes tiny slits. He was in shackles, around his hands and around his legs. As he was pushed up to the table, I thought about the fine black man

I'd saw dancing all them years ago. Moving like water on that stage. I thought about the boy Judd told me about who saw his mama in a whorehouse room with a man whose name nobody'd ever know.

Now Alfred was slumped in a wheelchair, barely able to lift his head. He didn't even want to pick up the phone at first. Judd tapped on the glass with the back of the receiver. Alfred kept staring into his lap like he didn't hear Judd. So he tapped again.

Slowly, Alfred lifted the receiver. He still wouldn't look us in our eyes.

"I got one question for you, Scooter," Judd said. "What make you stoop so low? Out of all the things you done done, what make you push that child?"

For the longest, Alfred didn't say a thing. Didn't grunt. Didn't hardly blink until he opened his mouth and his whole face started wiggling, straining to release the words. At first, nothing came out. Then the scabs that had crusted over around his mouth broke, sending blood pouring down his shirt.

"I did it," he said with that deep voice. He stopped to wipe his mouth and both of his palms turned beet red. "I pushed her."

Judd looked at him like he wanted to jump through the glass and strangle him, because he couldn't believe Alfred could fix his lips to say it so easylike. Like it was something that just happened, as simple as nightfall. Judd just stood there staring at him.

But Judd wasn't on that porch that night. I knowed right off that Valerie had jumped. I could see it in Child's face and Alfred's. Once I'd saw a boy about Li'l Beaver's age run out in the middle of the street right in front of a truck. People wanted to jump all over the driver for hitting him, but I saw that boy. Death by any way is hard to take. But there's something about watching somebody take their own life that makes the sight of it travel through you, from your eyes to your understanding, burning up a path.

Judd said, "What's it gone take for you to be a man, Scooter?

Will this make you stand up tall? Will this make you a man?" Judd didn't wait for an answer. He let the phone drop from his hand as they both stared at each other, both of them searching for the little boys that still jumped and played along their insides. In some dark upper room, we all hide from view.

Judd turned and walked over to the guard sitting by the door. "You see that man over there?" he said, pointing to Alfred. The guard rose a bit from his seat, peeking around the edge of the divider. "The news say some fancy psychiatrist supposed to be coming soon to say whether he fit to stand trial. You tell him I said he fit. And when they lock him up this time, make it last forever. Make it last so he can't do nobody else no harm."

Alfred sat crying like a baby as Judd began walking back down that long white hall. Alfred placed his hands over his face and his sound got real muffled and low like he was the one moving farther away. Like he was the one all the way down at the end of the hall, waving me toward him before turning out of sight.

On the bus home, I told Judd that I was 99.9 percent sure Valerie had jumped. That Alfred was there but that he didn't push her in that way. No more than all the other nasty men had laid their hands on her. All of them. But Judd didn't say nothing. Just kept staring into the falling snow.

But on the day of that child's funeral, none of that mattered. Not one bit. It wasn't long before Hump and Retha Mae arrived. Judd helped me with my coat. Fat Daddy cocked his hat to the side. And we all left O'Cala's together.

People was walking in the middle of Thirty-fifth Street. Like zombies. Cars, buses, cabs pulling around them without honking their horns. Everybody was patient that day. Everybody heading to the parlor. There was so many CLOSED signs in the windows. The beauty shop closed. The pool hall closed. And the whorehouse.

Them girls was busy sliding on Sunday dresses that had done dry-rotted or unraveled at the hem. Even Judd's smokestack—normally fluffy billows—was a little dab of smoke curling like a pig's tail and dissolving in the air. The pile of mail, normally all over the place, was stacked up next to the platform. Not that the mailman had done it, mind you. Some of Li'l Beaver's no-good friends had took a notion to make things neat, gathering all the envelops and placing them in three milk crates. One less thing for people to have to trudge through.

Everybody was moving like they was dragging something, pulling something behind them or toward them. Something heavy one minute, then wonderfully light. Something that the wind can snatch from your grasp and send tumbling down the street. And each time a baby died, more and more garbage was pressing against those buildings, the bricks, the metal doors. Sticking along the curbs. Each time, the place was looking more and more like the little storms was preparing for the big one that would wash it all away.

At the parlor, so many people came out that we had to stand at the back of the room. I looked and looked for Child, but I didn't see her. People was lined up along the walls. Every pew was full and spilling over. People was squatting at the end of the aisles. And by the time the service started, people was standing outside the parlor door, listening to the service over a loudspeaker put up for those standing out in the cold.

Another child had died.

A child that her own mother had throwed away; that in life didn't seem to belong to nobody, suddenly, in death, belonged to everybody. That's why so many people came. Thirty-fifth Street's biggest thieves, cheats, and lowest dope dealers. Even a few New Saveds trickled in, standing all the way at the back. That's why the basket that's custom to pass around was overflowing with bills in the vestibule. And that's why the stairs leading up to the parlor had been swept extraclean, and the floor mopped, and the pews shined with lemon oil.

I was staring at the altar, all them flowers, and the little white coffin sitting in the middle, when I felt a tugging on my arm.

"Miss J.," Li'l Beaver said, his voice a tiny whisper. "Do I look okay? I wants to be presentable."

"Oh, you look mighty fine," I said, stroking his arm. "Mighty, mighty fine."

It wasn't until he left me and walked back over to stand next to his no-good friends that I noticed how his suit hung like a choir robe over his little body and how his eyes was a sickly yellow, even though he could hardly hold his head up. Eyes had no life. Then a funny feeling shot through me and I began to wonder how long before I'd be standing in that same spot, with Li'l Beaver lying up there at the front of the parlor. How long before I'd have to look down on him.

The room had been so quiet that until the minister walked up to the podium, I didn't think it could get any quieter. He carried his Bible tucked under his arm and the sleeve of his robe hid most of it from view. He placed the Bible on the podium, then opened it, flipping the pages back and forth.

"In my Father's house are many mansions," he said, looking up to the rafters. "If it were not so, I would have told you. I go to prepare a place for you. The Bible says that we shouldn't be sad today. We should have been sad years ago when this child entered this world. The Bible says we should have cried then. But today, we should celebrate her homegoing. We should rejoice."

Oh Heavenly Father, I said to myself, ain't nothing for us to be rejoicing about. I looked down at the obituary. Seem so unfair for her face to be on such a stiff piece of paper. Didn't seem right either for them years—1963–1975—to have so little room between them. Not enough room for even a good breeze to pass through. Old folks used to say the first thing a mother place in her baby's hand is what that child has a lot of for the rest of his life. As I stood there, I wondered what old Ruth touched Valerie with. And what about John?

The preacher went on and on, sometimes seeming more concerned about adjusting his robe, fiddling with his collar. He talked and moaned and grunted for a few more minutes; then he opened the ceremony up to the people.

"Anybody else got something to say?" he asked. It was quiet— quiet, quiet. I thought to myself, I got something to say, but I don't know if I can say it. Don't know if I can make myself make sense standing over my own great-niece. I took a deep breath and leaned forward to walk, but Judd beat me to it.

The next thing we know, Judd walking down that center aisle, up to the altar. Bowing at the casket before walking up to the podium and looking out over the crowd. He was silent for quite a spell, so long that people started to stir and cough the way you cough when you need to pass the time. For a minute, I thought he had done forgot what he went up there for. That the words just disappeared from his head. Then the preacher rose from his chair to try to say something to Judd, and Judd just kept staring straight ahead. I can only guess, because I never got around to asking him, but I'd bet my life that as he stood up there, he thought about the day that child crawled up into his lap. About how he wasn't sure whether to wrap his arms around her. I can only guess he thought about his own children and the crackle of the fire. About their screams and the feeling, that willingness to give your whole life— not just this one but any one promised in the hereafter—if he coulda run back through those flames.

Wasn't until the preacher stepped back and everybody got quiet again—quiet, quiet—that Judd looked his most peaceful. Then, Lord don't you know, he pursed them lips of his in a good-bye kiss to the baby below. There was no doves or harps or angels. He closed his eyes and the melody just came. He started low, way down deep, in the part of your being that cups your secrets and disappointments and cradles them like a newborn child. Then he started to climb. It was a whispering, this gentle nudging, that spread out across the floorboards until they began to rumble and doors began to fly open. He moved higher and higher until that big old room swole up, making way for the flood tide. His humming surrounded us. Made us feel that little girl. It gave her a breeze she longed for and tied pretty bows across her soul. It showed us she was color and light in a darkness most people can't imagine. It showed us her strength and it showed us how her soul finally surrendered. And I began to cry like I ain't cried in years. Hump and Fat Daddy was nice enough to put their arms around me. Fat Daddy cried, too. Chitlin was nice enough to pat me on my shoulder. Oh, we wasn't the only ones. Everybody in there who hadn't been the least bit moved by that mealymouthed preacher was suddenly whisked away. If no one knew Valerie before, through Judd, an otherwise ordinary traveler—who himself knowed her for just a few hours—they knowed her now.

Even that preacher musta understood that nothing else could be said after Judd got up there. So as my old friend continued to hum, the preacher waved the two pallbearers forward. Then he turned the casket so that it was pointing down the center aisle. The two men stood on both sides and began to wheel it while Judd steadily hummed. People could hardly watch it go past. Some turned away.

Halfway down the aisle, one of the pallbearers lost himself. It was like the casket all of a sudden got too heavy for him. He couldn't move any farther. Don't you know, Chitlin threw down his cane. Didn't bother to hand it to nobody, either. Threw it right down on the floor. He hobbled over to the casket and grabbed one of them gold handles that stuck out the side like wings and walked with that other man on down the aisle. On out the door.

Part III

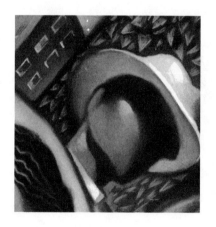

Miss Jonetta:
"All of us had to be gone come the New Year."

A few days after the funeral, the weather went and lost its mind. One minute, it was snowing big bulldog flakes. The next, it was warming up enough to rain, then freezing up again. The mud on them streets slicked over like Shinola, and the cars and buses was sliding into lightposts and traffic signs.

But that didn't trouble the city workers who came out in all that mess. Handing out notices about inspection dates and violations and penalties. They delivered them notices door-to-door. Such important papers wasn't allowed to sit stacked up in the mail pile, mind you. Yes sir. Delivered them door-to-door.

It was a young blond boy who entered my store, tipping up scarylike to my counter. I was sitting on that stool, reading the newspaper, when I cut him sideways with my eyes.

"Is the whereabouts of a Mr. Timothy Francis O'Cala or any of his relatives known, ma'am?" he asked. Lord, I had shoes older than that child. "He's the last known owner of the store. I'm from city hall, the Division of Building Codes and Regulations, and I have a notice for him regarding inspections."

"A notice?" I said, pretending like I didn't know nothing. "He's not in right now, but I'll make sure it reaches his hands."

When the boy left, I read the whole letter from top to bottom. It was short and to the point. Said in a few days, building inspectors would come out. The city knowed right off most of the buildings would be condemned for something—corroded pipes, or for plumbing that was no good, for cracked foundations, or for wiring that wasn't right, or walls that had dry-rotted or become rat-infested. And if any of the above fit, then your days was numbered. The next notice coming out was the one kicking you to the curb. You could leave on your own, the notice said, or with police escorts. Either way, if you was one of the cast-asides—which 99.9 percent of Thirty-fifth's lot fell into—by January first, you had to go. Everybody—from those of us in O'Cala's to Judd's ribs joint to Sarah Ann's beauty shop, the whorehouse, Mr. Felix's parlor, Fat Daddy's pool hall, the vacant lots. All of us had to be gone come the New Year.

I watched all the people get their letters. People coming in with them white letters sticking out back pockets or folded up, bulging from their breast pockets or the brims of their hats. Fat Daddy tore his up right away, trying to act madlike over something. After a spell of hell-raising, though, he collected the pieces like he had sense and went down to get his business in order.

But Judd was the one that kind of throwed us all off guard. When he got his letter, he sat in the chair for a while. Thinking, I reckon, looking back. Then seem like something shot through him. He got up and went down to his store. Fat Daddy and me followed him because we ain't never quite seen Judd like that before—sweat coming down his face in that cold weather, a pacing going on behind his eyes.

At the ribs house, Judd told Li'l Row to serve the last customers in the store, then lock the door. Bolt it down if he had to. When the last man shuffled out, Judd gave Li'l Row a piece of change, thanking him for his years of service, and told him to go home. Then Judd started cleaning. Fat Daddy and me wasn't gone just stand there watching, so he started sliding the broom across the floor. I pulled out one of my cloths I used to keep tucked in my pocket and started dusting off the counters. We cleaned out the back bathroom, the back closets real good. Judd boxed up all the extra meat and some heavy jars of sauce and set it out on the front stoop. He then dabbed at the grease on the walls and on the grill, working more to touch everything than to clean it. It was almost like he had to run his hands over that whole store one last time—the stools, the glass partition, where people made their orders. He wiped down the signs in the windows: ONE SLAB, $3.00; HALF ORDER WITH TWO SLICES OF WHITE BREAD AND COLESLAW, $1.35. Before Judd took over, you'd order a slab and wouldn't know what kind of meat you was getting. Wouldn't know how long the meat had been sitting or what had crawled over it in the dark of some corner, either. But Judd cleaned the place up. Made it respectable.

When everything was fixed to Judd's liking, he took a bucket from the closet, filled it with water, and lugged it over to the oven. He poured it onto the grill and it started to sizzle like nobody's business. Smoke and ashes started whirling around his face and into his hair. That fire put up a good fight, but Judd just kept pouring, dripping water over them hot coals, letting it take its time to seep down into the cracks and crevices until the three of us was sure, as sure as God sits on high, that nary a flame would ever jump out of that grill again.

Well, something shoulda told us after all them years Thirty-fifth Street wasn't gone shut down easylike. Judd and me was sitting in the store later that night, talking about where we planned to head once everything shut down.

"You know, Johnie," he said, "I been here all my life. All my life. I think I'll just start walking. Who knows where I'll end up."

"Well," I said, "if you do it that way, you can end up anywhere."

"Anywhere is better than here," he said, looking out the window, up to the sidewalk.

"Yeah, but I don't want you to land just anywhere, honey. I want you to find yourself a place you can call home. I reckon what I'm trying to say is, if you get someplace and it ain't worth putting roots down, then don't be afraid to leave it. Leave it and don't worry about looking back."

He smiled a bit. "Think you gone miss this place, Johnie?"

"I'm gone miss all my friends. But I won't miss O'Cala's or Thirty-fifth Street. No, honey. When I think back on it, I been here nearly all my life, too. And you know what? It's time for a change of address. I'm looking forward to finding me a porch swing. And a pretty sunset and rocking to it."

We was just sitting there when all of a sudden we heard shots fired. Sounded like firecrackers. Next thing we know, them boys running past my window.

Judd stood and ran out the store. I wanted to grab his arm so he wouldn't go out too fast. In case other bullets was flying. But I couldn't catch him. People was looking in the direction of the alley. And that's where we hurried to.

As Judd and me got there, Li'l Beaver was breathing hard, poor thing. Judd and me ran up to him, sliding twice through the mud and snow. We both fell to our knees beside that child. I pulled him to my bosom. "Li'l Beaver?" I said, barely catching my own breath. "Li'l Beaver?"

"Come on, Li'l Beaver," Judd said, shaking his arm. A old nasty needle stuck out the back of his hand and stayed there until a barrel of blood forced it from his vein. "C'mon, son. You can make it!"

I think both of us knowed yelling wasn't gone bring that child back. If he was coming back this way, he had to do it on his own. I kept rocking him. Judd kept rubbing his arm.

Then a trickle of foam started dripping out the corner of his mouth and his head went lazy, but he was still breathing. I could see it in his chest.

"C'mon, Li'l Beaver," Judd said again. I held my cloth over blood jumping out of a bullet hole in his stomach and I rocked him. Li'l Beaver coughed and his eyes opened wide. To this day, I don't know how many bullets was in that boy. I counted two just while I was holding him. So I don't know how he made it through.

When his eyes opened wider, and it seemed like there was still some hope, Judd got up and started pounding on the door of the building behind us. People was peeping around curtains, pulling down shades. But Judd kept on pounding and yelling, "Help us, somebody! Help us!" He was pounding and pounding against that green metal door and them old slick brick walls. Pounding and pounding, until finally the ambulance pulled up and Judd slammed his body against the wall and began to slide down, his head bumping against the bricks.

"Help us," he was still saying over and over. "Help us. Help us."

Then, as the ambulance men grabbed Li'l Beaver from my arms, I began to realize Judd wasn't asking for help for Li'l Beaver anymore. He was simply asking for help.

Lord, all the mess that'd gone on in that alley. If them old walls could talk. It was the same alley Hump had found me in years ago; same one Alfred Mayes had run through as a boy and the same one he'd later send them young girls through.

But if this old world was right, I said to myself as the ambulance drove away, the siren whining sickly and poorlike, if this old world was right, something, I don't know what, woulda made them buildings come together a long time ago. Woulda squished them side by side so that there was never no more room for a child to squeeze between.

Tempestt:
"They called it the Nicholae Plan."

After what administrators called a proper mourning period, school reopened on a Thursday. Standing outside the classroom, I saw my peers stringing orange and black streamers on the walls and measuring one another for Halloween costumes. A box of costumes sat in the center of Mrs. Jackson's desk. One after another, students were reaching in for capes and ghoulish masks, holding them up to measure, then returning to desks where softball-sized pumpkins sat next to carving knives and candles. Every desk had one except one desk, which was pushed off into the corner, facing the wall.

I couldn't understand how they could think of celebrating when everything I did or saw or thought about seemed to revolve around Valerie. How could they be so unconcerned? Maybe Valerie hadn't come to school enough for them to miss her.

Before Mrs. Jackson could see me, I backed out of the doorway and ran down the hall to the stairs. Outside, I ran, choking, all the way to the south gate.

A row of fallen leaves had begun to gather at the bottom of the fence. The wind lifted more leaves onto the grass, over the barbed wire, and into the lake. So many leaves had fallen off the fence that for the first time I could see shards of Thirty-fifth Street breaking through the vines—a semblance of red bricks or battered cars. And then up closer, there was the fence itself—tall shafts of black iron, peeling and flecked with rust.

I ran my hands against the gate and more of the leaves started crumbling into tiny pieces. I searched and finally found the latch, but when I pulled on the gate, nothing happened. I kept tugging until I pulled back layers of vines and I could see the gate had been padlocked—one lock, a gleaming steel that separated me from all my friends.

A breath swelled inside me and I slumped against the ivy. I sat there all day it seems, shivering in the cold, crying until my sides hurt, before finally falling asleep on the wet lawn.

Three weeks passed and nearly every day Miss Lily came up to our apartment to confirm, report, or simply discuss news about Alfred Mayes.

On the day he was deemed mentally fit to stand trial, Miss Lily walked into the kitchen with the newspaper plastered to her face, sipping her morning coffee.

"One thing is sure," she said, squeezing in between my parents at the kitchen table. "He ain't mentally fit for nothing. But if that makes it so justice can be served, then I'm all for it."

But on the morning the state's attorney announced that Alfred Mayes had plead guilty to Valerie's murder, Miss Lily came bursting through the back door, huffing and puffing down the hall.

"In exchange for his plea," Miss Lily said as she read the newspaper, "he will not face trial or a possible death sentence. He likely will spend the rest of his natural life behind bars."

Natural life behind bars?

I wondered what exactly "natural life" meant, how it differed from regular life. Hearing it caused a pulling on my stomach; made me swallow back breaths. I thought about it, and about what I had seen. I ran it past reason and logic and sat on it, until two mornings later when we got yet another news flash.

In a late-night city council session, aldermen had passed the coveted ordinance for which Lakeland's residents had long been waiting: The new law would allow the city to expand Lakeland and evacuate Thirty-fifth Street's stores. They called it the Nicholae Plan.

"Ain't really news," Miss Lily said, leaning against the counter as my mother cooked. "Them inspections wasn't nothing but a formality. I hope people wasn't thinking they was gone figure out what was wrong with the stores, then rebuild them. If they did, they had another thought coming. Only a fool didn't know this was heading our way."

But what was news was that Thirty-fifth Street's rebirth would begin as early as the spring. Placards would be printed. Soon architectural renderings would be posted to show everyone how the new Thirty-fifth Street would look: a hotel, quaint boutiques, elegant eateries.

"But how can they just up and move people out of their places like that?" Mama asked.

"Girl, if you only knew Thirty-fifth Street, you'd know it wouldn't be that hard. The mayor acting like he just now noticing them people living in unsafe conditions. Living like swine is what they living like. It's not just the projects. Them stores ain't nothing but shells over there. Wires strung from building to building, stealing electricity. Holes in walls, bigger than my head. In the winter, they say you can stand in one store and feel the wind straight through to the next."

"It can't be that bad," Mama said.

"No, it's worse. But until they fixed Lakeland, wasn't much better over here. We just looked better."

Out of all the news that cropped up, the bit that concerned me most was the possibility of O'Cala's closing. Forever. Where would Miss Jonetta and the men go? I was determined to get back over to see them. I thought about my father's toolbox. He hadn't used it since we'd been in Lakeland. There was nothing to spackle there. No screws to tighten. During our entire two-month stay the toolbox had lain dormant in the back of his office closet. I went to the box and reached for his keyhole saw. God only knows how I'd planned to saw through the wrought iron. But, for now, that was the goal.

I got down to the back gate and peered through the fence. To my surprise, I saw Fat Daddy on the other side, pacing under the tree that blocked the opening.

"Hi, Mr. Fat Daddy," I yelled.

He looked over his shoulder.

"Hi, Mr. Fat Daddy. Over here."

"Well, shut my mouth wide open," he yelled, adjusting his hat from the wind. "Just shut my mouth." He knelt into the dirt. "Miss Johnie was feeling kind of low, missing you and all. So I told her I wasn't gone come back today until I found you. I didn't know how I was gone do it, but I wasn't gone come back until I found you. You told me you was lucky and I didn't want to believe it."

"They closed the gate," I said.

"I know," he said. "Been pulling on it for a few days now. Don't worry none about that, though. You wait right there and I'll go get Miss Johnie."

After a few minutes of watching the **S** curve darken behind me, and Christmas lights that swung from lamppost to lamppost blink on, a faint voice called through the fence.

"Child?" Miss Jonetta said, out of breath.

"I'm here," I said, trying to rip through the ivy. "I'm right here."

I stuck both hands between the wrought-iron poles and Miss Jonetta quickly threaded her fingers through mine, our hands clasping against cold metal and nearly barren vines. She stooped a bit so she could see me through the slender openings.

"Child," she said. "It's so good to talk to you again. Not a day's gone by that I ain't thought about you, wondered how you was getting along. Not a day's gone by."

"They locked the gate," I said, breathing hard. "It won't open at all."

"Oh, Child," she said, "we ain't thinking about no fence. This old ugly thing can't keep us apart. We can talk just like there ain't nothing here. I want to know how you handling things. How you handling what you saw."

I was quiet for a second. I could feel the tears burning the corners of my eyes. Beyond the rocks, I could see the light on the lighthouse begin to fade away as the water fanned up over the shore, dissolving into the air.

"I miss her," I said finally. "Every day I think about her. At night I dream about her. I try not to. But that's all I do. Every time I close my eyes, I see her. I keep thinking that if I hadn't gone up there, then maybe . . ."

"Oh, Child," she said. "It was gone happen. That's what I want you to know. That's why I wanted to talk to you. Can you see me, Child?"

"A little," I said, here and there catching glimpses of her eyes, her bracelets, her ruby red lips.

"I want you to know that it wasn't your fault. It was gone happen. That little girl wasn't meant for this world. I don't always explain things too good, but you have to understand that she never wanted you to be there. Some things just happen. Can you hear me, Child?"

She paused.

"Let me put it this way. At the same time I came into this world, lo them many years ago, my mother left me. My papa said her heart just stopped. As I got older I began to feel that my mother's passing was my fault. Sorta like you feeling right now.

"You see, we lived on a hill and at the bottom was a small river. From time to time, I used to go sit on the banks just to think on things a piece. On the other side of that river was a small cemetery where my mother was buried. My father would see me sitting, staring across the way, and every now and then he would scoop up a handful of daisies, come get me, and we would wade through the water to get to the other side.

"Always, as soon as my father crossed over, he snatched his hat off and tucked it under his arm. Then we'd bow down on the dusty mound that marked my mother's grave, lay the flowers nice and neatlike, and Daddy would commence to talking. 'Mrs. Goodings,' he'd say. He said he called her Mrs. Goodings and she called him Mr. Goodings 'cause nobody else would give them that kind of respect in Annington County, Mississippi. So they gave it to themselves. 'Mrs. Goodings,' Papa would continue, 'your daughter here still ain't got it through her head that she had nothing to do with you being where you are.' He'd look over at me. As always my face would be a mess, wetter than wet. 'Mrs. Goodings, I've told this child over and over that some things we can't put ourselves in. Some things ain't about us, though they looks like they might be. Some things—like night turning to day, or that there river flowing downstream—gone happen with or without us. And ain't nothing we can say or do to stop it even if we just happen to be standing there at the time.' "

Miss Jonetta adjusted herself against the fence but at no time did we dare let go of each other's hands.

"What I'm trying to say, Child, is that this was gone happen. I swear to you. I ain't never lied to you before, ain't gone start now. Believe me honey, it was gone happen. Knowing that won't make anybody one bit less sorry. But it reminds us that we don't always get a say in the way folks come into and leave this world. The trick is, we can't let it take us under."

Once again, my throat felt as though it were closing, turning inside out. "And now," I said, "Thirty-fifth Street is about to change."

"Well," she said, her voice low, "that's good news."

"Good news? But you'll have to go away. And Mr. Judd once said O'Cala's and all the stores would be around forever. That's what he said, forever."

"Honey, as far as that old street is concerned, it's time. Truth be told, it's time that somebody tear down all them stores, clean the place up." She paused. "Maybe it'll give folks a chance to start over. Sometimes folks need to be turned in another direction before they can see their way through."

"Aren't you going to fight it?"

She laughed to herself. "I'm too old to fight, honey. That's what I had to explain to Fat Daddy—I just don't feel like fighting. Did I tell you Hump and Retha Mae left?"

I shook my head; then I remembered she could hardly see me.

"Where'd they go?"

"Retha Mae is from New Orleans originally and they said they was going back there. We took them to the train station a couple of days ago. Lord, we got so much catching up to do. But none of that is important now. What's important is that you know this whole mess ain't your fault."

A police car with its sirens on passed by. We both knew others would follow.

"I better get going, Child," she said. "But I'll be back tomorrow, around the same time you used to come to the store. And me and you gone work this thing out. I promise. We gone make all this stuff try to make some sense. Ain't gone happen overnight. You hear me, Child? But we gone turn it into something worth holding on to."

Miss Jonetta:
"I hoped with all that was in me that one day the words would rock her."

I walked away from the fence feeling like I was hanging from a ledge, holding Child's hand but barely holding on myself. There was so many things I wanted to tell her but didn't. So many things I wanted to squeeze in but couldn't.

I just felt like walking that night, so when I got to the store, I walked myself right on past the steps. I was gone walk till I found an answer. How could I help that child? How could I save her from this hole I could feel her sinking into?

The streets was slick and the wind heavy. At first, I thought it was them pigeons gone that made Thirty-fifth Street seem a little different. But then I realized it wasn't just them pigeons. Already that old street had changed.

Instead of the regulars, undercover police officers was busy at nearly every intersection. It was almost like there hadn't been a time when the city had forgot about us. Like them coppers had always rode up and down that street. Stopping young boys from passing elastic bands and white packages from hand to hand, or them young girls from flaunting themselves in front of wet, speeding cars.

On each of the buildings, city workers had slapped bright orange CONDEMNED stickers, clearing the vestibules of men and women who had sat there for years, sipping from their brown paper sacks. Workers had also cleared out the vacant lot next door to O'Cala's. I hadn't ever walked past that place and there wasn't at least one plaid suit huddled around a burning garbage can. Or at least one little boy or girl rubbing their hands near the flames. Well, that was until that night I left Child.

And if that wasn't enough, for the first time since Creation, city plows was roaring up and down the street, clearing a path of mud and snow that stretched from the projects as far as I could see. Causing a rumbling underneath, a stirring, that seemed like the ground was peeling apart. Nobody and nothing was where they used to be. All that snow and mud turning over a new day. Right before our eyes.

I stopped at the ribs house to look at all them buildings. Some vacant, or burnt out, others just standing. Been standing for so long—tired for so long, wasn't nothing else for them to do.

At the whorehouse, girls was trickling out, one by one, leaving in cars, or cabs. A New Saved preacher, one of the last, stood near the door, holding a sermon. I guess the police felt sorry for him, so they let him stay for a spell. Lord, the child was preaching like he had a whole congregation in front of him. Pointing to the concrete, asking for a amen. Pointing to broken-out second-floor windows, waving his hands. I felt sorry for him, so I dropped a dime into his gold-plated canister.

I was walking, looking for me a answer. How could I help that child? How could I spare her from losing her way? Oh, you can't stop the pain, I knowed that. Honey, once it comes to rest on your front stoop, it moves on in, easylike, and lets you know it's gone stay for a while. But I wanted to find a way to let her know that the hurt wouldn't be so hard or so heavy forever. That one day she'd open her eyes wide and see more than darkness. Oh, I tell you, I was praying good.

I started to walk back to the store and, don't you know, a strong breeze whipped right through me. It was a June breeze, a porch swing breeze, that came out of nowhere. Snatching my breath and making my coat fly back. It was like nothing I'd felt the whole time I'd been walking that night. I had to hold on to one of them parking meters to steady myself. For a second, my whole body tingled and all around me I could smell wildflowers and lilac soap tickling at my nose, fanning against me like a rush of butterflies.

That was when it hit me. Made me smile to myself. Hit me like somebody was tapping me on my shoulder, whispering right into my ear: Before there was all these buildings, Johnie, dry-rotting walls and corroding pipes, before the bricks and concrete and plaster walls, and before hairline cracks became gaping holes, there was fields, wide and open and light. There was wildflowers and tall prairie grass and sticky bugs that little girls and little boys once ran through.

When I got back to the store, Judd, Fat Daddy, and Chitlin was sitting at the table. Judd and Fat Daddy had been clearing out my closets. Had done pulled out a mess of old cans of Wild Rose sugar corn and Snider's soup and throwed them into a barrel in the center of the store.

"How's that little girl doing?" Judd asked. Chitlin clicked off his radio. He and Fat Daddy turned to listen.

"She gone be okay," I said, nodding.

"How can you be so sure, Johnie?" Chitlin said. He eased back away from the table the way he used to so he could study the board for his next move.

"Ain't no guarantees," I said. "It's just a feeling I got is all." To Judd, I said, "Honey, could you watch after the store for a spell longer? There's something upstairs I need to do."

He winked at me and got up and walked behind the counter.

"You sure you okay, Johnie?" Fat Daddy said. "You looking a little red in the face."

"I'm fine, honey," I said, pulling the curtain behind me. "I'm just fine."

I got upstairs and sat down on my sofa. I thought about all them cans of food downstairs in the store—cans so old, I was sure they was filled with worms and vermin by now. No good for eating or nothing else. But you can't tell that to somebody who had held on to them for all them years, fearing having to stare down hunger pangs again.

I thought about the night Judd and me brought Valerie and John up. Tears started tugging at my eyelids. Right across the room, that pretty little girl had crawled into Judd's arms. Then I thought about Child. Even through all that mess on the fence, I could hear the sorry in her voice. So much sorry and pain. Strange how everybody walks down a road and how paths crisscross, overlap, and run into one another. And people are changed by it. Forever changed.

Now one baby was gone and the other was near so, feeling ripped apart. I wanted to tell Child that peace wouldn't come overnight. She had some long, long days ahead. A lot of ground to cover. Just ain't fair for a eleven-year-old to have to make up so much ground. One day, your biggest worry is having red hair, and the next, you trying to find ways to forget. Tell your eyes they didn't see what you know you saw.

I went over to my bureau and pulled out a stack of paper, some envelopes, and a pen. I decided to write Child some letters, a group of letters with particulars that I knowed she couldn't understand right off. For some of it, she'd have to wait on time. But I hoped with all that was in me that one day the words would rock her. Hold her tight.

I didn't know where to begin at first and how much of the story to tell. But it seem like as soon as the ink started spilling good on that paper, something inside me took over. And I did like the good Lord did and just started at the beginning.

First, I told her about Papa, Essie, and me back in Annington County. I told her about our move to Aunt Ethel's, and how I made it to Thirty-fifth Street, stumbling into Alfred Mayes. I mentioned Aunt Ethel's basement, and Chloe's birth, and that back alley Herbert Fastile Porter found me in. Mr. Hump, she knowed him as.

I told her that I, too, knowed what it was like to have someone precious snatched away. I knowed what it felt like to hurt so bad that you don't know whether you coming or going. You let the years sweep by and your insides shrivel and you force your outside to numb over. Oh, I knowed that well.

Some days, you pray for God to let the hurt stop. You scream to him. From the pit of your being, you scream, thinking he can't hear you no other way. But he hears you, Child, I wrote. Then he moves you—little moves that you can't recognize right off. Until one day you pulling into the station. And you find yourself in a place, a little hole-in-the-wall, surrounded by friends who bring you flowers by way of kind words and remind you that you once ran through fields of corn and wheat and believed you could find all kinds of treasures in the stalks.

I told her some day she, too, was gone find a place—a safe place where she could feel like she belonged. Wasn't gone happen when she wanted it. But one morning, she'd wake up a little lighter. One day, she'd go some minutes, then some hours without thinking so hard about Valerie. One day, she'd be able to look at a little girl who resembled Valerie and her heart wouldn't bleed rivers and feel like stopping.

The last letter I wrote, I shared with her what I'd just learned myself about secrets. Honey, secrets wasn't ever meant to stay down. Ain't part of their constitution. That's why as much as I didn't want to tell Child about my past at first, as much as I was so afraid she couldn't love a ex-whore and fool, I had to tell her my story. I had to let her know that in life we see things and do things that seem to want to take us under. But they ain't got to. I knowed she was holding on to a secret so big that it alone could swallow her up. I told her that early on she'd hold on to it. But one day, she'd have to share it, set it free. She'd have to tell what she saw, even if it wasn't no more than to tell somebody that she knowed what road they was headed down. Because she herself had done been down that same path before.

Well, don't you know, I wrote until I got tired, until the age in my fingers started to catch up with me and this old soul couldn't find nothing else to give. I licked all them envelopes, then tied pink ribbons around each. Funny how writing about the hurt can release pieces of it. Bits and pieces into the wind. I lined the letters up across my bureau, counted five in all. I went back and sat down on my sofa and just stared at them. The way they cut across the years, the ones behind me and the ones straight ahead.

C H A P T E R 2 9

Tempestt:
"South till your hat floats."

The next morning, Miss Lily came running in through the back door, huffing and puffing down the hall. She had to sit at the kitchen table for a second to catch her breath.

"Are you okay, Lily?" Mama said. She turned to the faucet and poured Miss Lily a glass of water.

"Leesha," she said, "that husband of yours is over at the coffeehouse on Baldwin and Tubman." Each word sort of shot out at first, broken up by intermittent gasping and wheezing, and her taking a second to wipe sweat from the back of her neck. "They holding a celebration toast to the end of Thirty-fifth Street. Mary Helen just called me to say somebody done stirred his colored good. She said he just announced y'all leaving Lakeland."

Mama ran over to the hall closet and grabbed her coat. "Tem, I'll be back soon," she said.

I counted to twenty—slowly—then I ran out behind her.

I could hear Miss Lily calling me. But I couldn't stop. I ran all the way north to the main gate. I slipped through when a car entered and ran almost endless blocks back south to Thirty-fifth Street.

By the time I arrived at the store, my throat was on fire. I was dizzy and sweating. My hands were shaking.

"Miss Jonetta, Miss Jonetta," I yelled, bursting through the door. She was standing at the table with her hands on her hips. Judd, Fat Daddy, and Mr. Chittey were sitting. I fell—as though dropped—right into her arms.

"It's so good to see you, Child," she said. She hugged me, pushed me away to look at me, then pulled me toward her again. "So, so good to see you, Child."

"I knew you'd come back," Mr. Chittey said, slapping his thigh. "And just in time, too." He was smiling so broadly that for the first time I noticed he was missing his two front teeth. I was still holding on to Miss Jonetta and I could feel him patting me on my back.

"My father says we're leaving Lakeland," I said, looking up at her, then over to the men. "We're leaving Lakeland because nobody came to Valerie's funeral."

"Nobody?" Mr. Chittey said, his face now a scowl. "Y'all should leave. Niggas over there ain't no good these days." He patted me on my shoulder. "Fat Daddy and me is leaving, too. We heading to . . ." He stopped to scratch his chin. "Where we heading again?"

Fat Daddy reached over to muss my hair. "If I have to tell you one more time," he said to Mr. Chittey, "I'm gone leave you right here." To me he said, "We going to Paducah, Paducah, Kentucky. About nine hours from here, south on I-Fifty-seven. South till your hat floats."

"They was just about to leave," Miss Jonetta said. "They wanted to get on the road before nightfall. I'm so glad you're here, Child."

"I am, too," Fat Daddy said.

Judd simply winked.

"Me, too," Mr. Chittey said. He struggled to stand without his cane; then he hobbled over to the door. A couple of worn suitcases sat next to the hat rack, along with a duffel bag and some A&P shopping bags. Mr. Chittey reached into one of the shopping bags, pulling out his radio. He stared at it for a second until he was certain of what he was about to do. "If I give you this, it's only a loan, you hear?"

I nodded.

"It's just that . . . well, there's a radio in the car. We just put it in, so I better use it." He jerked his head up to the window, to the car parked by the curb. I could see only one of the tires, thick whitewalls, with snow dotting the chrome. "You never know when I might need this back, you hear?"

His hands trembled as he handed me the radio. "Jiggle this knob if the reception is bad. Tap the back like this if it don't come on right. Battery connection sometime ain't worth a dime."

When I took the radio, he slapped the back of my hand twice and turned to get his coat and cane from the table.

Miss Jonetta walked over to the counter and grabbed two medium-sized bags that were sitting on top, hiding the second shelf of liquor in her cabinet.

"I got you both some shaving cream and some sandwiches and some other notions for your trip," she said. Judd jumped up to help her with the bags.

In putting on his coat, Fat Daddy's collar had gotten twisted, so she reached out to fix it. And he smoothed the purple flower in his kelly green lapel before cocking his kelly green hat to the side. Then all of a sudden, he sat back down.

Miss Jonetta sat down, too. Mr. Chittey was bundled up, standing at the door, leaning on his cane.

"I'm gone miss you, Johnie," Fat Daddy whispered. We could barely hear the words, but everybody knew what he said. His face said it, the way he looked past her, up toward the window.

"Now, now, honey," Miss Jonetta said, leaning forward to rub his face. "We said last night we wasn't gone do this. We said we each was going our separate ways just for a spell. You know we can't stay away long. We too old. Been knowing each other too long. What'll you think life'll be like without me having to say, 'Watch your mouth, Fat Daddy,' or 'This don't concern you, Chitlin. Just mind your own business'? So that's why this is only temporary. We ain't saying good-bye. No, no. We just saying, 'I'll see you later.' Besides, honey, you know me. You could be shooting some pool one day, look up, and see me standing in the doorway."

Fat Daddy smiled a bit, straightening his back out. Miss Jonetta put her arm in his as she pulled him up and we all walked toward the door. Outside, she put her arms around both Fat Daddy and Mr. Chittey. "Now, watch your speed," she said. "Remember, this car been sitting up for a while. It's old and a little rusty like both of you and gone take some time to get moving right." She smiled. "And don't forget Chitlin's sugar. Make him take his pills."

Miss Jonetta held her arms around her body, protecting herself from the cold. Judd took his sweater and draped it around her shoulders and we watched as Fat Daddy motioned for traffic behind him to go around and that 1960 Le Sabre U-turned in the middle of the street.

"I'll see you real soon," she yelled, waving. We watched them for a while until the red lights and the smoke trailing them, even in the light of late afternoon, was lost amid dump trucks and bulldozers and mounds of concrete ash.

Then we turned and went back into the store.

Miss Jonetta pulled a chair out for me at the table. She sat down next to me.

"I'm going upstairs to finish moving them boxes for you, Johnie," Judd said. And he slipped behind the curtain.

"All this stuff," she said, looking around the store. "We just gone leave it right here. Didn't bring it. Ain't gone take it with me. But my belongings upstairs is something else."

"Where are you going?"

"Well, that's funny that you asked that, Child. I still haven't really decided. I reckon I'll spend some time in Annington County. I'll go down there for a spell and find the land I was born on and reminisce for a while. Then after that, I don't know. I can't tell you where I'll finally hang my hat. I just know it's time to pull up from here. Been here too long. Too long."

"Miss Jonetta," I said, "I have something to tell you about Valerie and Rev. Mayes."

She put her finger up to her mouth. "Shh, Child," she said. "I know. I know." Standing, she said, "Wait here for a second. I got something for you. Sort of a going-away present. I won't be long."

Viewing the store from the table gave O'Cala's a totally different perspective. Part of it, I know, was that the aisles had been cleared during what Miss Jonetta called her "fire sale," although much of the food and liquor had been given away instead of sold. The refrigerator was open and defrosting. And the piano had been turned so that the keys faced the wall. The barrel of candy was gone, but the ring on the floor assured me it had been there. And the Pepsi-Cola clock had been unplugged, its cord folded and wound around itself and swinging against the back wall.

I tried to remember every chipped piece of paint, every cobweb that hung in places too tight for even Miss Jonetta's cloth to reach.

Once again I was leaving home.

When Miss Jonetta returned, Judd was with her, and she handed me a large envelope. It was thick and bulging. She'd sealed it, but barely so. Then she handed me a pair of earrings and a bracelet.

"You'll have to wait a few years before you can wear the earrings," she said, dangling them up to the light. "But that's okay, since they ain't the type that turn green on you when you ain't looking."

Behind the counter, she grabbed a paper bag, in which she placed each of the items, including Mr. Chittey's radio.

Judd left to get the car.

"I love you, Miss Jonetta," I said, hugging her.

"Oh, Child," she said, her voice cracking. "Honey, you ain't telling me nothing I don't already know. I feel like I've known you for a lifetime. A couple of lifetimes." We didn't say anything more. We couldn't. We simply held each other until Judd's car pulled up in front of the door. He beeped twice.

Judd and Miss Jonetta drove me home that night. Miss Jonetta and I sat in the backseat holding hands. When I looked up at her, her back was straight, her pillbox hat sitting just above her forever-black bun. I looked at her, trying not to stare. Just to remember her face. Seal it into my memory so I would never, ever forget it.

At the gate, Judd didn't pull into the driveway. We sat by the curb. Judd turned around. "Remember, this ain't good-bye," he said, placing his hand on my shoulder. "This is 'I'll see you later.'"

I nodded. I kissed Miss Jonetta and I leaned forward to kiss him.

They waited in the car as I walked the slight incline up the drive to the guard's station. I turned several times to wave. The guard called my parents. And it wasn't long before the Volvo came speeding toward the gate, my parents jumping out and running toward me. When I turned around the last time, Judd's car was gone.

Mama and Miss Lily packed three suitcases. Mama told Miss Lily to pack only the things we had brought to Lakeland. But Miss Lily slipped in a few white towels and some crystal Christmas ornaments when Mama wasn't looking.

Daddy spent most of the following morning in his office, going over our contract. He explained to those concerned that the Saville family was breaking it and he didn't give a damn what the repercussions would be. Afterward, he went down to the garage to put the suitcases in the car, check the oil, the gas, the tires, preparing it for the three-thousand-mile trip to California.

Mama called Aunt Jennie to tell her we were coming. The length of stay, she said, was undetermined. But we'd arrive in a few days.

Mama told Miss Lily, "Auntie's so happy, she said she could wet on herself. I'd love for you to meet her, Lily. She's a character. She says she's got a new boyfriend who's ten years younger and Nigerian. Emeka is his name. And she's thinking about changing her name to Ayana. Means beautiful flower."

"Oh, I'll be out there," Miss Lily said, rubbing her hands on her uniform, shifting from side to side. "I'll be there. Don't you worry about that. This ain't the last you seen of me. Besides, I been hearing rumors that when they finish remaking Thirty-fifth Street, they gone build some new projects on the border. A whole bunch of them. Wait until these Negroes hear about that. Lord knows, I don't want to be nowhere in sight."

My father didn't come back up to the apartment. When it was time, he called up and told us to meet him in front of the building.

"Leesha," Miss Lily said to my mother in the elevator. "Now, I want y'all to just keep driving and don't think about us back here. These people was acting a fool before you got here and they gone still be acting a fool after you leave."

Mama nodded as she leaned forward to give Miss Lily a kiss and a hug. Miss Lily's arms must have weighed thirty pounds each. But she lifted them easily, lowering them around both of us.

As the car wound its way back through Lakeland's streets, we turned onto the path by the lake. In front of us, the snow and ice stretched across the rocks that jutted into the water. The sunrise against the stark white floor made my eyes burn when I looked at it straight on. And the water simply flowed into the sky. It was interrupted only by the lighthouse sitting on the horizon, its light blinking as though nothing, not even the earth stopping, could ever make it lose its timing or pale yellow cast.

Tempestt:
"I'll see her letting go."

This Sunday, my husband, daughter, and I will drive the forty-five miles up the coast to Justin Bay to have dinner with my parents. They still live in that small house we moved into all those years ago. It's an oceanside combination ranch-bungalow with ten bird feeders that I begged my father to build and plant around the yard. Each year until I left for Berkeley, the yard seemed to need a new one. That first year, the finches came, then robins and beautiful sparrows, and suddenly my father was turning ground for bird feeders as fast as he was for his beds of dahlias and petunias and daylilies.

Frank and I have made this drive countless times. Still, this Sunday, something in me will dissolve like cotton candy as I look over my shoulder at my two-year-old in her car seat as she strains to see where the seagulls disappear to when they dip down into crashing waves or dart behind jagged cliffs. Pretty soon, her eyes will widen and she'll start to bounce as we pull into my parents' driveway and she sees Grandpa flopping around the yard in tight shoes only fit for pulling weeds, and Grandma reading under a palm tree.

Later in the evening, after the dinner dishes have been dried and stacked and Kim is sound asleep in my old bedroom, my mother, father, and Frank will gather around the television to debate some national or local bit of news. My father will disagree with Frank, whom he loves dearly, and my mother will say, "Pay no mind to Thomas, Frank. He'd argue with the wind if it stood still long enough."

Me? I'll sneak off to the rocks. I'll bring along a cup of mint tea and, as I have for years, I'll unfurl a stack of letters whose ribbons are yellowing now and whose pages are tearing at the folds. I've read them many times. But I'll read them again and again as though the words are new and still vibrant, still capable of casting memories out into the water.

Before me, the sky will darken into a deep purple and the gulls will squawk and come to rest against the rocks at my feet, and once again I'll see Valerie in her final moments. I'll see her unwrapping all of her secrets, untucking them from her bosom, releasing them from her wings. I'll see her letting go. And with each letter, I'll remind myself that this colorful sparrow, once trapped, is no longer desperate, no longer wanting, but finally, finally free.